Forrester Square

LEGACIES . LIES . LOVE .

MINDY NEFF
TOO GOOD TO REFUSE

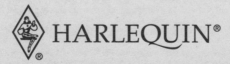

HARLEQUIN®

TORONTO • NEW YORK • LONDON
AMSTERDAM • PARIS • SYDNEY • HAMBURG
STOCKHOLM • ATHENS • TOKYO • MILAN • MADRID
PRAGUE • WARSAW • BUDAPEST • AUCKLAND

To Mary Ray

For late-night e-mails, encouragement and hand-holding.
We birthed this one together.
Thanks, my friend

HARLEQUIN BOOKS
225 Duncan Mill Road, Don Mills,
Ontario, Canada M3B 3K9

ISBN-13: 978-0-373-61275-8
ISBN-10:   0-373-61275-3

TOO GOOD TO REFUSE

Mindy Neff is acknowledged as the author of this work.

Visit us at www.eHarlequin.com

Printed in U.S.A.

Dear Reader,

I've always had a desire to write about a sheikh, and after twenty-three published books, Harlequin has presented me with the perfect opportunity.

Jeffri al-Kareem is a man with a wounded heart who is used to order and decorum. When Millie Gallagher shows up on his private island, she takes charge of his life, his house, his son…and his heart. Come along with me as coffee-barista-turned-nanny Millie Gallagher throws the life of Sheikh Jeffri al-Kareem into total choas!

I hope you enjoy my addition to the Forrester Square series, that Millie and Jeff will make you laugh a lot and cry a little, and that their story will touch your heart.

All my best,

Mindy Neff

P.S. I love hearing from readers. You can write to me online at www.mindyneff.com or by snail mail at 8502 E. Chapman #355, Orange, CA 92869.

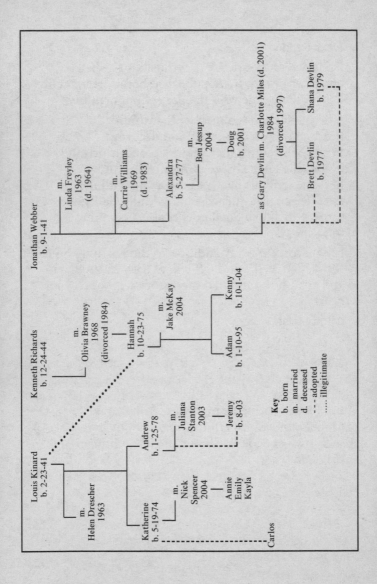

Louis Kinard
b. 2-23-41

m.

Helen Drescher
1963

Katherine
b. 5-19-74

m.

Nick Spencer
2004

Annie   Emily   Kayla

Carlos

Andrew
b. 1-25-78

m.

Juliana Stanton
2003

Jeremy
b. 8-03

Kenneth Richards
b. 12-24-44

m.

Olivia Brawney
1968
(divorced 1984)

Hannah
b. 10-23-75

m.

Jake McKay
2004

Adam
b. 1-10-95

Kenny
b. 10-1-04

Jonathan Webber
b. 9-1-41

m.

Linda Freyley
1963
(d. 1964)

m.

Carrie Williams
1969
(d. 1983)

Alexandra
b. 5-27-77

m.

Ben Jessup
2004

Doug
b. 2001

as Gary Devlin m. Charlotte Miles (d. 2001)
1984
(divorced 1997)

Brett Devlin
b. 1977

Shana Devlin
b. 1979

Key

b. born
m. married
d. deceased
- - - adopted
..... illegitimate

CHAPTER ONE

MILLIE GALLAGHER looked out at the Seattle skyline from the Space Needle's observation deck. All her life, she'd been drawn to this monument as though it held the secret to her destiny. She felt a sense of anticipation every time she stood here gazing at the endless horizon.

This was a place where she could let her eyes roam and her mind wander, let the responsibilities sitting on her twenty-three-year-old shoulders melt away for an hour or two.

High above the city, she could dream silly dreams, imagine herself falling in love with the perfect man—a man who would be the father Lindscy so desperately wanted, who would love her as deeply as Millie did. The three of them would be a family, and live in a stately old Victorian house in the Queen Anne neighborhood that draped across the tallest of Seattle's seven hills. And Lindsey would have a tree house with a bird's-eye view of the ferries scurrying in and out of Elliott Bay and the ocean-going freighters resting at anchor farther out in Puget Sound.

Adventure, possibilities, new worlds. They were only wishes right now, but maybe someday…

"Mimi, I can see the whole world!"

Millie smiled down at her five-year-old sister. Lindsey's blond hair was a riot of curls, much like her own, and the absolute love she felt every time she looked at the sweet, energetic, happy child made her realize that she was pretty darn lucky. Lindsey had called her Mimi ever since she'd learned to talk and couldn't quite get her tongue wrapped around the *L's*. The name sounded enough like Mommy that most people assumed Lindsey was her child. She rarely corrected the assumption anymore.

Because Millie was the only mother Lindsey remembered.

"You say that every time we come here, sweetie."

"So do you. Can we go to the kids' museum next? And we could take off our shoes and play in the fountain."

Millie passed a hand over Lindsey's soft curls. "It's only March, kiddo. It's still way too cold to stick our feet in the water. And we'll have to save the museum for another time."

"Aw, Mimi."

With her hand on Lindsey's shoulder, Millie urged her forward. "I have to work this afternoon. You know that."

"Hy knows how to make lattes."

"Yeah, but nobody makes a double-chocolate skinny foam like I do." She shook her head and grinned. "There'd be a mutiny. And after work there's the bridal shower for Hannah, remember?"

Lindsey nodded, but deliberately looked away from the closed doors of the gold-and-glass elevator that would shoot them five hundred and twenty feet down to ground level in a matter of seconds. Millie understood Lindsey's reluctance to end their special time together. It was rare for Millie to have a free morning. Any other day she'd be working at Forrester Square Day Care preparing fresh lunches and snacks for the children before she started her shift at Caffeine Hy's.

"How come the mountains have snow on them?"

"Because they're very tall and it's cold up there."

"Can you teach me to ski, Mimi?"

"Yes." Unexpected tears burned the backs of her eyes as she punched the button to call the elevator. "Next year. I promise."

Every once in a while, the ache of missing her parents sneaked up on her. She remembered how stunned—and then excited Cleve and Selma Gallagher had been when they'd found out they were expecting Lindsey, a late-in-life baby. Millie, too, had been thrilled.

Her parents had been wonderful people, and they'd made sure Millie's childhood was full of new experiences, that she always knew she was loved, and looked after, and safe. A senseless automobile accident had cheated Lindsey out of knowing Mom and Pop and feeling that security.

But Millie was determined that Lindsey would have the same advantages that she'd had—the childhood memories that stuck with you forever, the friends, parties, dance lessons, field trips and vacations.

Although she worked three jobs to make ends meet, Millie counted her blessings. They had a roof over their heads and enough money in the bank to take care of their needs. Her dream of someday opening a catering business seemed unattainable just now, but she wasn't a person to ever give up hope.

"Hi!" Lindsey chirped. "What's your name?"

Caught daydreaming again, Millie glanced down to see who Lindsey was talking to. It was sometimes frightening how friendly her little sister was.

A boy, taller than Lindsey, but looking pretty close in age, stood with his hands in the pockets of his nicely creased slacks. His shirt was buttoned to the neck, his kid-size bomber jacket was pure leather, and his dark hair was neat and trimmed. Mighty dressed up for a little guy.

"Sam," the child said, his dark brown eyes darting behind him, then at one of the game stations on the Space Needle's O deck. "Did you play any of the games?" He spoke as properly as he was dressed.

Lindsey rolled her eyes. "Of course. We come here *all* the time. You want to play? I'll show you. We could do the one about the candy bars."

"Lindsey," Millie interrupted. "We really have to go." She glanced around, wondering where this child's parents were. "You're not lost, are you, Sam?"

"No." Clearly indignant, he puffed out his chest, and Millie struggled not to smile. Still, she didn't like to see a small child alone.

"Silly question," she agreed for the sake of his pride, yet alert for a frantic mother who'd lost track of her kid. "I'm sure your mom and dad are here with you."

"My mother died when I was five. I am six now."

"Oh, Sam." Millie dropped to one knee in front of the little boy. She was a nurturer—couldn't help it and didn't want to change. "That's very sad. I lost my mom, too."

He frowned. "Why do you not find her?"

She smiled. His speech was so grown-up. "Not *lost* as in playing. She died, too. Are you here with your father, then?"

"Yes. He is talking business on his telephone." Sam gestured with his head, his dark, silky hair shifting, then falling right back into place. "He does that a lot. He is a very important man. But I saw this cool tower when we flew into Seattle, and Father promised we could come."

Millie smiled. Little Sam was loosening up a bit. "Yeah, the Space Needle's pretty cool," she echoed.

Lindsey slipped her arm around Sam. For a moment he

seemed startled, as though he wasn't used to affectionate displays.

"Don't be sad about your mom," Lindsey said. "We could go get some candy bars. They got 'em over there at the coffee place. We could stack 'em up and pretend—" She glanced at Millie. "How many candy bars tall are we, Mimi?"

"One thousand three hundred and twenty from the ground to the top of the Space Needle." The little stinker. She was deliberately trying to stall so they wouldn't have to leave. But Millie had obligations, and she didn't blow them off lightly, even when it meant cutting short Lindsey's and her "special days" together.

"It says so in one of the trimmea game things—"

"Trivia," Millie automatically corrected, "But we really have to—"

"Yeah." Lindsey nodded. "One of those." She removed her arm from around Sam and faced him, her expression earnest. "If we were rich, we could buy that many candy bars and see. But we don't have lots of money for extra stuff, so we pretend."

"Lindsey—"

"My father is rich," Sam said. "I could ask him to buy the candy."

Millie had to put a stop to this. She checked her watch. There was plenty of time to get Lindsey to Forrester Square Day Care and herself to Caffeine Hy's. But not enough time to do a load of laundry before she left— which meant she'd be up well past midnight tonight.

"Sorry, kids. I don't think the café stocks that many candy bars. Sam, can we walk with you back to your father?"

"It is not necessary. I can see him."

Millie looked, but had no idea who she was looking

for. There were lots of people around, peering through telescopes, sipping coffee or simply gazing out at the awesome view. Several of the men within sight had dark hair like Sam's.

That was fine and dandy, she thought, but Sam was standing right next to the elevator with two total strangers. A person could snatch this child and be gone before anyone could get to them—she knew that only too well after young Lily Marshall's kidnapping at the day care a few months ago. Thankfully, Lily had been rescued.

Still, the irresponsibility of Sam's father made Millie mad, but what could she do? It was none of her business.

"Well then, it was very nice to meet you, Mr. Sam. You run on back to your dad while I watch." She held out her hand for a cordial shake.

Sam's brown eyes sparkled at being called Mister. He took her hand and pumped it up and down. The exuberance was in direct contrast to his formal speech.

"You could shake my hand, too." Lindsey didn't like to be left out of anything.

"You're a girl," Sam said.

"So. Girls can shake hands. Girls can do anything boys can do!"

Oh, dear. A potential squabble already. Millie had deliberately raised Lindsey to be independent. Their parents' death had made Millie all too aware of her own mortality, and she was determined that Lindsey would grow up strong, capable and independent so she could manage on her own if anything happened to Millie.

Before she could intervene in the girls-versus-boys disagreement, Sam stunned her by picking up Lindsey's hand and placing a gallant kiss on the back of it.

Millie's heart melted. A little man in a child's body.

Lindsey wasn't quite so romantic. She snatched her

hand away and wiped it on the seat of her jeans. "How come you did that?"

Sam shrugged.

Making another great effort not to smile, Millie steered Lindsey closer to the elevator. "Have fun while you're in Seattle, Sam." When the door swished open, she turned and stepped in, intending to hold the door until Sam made it safely back to his father.

But Sam followed them right onto the car.

"Oh, no, little man. You need to stay here." She quickly pushed the button to keep the automatic doors open and rested her hand on Sam's bony shoulder. "Your dad would be frightened if you went joyriding on the elevator and he didn't know about it. Come on, we'll go find him together, okay?"

Sam didn't budge. "He won't care if I ride with you. He talks on the phone a long time. The lift will come back up. And you are a grown-up, so you can watch me." His words came faster now as he attempted to convince her with his little boy charm. "Amala came to America to chaperone, but she was lazy and Father sent her home. I didn't like her, anyway. Her hands smelled like fish."

"Yuck," Lindsey said. "Fish are icky."

"Fish are very healthy for you," Millie interjected. Their father had made his living on a fishing boat. "Though fishy hands are a bit difficult to take. However, Sam, we have to go find your dad, because I could only keep you company on the way down. You'd have to come back up by yourself, and I would worry myself silly over that."

Sam giggled. "I like you better than Amala. You smell like apples."

She couldn't help herself, she thought, crouching down. He was so darn cute, she just had to hug him.

A large masculine hand slapped against the door of the elevator, holding it open even though Millie was still pushing the button.

She glanced up and nearly fainted. "Oh! You must be—"

"What the hell do you think you are doing? Take your hands off my son." The man reached in and swooped Sam out of the elevator and into his arms. The boy's feet dangled nearly to the guy's knees, but he held his son as though he were a toddler, passing his palm over the child's face, his hair, his back, as though checking for injuries.

Despite the man's less than cordial manners, he obviously cared deeply about his child.

Fury and worry creased his swarthy, oh-my-gosh-handsome features, and it took a minute for Millie to realize she'd automatically risen and stepped forward out of the elevator, while Lindsey gripped the tail of her jacket.

She might as well have been in a trance, because all she could do was stare. The man was impeccably dressed in a dark business suit, with a duster-style overcoat open at the front. She had a wonderful view of a sedate tie— silk, probably—a white shirt covering a nice broad chest and a black leather belt with a platinum buckle emphasizing a lean waist and hips.

"There are laws against kidnapping." His voice, soft and subtly accented, lashed out like a whip.

Never mind that he looked like a male centerfold or movie star, his words ignited Millie's temper. She could only be nice to a point. How dare he make accusations when *he* was the one at fault.

"Kidnapping?" Her heart thumped and her hands trembled. "You know, it just figures a man like you would automatically put the blame for his own shortcomings on someone else.''

He drew back his shoulders, looking utterly appalled that she'd spoken to him in such a forward manner.

''Going on the offensive will not confuse the issue, as I am sure you intend.'' He removed a small cell phone from his pocket and flipped it open. ''I should report you to the police department.''

Oddly enough, she realized that his hand wasn't all that steady. She nearly reached out to him. He'd clearly had a scare to find his son had wandered off. But his terse voice and piercing obsidian eyes nixed her sympathy like a splash of ice water.

Millie perched her hands on her hips. ''You go right ahead and call the police, buddy. In fact, I'll be happy to do it for you. I'm sure they'll be as interested as I am to know where the heck you were all the time your little boy was wandering around on his own. Do you think the Space Needle is anyplace to just let a child run free? What's the matter with you anyway? And how do I know this is even your child?''

Although it was obvious Sam was perfectly comfortable in the tall man's arms, she nevertheless directed her attention to the little boy.

''Sam, is this your father?''

''Yes.'' He nodded as he answered, pride evident.

''How do you know my son's name?''

Several people looked their way when he hurled the question at her.

''Would you lower your voice? If you keep standing there acting like a big brute, someone's liable to think you're threatening me.''

He took a deep fortifying breath, then set Sam down on the ground, keeping his hand on the boy's shoulder.

"I said you could not confuse me by going on the offensive, but I stand corrected. I am thoroughly confused. And for the record, I do not threaten. I generally do what I say. Now, you will enlighten me as to why you were attempting to leave with my son, and how you came to know his name."

"I wasn't *leaving* with your son. He followed us onto the elevator, and if you'd given me a half a second, you would have known I was coming right back off the elevator to find Sam's missing parent. And I know his name because he told me…well, actually, he told Lindsey, but that doesn't really matter. The fact is, you were too busy talking on the telephone, or whatever it was you were doing, and your child wandered off. You're just darn lucky it was me he hooked up with and not some crazy person."

He stared at her for so long she nearly squirmed. Stubborn man. Hadn't he ever heard of an apology? Or gratitude? Obviously not.

"Do you always speak so quickly?" he asked.

"When I have something to say, I say it." She stabbed the elevator call button, pleased when the doors opened immediately. Beneath the scowl, she could have sworn she saw a hint of amused indulgence in his deep brown eyes. It set her off balance.

Darn it, this man had been negligent with his kid and downright surly with her!

Surely he wasn't *flirting*.

"Look, I'm late for work, otherwise I'd be happy to spend the day in your charming presence." She drawled the last two words in case he was too full of himself to catch the sarcasm. "That boy is precious cargo. Try to remember that when you get wrapped up in your little cell phone dealings.'' Taking Lindsey by the hand, she stepped into the elevator.

"And you're welcome," she added sweetly just as the steel doors swished closed.

Millie leaned against the elevator wall, her body quaking like an aspen in the wind. She wasn't one to run from confrontations, but they took all the stuffing out of her.

"Wow, Mimi," Lindsey said in awe. "I thought you were gonna give Sam's daddy a time-out."

She found the energy to laugh. "If I'd thought about it, pet, I would have."

JEFF STARED at the closed elevator doors, not quite sure what had just happened. Had the world gone mad, or was it just him? His insides still shook from the terror of realizing his son was missing. Then to find him on an elevator in a strange woman's arms... How could the woman possibly question his reaction? He had every right to behave exactly as he had.

He glanced down at Sam. His son's small hand, clutched tightly in his own, felt so fragile.

An ache built in his chest and pushed upward to his throat, surprising him. He'd been emotionally numb for so long, he'd begun to accept it as normal. The gut-wrenching panic he'd felt when he couldn't find Sam proved that he had jarred loose another layer of the ice that shrouded his battered soul.

He crouched beside his son and brushed a hand over his hair, needing to touch him. "Are you all right, son?"

"Yes. They were nice, weren't they?"

Nice and feisty, Jeff thought. As well as disrespectful, bold, outspoken...protective. He hadn't been so thoroughly confounded—and *intrigued*—by a woman in a long time.

"You know better than to wander off and talk to strangers, Sam."

"I didn't wander far. I could still see you...mostly." Sam scuffed the toe of his loafer against the floor. "I just wanted to talk to a kid my age."

Jeff pulled his son between his thighs and held him against his chest. Although this trip to Seattle was for business, he'd brought Sam with him, intending to reaffirm their father-son bond. He'd also hoped to find a way to draw Sam out of the pensive mood he too often slipped into.

They'd planned to stay at his penthouse condominium in the city so Jeff could show Sam the sights in Seattle between business meetings. But someone had breached the security system in his home, then flaunted the cunning feat by leaving a note on the desk in Jeff's study. The words made no sense: "I will be you."

He and Sam were traveling only with Amala, Sam's nanny, and Zaki, who was more of a family member than an employee. All four of them had been asleep and vulnerable while a deranged trespasser left a cryptic calling card. That thought sent icy fingers up his spine.

Vulnerability was inexcusable. Caution and unblinking control were the only way a man could protect himself and his family. He'd forgotten that lesson once, and it had cost him dearly.

So, he had summoned his minister of security, who'd flown out immediately and taken charge, insisting they relocate to a more secure residence. Sadly, that protective move only increased Sam's loneliness. The most secure piece of real estate Jeff owned in Washington was too far from the city to allow for spur of the moment sightseeing.

Watching his son's quiet acceptance of their change in plans had been difficult. Jeff felt as though he'd advanced two steps, only to be knocked down another five. He'd wasted so much time over this past year and was trying like hell to make up for it. Although he was getting the hang of single fatherhood, he stumbled on occasion. And he still had business obligations.

The breakdown in security had been a wake-up call, and when he'd taken a good look around, he'd realized that Amala paid more attention to her needlework than she did to Sam. She was a member of his late wife's family, but the woman was lazy. He no longer trusted her with his son's care, so he'd sent her home.

He'd managed well enough these past four days by rescheduling meetings and appointments, but he could no longer put off the inevitable. He needed to find a replacement nanny. And Sam needed a child his own age to play with.

He kissed the top of Sam's head, wondering how a man whose spirit had been ripped away could possibly feel his heart swell with such love for his boy.

Reaching in his pocket, he retrieved his cell phone.

Sam eased back, still standing between Jeff's thighs. "Do you have more business to take care of?"

"Business for you." He straightened Sam's shirt, an excuse to touch. "I have a friend who lives in Seattle. Her name is Katherine Kinard. We attended a year of college together, and we keep in touch when I am in town. She happens to own a day-care center."

Sam frowned. "Are you going to send me to baby-sitting school?"

"No way, champ. You are staying with me. But I would like to see if she has a nanny available. One who has a son or daughter around your age so you will have someone to play with. How does that sound to you?"

Sam's smile lit up. "I liked the girl on the elevator."

Jeff merely raised a brow and checked the stored numbers in his phone. He wasn't sure if Sam meant the little girl or her mother. Either way, the boy was out of luck.

Even if Jeff *did* know the woman's name, and she *did* by some miracle work as a nanny, there was no way in hell he'd hire her.

Something about her spelled trouble with a capital *T*. Shoulder-length curly hair, compact sexy body, intriguing gray-blue eyes and a mouth that could make a man forget his own name.

Exactly the kind of trouble he didn't want or need in his life. Not now. Not ever again.

He located the entry for Forrester Square Day Care and pushed the call button.

The type of woman he intended to hire would *not* be a temptation like that little blond vixen.

CHAPTER TWO

"THIS WAS the best shower, you guys. Thank you." Hannah Richards kicked off her shoes and settled comfortably on the plump, chintz-covered sofa in Katherine Kinard's living room.

Millie smiled and put away a crystal bowl in the china cabinet. The bridal shower guests who'd come to honor Hannah had left, and Katherine's small home was restored to order—aside from the stack of gifts spilling over the lace-covered dining-room table. It was still early, and Lindsey had fallen asleep on Katherine's bed, so Millie was looking forward to unwinding for a few minutes with her three closest friends.

Katherine Kinard, Hannah Richards and Alexandra Webber were co-owners of Forrester Square Day Care and had known each other since childhood. Millie had met Katherine and Hannah the day of her parents' funeral, when the two women had come to pay their respects to Selma Gallagher, who'd been catering for Hannah's family for years.

Millie had been clutching her baby sister, trying not to think too far past the moment. She'd been eighteen, racked with pain and terrified over what lay ahead. Yet at the same time, she'd desperately wanted to dump her interfering Aunt Flo into an empty casket in the storeroom of the mortuary. Katherine seemed to pick up immediately on what was going on and had smiled in understanding from across the room. Both she and Hannah had simply reached out their hands in friendship to Millie and she had gladly accepted.

They'd been an absolute godsend. They'd helped her wade through the red tape of insurance policies, dragged her out of the house when she'd worn the same sweatpants four days in a row, linked arms and formed a human blockade when Aunt Flo had tried to bully her way into the house to take Lindsey. And when Katherine had talked Alexandra into coming back to Seattle last year to be a partner in the day care she and Hannah had started, Millie and Alexandra had clicked as though they'd known each other for years.

"Your mother did most of the work," Katherine said to Hannah now as she breezed through the dining room and snatched the dish towel off Millie's shoulder. "I just supplied the house."

"Nonsense," Olivia Richards said. Sitting in one of the overstuffed Queen Anne style chairs flanking the coffee table, she reached for her cup of tea, looking secretly pleased with the acknowledgment. "Although I was delighted to help out. It was a wonderful turnout."

Sometimes Millie wondered how Hannah could be related to Olivia. Hannah was so warm and down-to-earth, and though she'd had a financially comfortable, privileged upbringing, there wasn't an ostentatious bone in her body.

Her mother, on the other hand, was a tough one to figure out. At fifty-six, Olivia Richards looked every inch the wealthy lady of the manor—even though she was technically in *Katherine's* manor just now. With her perfectly styled light brown hair, flawless skin and trim figure, she could almost pass for Hannah's sister. A ruby ring with diamond baguettes sparkled on her finger, drawing attention to acrylic nails painted in a glossy French manicure.

Olivia's correct posture and somewhat formal manner of speaking reminded Millie of the man and boy she'd met at the Space Needle earlier today.

Oh, great. Why in the world couldn't she stop thinking about him? He'd been rude, scowling, rigid—not to mention lax in his parental duties. Certainly not the kind of man she'd go for. If she had the time to even *go* for a guy. Between work and Lindsey, romance didn't fit into her life right now.

"Let's all take a load off our feet," Alexandra said, plopping down onto the sofa without an ounce of grace, earning a disapproving glance from Olivia. Clearly unconcerned, Alexandra gave her short red hair a quick fluff with her fingers. "And don't even think about cutting out early, Millie. Lindsey's asleep, you have the rest of the night off and you're *ours*. So get over here and park your skinny butt."

Millie had been looking forward to an evening of girl talk so she only gave a fleeting thought to the dirty laundry she'd left sorted in piles on the floor of the laundry room, and the bills waiting in the antique secretary desk that still needed checks stuffed into the envelopes.

"My butt's no skinnier than yours is," she said, pushing up the sleeves of her green sweater as she crossed the living room of the small cottage. "You're just jealous because it's *younger*."

"I swear, you two need a referee," Katherine said, sitting down in the overstuffed chair opposite Olivia.

Millie folded her legs as she lithely sank to the floor and leaned her back against the sofa, giving Alexandra's leg a playful whack. She noticed that the thick, chintz-covered photo album on the coffee table in front of her had a smear of frosting on the edges of the plastic inserts.

"Now, look what someone did." She flipped open the album and used a cocktail napkin to wipe off the mess. "This is going to be sticky. Too bad *someone* snatched away my damp dish towel."

Katherine laughed and scooted forward to get a better look at the photo Millie had just rescued from buttercream icing. "Check out those bell-bottom pants. Isn't it crazy how styles go in and out?"

"Don't be picking on those pants," Millie warned as everyone shifted closer to study the picture. "Alexandra's mom clearly stole them from my closet. They look exactly like the ones I'm wearing." Sure enough, Carrie Webber wore lace-up hip hugger jeans with a ski sweater that barely reached the waistband. "I might not have gone for the cropped top in winter, though. Good thing her jacket had a zipper or she'd have gotten frostbite."

Alexandra smiled wistfully. "My mother never grew out of her flower child phase."

"Look at *my* mother's hair," Hannah commented with a laugh. "You look like a pampered poodle who's just come from the groomers, Mom."

Olivia leaned forward to study the tightly curled perm. "I should have fired that hairdresser."

"Was this photo taken in the San Juan Islands?" Millie asked. A rare snowfall covered the ground and frosted the needles of juniper and spruce trees.

"Mmm," Hannah said. "We had a vacation house there. Our families used to get together a lot."

Millie glanced over her shoulder, waiting for Hannah to go on. That's when she noticed that Alexandra had suddenly gone still and pale. She shifted the album and reached out to her friend.

Katherine noticed, as well. "Alexandra? Are you okay?"

"I'm fine. It's just…no, never mind."

"What?" Millie prodded.

"It's these nightmares about the fire. They're becoming more vivid. Looking at the picture just now, I got a flash and—"

The cup of tea in Olivia's hand crashed to the table, splattering hot liquid over the wood surface. Everyone jumped up like scalded cats. Millie ran to the kitchen and grabbed a towel and a bottle of club soda in case any of the brew made its way to the carpet.

Millie had been too young to remember the fire in 1983 that had destroyed Alexandra Webber's home and taken the life of her parents. It had been a horrendous time for the families of all three women—Katherine, Hannah and Alexandra. Their fathers were partners in Eagle Aerotech, a computer software company, and they lived close to one another in Forrester Square, a prestigious neighborhood in the Queen Anne district.

There was barely time to mourn the deaths of Jonathan and Carrie Webber because Katherine's father, Louis Kinard, was arrested and sentenced to jail for embezzlement and the sale of classified information from Eagle Aerotech.

Alexandra, who was sent to live with relatives in Montana, had been plagued with nightmares since the fire.

Now that she'd returned to Seattle, the dreams were becoming more disturbing. Millie knew that Hannah and Katherine were worried about the effect this was having on Alexandra's health and happiness.

Once the spilled tea was cleaned up and Olivia had sufficiently expressed her embarrassment and apologies, Millie waited to see if Alexandra would say any more about the memories the photo had triggered, but the moment was lost.

Hannah decided to call it an evening, and that prompted a gathering of purses and several trips to the cars to load up gifts. Millie brought out the leftover cake she'd wrapped up and put it in Hannah's car, then hugged her friend close.

"I'm so happy for you and Jack," she said. "It's like a fairy tale, that you loved him all those years ago, and now you've found him again, and your son, and a new baby's on the way. You deserve every bit of the happiness I can see in your eyes."

When Hannah was unable to speak past her emotions, Millie lost the battle with her own tears.

"Oh, would you just look at us," she said. "Why do we get all drippy when we're *happy?* It's ridiculous." She laughed and swiped at her eyes. "Take your pregnant hormones home before we find something else to cry about. And do me a favor. When you're done with that fairy godmother, would you send her my way? I could use a fairy tale myself."

Hannah laughed and opened her car door. "I'll give her directions to your front door."

Millie linked arms with Katherine as they waved off Hannah, then Olivia and Alexandra. When only Millie's Volkswagen remained in the driveway, they turned and walked back to the house. "I should get Lindsey and head home, too."

"I need you to stay for a few minutes," Katherine said. "Let's go sit in the kitchen."

"Sure." Millie felt a slight quiver of unease as she joined Katherine at the table. "What's wrong?" Millie asked.

Katherine grinned. "Nothing's wrong. In fact, it's very right. I have a job for you—"

"A job? I have three of those already, if you count my nighttime baby-sitting jobs. And since I sit for different families—"

"Would you hush and pay attention? It's for two weeks. You'll be the nanny for a visiting businessman's six-year-old son. It's out on a privately owned island near the San Juans. He requested a single mother because he wants his son to have a playmate while he's here. Lindsey fits that bill. And the pay is a flat forty thousand. So, what do you think? Do you want the job?"

Millie blinked. Her head whirled and she could hardly think at all. Forty *thousand* dollars? Just to be certain, she glanced behind her to make sure Katherine wasn't speaking to someone else. The room was empty.

She finally found her voice. "Forty…thousand?"

"Twenty grand per week." Katherine pressed her smiling lips together. Clearly, she was having a difficult time containing her glee.

Millie didn't know *what* she was feeling. Stunned. Bewildered. Confused. Excited. She knew she was in danger of jumping on top of the table and doing the Snoopy dance.

"Who the heck can afford to pay that kind of money?"

"Jeffri al-Kareem. He's an oilman. Forty grand is chump change to him."

"Good grief. That's way beyond *my* scope of imagination." She needed to think logically. For the life of her, she couldn't formulate all the questions she should ask. "Do I even know how to be a nanny?"

"It's just baby-sitting, Millie, with room and board included."

"Will there be anyone else out there on the island?"

"Oh, yes. You won't be alone in the house with him. He'll have others on staff. I wouldn't offer you a job I thought was risky, Millie. I happen to know Jeff, and he's a good man. I met him years ago when he spent a year at Washington State University. His wife died a while ago, and he's turned into a workaholic. His boy needs someone to look after him. And frankly, Jeff's gotten a little stuffy lately. I think you'd be just the one to shake up his household a bit. Your personality and your love of life are irresistible, and you're a natural with kids. Who could resist you?"

"I'd be there to take care of the child, Katherine, not shake up the man. But how am I supposed to accept a job when I already have two? Or three?"

"I've got the ball rolling on that. I asked Tansho if she could cover for you if you took the assignment." Tansho was the Japanese woman who came to the day-care center every morning to deliver fresh produce from the International District. "That baby looks like it's ready to pop out, but Tansho keeps assuring me it's not time yet."

Millie simply nodded because her head was spinning.

"As for Caffeine Hy's," Katherine continued. "All you have to do is explain the circumstances to Hy, and he can have someone take over your shift for two weeks. You've been a loyal employee, Millie, and Hy adores you. He's not going to stand in the way of an opportunity like this."

The butterflies in Millie's stomach were multiplying, and her mind kept dipping back into the same groove. Forty thousand dollars!

Thankfully, a mortgage insurance policy had paid off the loan on the house when her parents had died, but there were still everyday things like taxes, utilities, food and medical expenses to cover. With her tips and salary combined, she made surprisingly good money working at Caffeine Hy's, but in order to make ends meet, there wasn't room in her budget for too many extras. Certainly not enough to reopen her mother's catering business, which she dreamed of doing.

"There's a hitch," Katherine said.

"A hitch?" Great, she was a parrot now. But darn it, she felt like Alice stumbling into Wonderland, except nobody had told her it was pretend. Emotions were swirling so fast she couldn't identify them.

Forty thousand dollars would mean so much to her and Lindsey. Besides allowing her the financial leeway to start her own business, she could get a jump on Lindsey's college fund—something she'd never be able to do working at a coffeehouse and baby-sitting.

"He wants you to start tomorrow."

Millie's head snapped up. "One night to pack and put two weeks of my life on hold?"

"I persuaded him the afternoon was better than the morning."

"You're such a pal."

"As a matter of fact, I am. And I happen to know that you move faster than all of us put together, so that deadline's doable. His boy's lonely, Millie. You'd be so good for him."

"Oh, you know just how to get to me. Why were you so sure I'd take the job? I mean, it sounds like you practically told him yes before you even approached me. You talked to Tansho—"

"Millie, it's forty grand! *I* was tempted to take the job. But Carlos isn't a young child." Carlos was Katherine's thirteen-year-old foster son, who'd been hiding in his room all night to avoid the invasion of women. "When Jeff called this morning, I honestly didn't think we could help him. Then Tansho stopped in my office, and when I saw her, it dawned on me that *you* would be ideal.''

''Pregnant women remind you of me? Did you forget a person has to have *sex* in order to develop that watermelon shape?''

''Not with artificial insemination, smarty. And the association I made between the two of you was the kitchen.'' Katherine reached across the table and put her hand over Millie's. ''You're great with kids, Mil, you could use the money and you can get two weeks off without jeopardizing your regular job. It's perfect.''

''That's what's scary. Perfection is usually hiding a thorn.'' Millie sighed. No way could she turn down an opportunity like this. ''Write down the details and I'll talk to Hy.''

''Super.'' Katherine sprang to her feet like an eager cheerleader celebrating the victory point. ''I'll call Jeff back and tell him it's a go.''

''Shouldn't you wait until I get the go-ahead from Hy? The coffeehouse is closed and I'm not even sure I can reach him at home.''

''Millie, Hy isn't capable of denying you a thing. He'll give you the two weeks—and two more if you asked.''

''Yes, well, I want that in writing. I'm not taking a chance that I'll flunk the interview with this guy or something, and end up coming home without a job to go to.''

''You're not going to flunk an interview. I've practically handled it for you.''

''Still, I need to do this my way. And I'll want to run it by Lindsey, as well.''

Katherine's eyes softened in understanding. With the exception of Aunt Flo—who had technically been her father's stepsister—Lindsey was the only family Millie had left. She was fiercely devoted to her sister, determined to provide stability and safety in a world she knew all too well could unravel the fabric of a person's life with one swift, devastating pull. Millie had learned to temper her need to overprotect, but she was scrupulously cautious and didn't take risks lightly.

"I'll wait until I hear from you, then," Katherine said.

Millie stood. Now that she'd put up a fuss, indecision plagued her. Mr. Kareem was clearly in a hurry to fill this position. What if he found someone else for the job before Katherine got back to him? Granted, it was well past business hours, but what if he had other personal contacts in the city?

She was being ridiculous. Lindsey would be thrilled to go on an adventure. School wasn't an issue because she'd just turned five in January and wouldn't start kindergarten until this fall. And Hy would give Millie his blessing in a snap. Heck, he'd try to tease her out of ten percent of the money.

It would be foolish to risk jeopardizing a once-in-a-lifetime deal like this. She had Lindsey's future to consider.

The decision made, her heart battered against her chest. She glanced down at Katherine. "I assume transportation is part of the package deal?"

"Yes, he'll send his yacht."

"His yacht." This time her stomach joined in the heart aerobics. Two weeks on a private island, probably living in a mansion, getting paid an obscene amount of money to care for two children—one of them her sister. This didn't feel like a job. It felt like she'd been tapped on the head by Hannah's fairy godmother.

"Call your oilman, Katherine. Tell him I'll be ready by one-thirty tomorrow afternoon."

ALTHOUGH SPRING sunshine had burned away the mist, Millie's teeth still chattered as briny wind whipped through her hair and chapped her cheeks. Lindsey had insisted they stand on the outside deck of the elegant yacht, which could have been a much more pleasant experience if Captain Mike wasn't such a hot dog behind the wheel. The temperature was a comfortable sixty-nine degrees, but at this speed it felt like minus ten.

At last, the yacht slowed and veered toward an island that looked like a small forest growing right out of the ocean. As they neared, the illusion transformed into a beautiful sandy beach, lush greenery and a private marina with its own twin-engine seaplane.

"Are you scared, Mimi?"

"Of what, sweetie?" Automatically she drew her sister close, cupping her hand over Lindsey's cold cheek.

"Baby-sitting for Mr. Cream and Samaal."

"It's Mr. Kareem," she corrected. "And I might be a little nervous, but not scared. Remember, I told you they're friends of Katherine's. And it's only for two weeks. It'll be a fun adventure. Check out this island, pet. Doesn't it look wonderful? Think of all the places we'll be able to explore."

The yacht eased alongside the dock and a crewman leaped off to secure thick ropes to sturdy metal cleats. Another man took their bags and disappeared through the trees. Watching the guy carry Pop's old Navy-issue duffel bag and Lindsey's small Scooby-Doo overnight case gave Millie a moment of panic.

Either she'd done an excellent job at packing light, or she'd forgotten a whole lot of stuff. In little more than twelve hours, she'd managed to attend to the details of putting a fully scheduled life on hold. Frankly, she felt like she'd been tossed into the stainless steel latte blender at Hy's, and her head was still whirling.

The yacht's skipper poked his head over the railing on the upper deck. "The house is just through those trees about a hundred yards, Ms. Gallagher."

She looked up, shading her eyes with her hand. "We'll find it. Thanks for the ride, Mike. It was fun."

The guy who'd tied up the boat held out a hand and helped them disembark.

Birds sang in the juniper and spruce trees that shaded the pathway leading away from the dock and the beach. The island was as lush as a tropical paradise, but the air had a crispness to it, a mix of tangy sea and icy mountain, and there wasn't a palm tree in sight. Millie was glad of her hooded pink parka. It wasn't fancy, but then, one didn't go baby-sitting in fancy clothes. That'd be pretty silly. Then again, maybe there were different requirements for nannies.

When they rounded the corner past the thick border of evergreens, Millie drew up short, automatically putting her hand on Lindsey's shoulder.

"Good grief. Why would someone hide a mansion behind a tacky wall when they live on a private island?" What she could see of the house beyond the stone wall was heavy stucco, tile and arches, with wrought-iron gates and security cameras discreetly placed to monitor movement. A bodyguard three times her size was obviously the gate patrol. "Guess there'll be no sneaking out in the middle of the night."

"Why do you want to sneak out?"

"Just kidding, pet."

"There's a little bridge over there," Lindsey said, pointing to a decorative wood arch that spanned a koi pond. "Maybe that big man is really a mean old troll and he's—"

Millie clapped her hand over her sister's mouth and bent close to her ear. "Shh, trolls don't live in a koi pond, and I'm sure the man is just a security guard." She uncovered Lindsey's mouth. "And shame on you. What if he heard you calling him a troll? Wouldn't it hurt your feelings if someone called you that?"

Lindsey's shoulders bobbed, her eyes guileless. "No. I like trolls."

Taking her sister's hand, Millie moved toward the stoic guy blocking the front gate. Tall, with a massive chest and bald head, the man was wearing a black suit that had to have been custom-made to fit his breadth. His skin was the color of rich caramel, quite striking against his snowy white shirt. He looked like a member of the Secret Service guarding the president.

"Hi." She smiled to cover her nervousness and to put him at ease. He probably had a gun under that jacket, and she didn't want him using it on her. What in the world had Katherine gotten her into?

"I'm Millie Gallagher, the new nanny. And this is Lindsey. I believe Mr. Kareem is expecting us…?" She laughed and a robin flew from the juniper tree. "That was pretty silly. Of course, he's expecting us. He sent that gorgeous boat to pick us up. Did you know it has teak on the floors, and marble in the bathrooms? That thing's furnished better than most homes. And…I'm talking too much. It's a curse, but what can you do? It's my first day—which you probably know."

The man's shoulders relaxed and he nodded. "My name is Sadiq. You may call me Deke if you wish."

Millie stuck out her hand. "I'm pleased to meet you, Deke. Should we just go on in, or what?"

Deke shook her hand. "Yes. You are expected." He unlocked the front gate and held it for her. She noticed that he smelled faintly of peppermint, as though he'd just bitten into a hard candy. "I will give you a full briefing on security and the layout of the island once you are settled in."

Security briefing? On a private island?

She and Lindsey walked through a courtyard that could have easily become an overgrown mess if some clever landscaper hadn't been so meticulous in its design. Hints of color sprouted among exotic greenery draped in pots and beds and even in a whimsical statuary frog. A cherub fountain splashed water in a serene flow over tiers of stone. The entrance smelled like a flourishing nursery, all damp earth, cool shade and wet stone.

At the double-door entry to the house, Millie pressed the button beneath an intercom box, and smiled down at Lindsey as the doorbell chimed eight notes.

The door swung open. She'd expected a butler or a maid, but...

Oh...my...gosh.

For an endless moment she stood paralyzed, stunned.

Scowling down at her was the incredibly virile, deliciously gorgeous, majorly surly man she'd had the misfortune to encounter at the Space Needle.

Peachy.

Good thing she hadn't burned any bridges with Hyrem.

"Mr. Kareem, I presume?" she asked when she found the wherewithal to unstick her jaw.

"*Al*-Kareem," he corrected. "Sheikh Jeffri al-Kareem from Balriyad. And how did you find my home?" he demanded.

Sheikh? *Oh, Katherine, you are toast.*

CHAPTER THREE

LINDSEY SLIPPED behind Millie's legs, clutching the ends of her coat. This wasn't going well at all.

"I didn't *find* you," Millie said. "I believe you sent your very charming man, Mike Brunelle, to pick me up in that really rad yacht."

His brows slammed down. "*You're* the nanny?"

Did he have to say it like *that?* She was feeling shaky enough because she couldn't honestly claim experience for that specific title. Straightening her shoulders, she tried to at least give herself the illusion of strength and height.

"My name is Millicent Gallagher, and I happen to be very good with children. Otherwise, Katherine wouldn't have sent me." *Lord, let me at least get in the front door!* Afraid he'd send her packing before she could overcome his objections, she took a calming breath and concentrated on speaking in a more subservient tone. Not an easy task, but she needed this job.

Sam darted out from behind Jeff, saving her from having to blatantly misrepresent herself.

"Lindsey! Millie!" He grabbed their hands, dragging them over the threshold into the foyer. "I did not know you did nannying! Remember, Father? I told you. She does not smell of fish like Amala—"

"Sam—"

"She smells like apples. Have a sniff, Father, and you will scc— "

Millie quickly knelt in front of Sam and grinned, which for some reason hushed him in midsentence. She had to distract herself from the fact that she was facing a sheikh, a small detail Katherine had neglected to tell her. Plus, little Sam was going to turn blue if he didn't take a breath.

"Goodness, Sam. You're going to wear us out before we've even said hello." She ran her fingers through his silky black hair, pushing it off his forehead, though it did little good as short strands fell forward again.

Sam's scowling father appeared a tad shell-shocked at his son's innocent suggestion to sniff the nanny. She didn't want the man angry. And she didn't want him embarrassed or befuddled.

She wanted him to honor his commitment and give her the job.

"I know you guys hate it when grown-ups send you out of the room," she said, "but could you do me a big favor, Sam, and go show Lindsey some of your toys while your dad and I have a talk? We need to discuss some business before anybody gets ahead of themselves."

"But you are staying, aren't you? Father sent Mike in the boat to pick up the nanny, and here you are."

"Yes, here I am. But I haven't even interviewed for the position yet. There might be complications."

The look on Sam's face nearly broke her heart, but she couldn't allow him to build expectations when she wasn't even sure Mr.—*Sheik* al-Kareem would want her to stay.

"Hey. No long faces, now. You never know when the frown grinch might be hiding around the corner, waiting to freeze unhappy faces. We have to be on guard at all times and remember to smile. Besides, smiling makes your insides tickle." To help him along, she gave his ribs a gentle squeeze, which sent him into a peal of laughter and caused Lindsey to join in.

"That's better." Millie stood and Sam darted over to Lindsey.

"C'mon," he said with typical six-year-old exuberance, "I will show you all my toys. You might not like them because they are boy toys."

Lindsey poked out her chin. "I play with boy toys all the time."

Uh-oh, Millie thought. Less than five minutes and the kids were headed for a sexism skirmish. She looked up at her potential employer. *They* might well have a battle, too.

Evidently Sam had a pretty healthy ego, because he didn't seem disturbed by Lindsey's pique. "I will race you," he challenged, and the kids were off like yard dogs turned loose on a rabbit.

"Stop," Millie said. It wasn't a shout, merely a change in tone. Lindsey skidded as though she'd hit an invisible barrier. Sam halted a few paces in front of her, both children turning to face Millie.

"Are we animals?" she asked, brows raised.

The kids giggled and shook their heads.

"I didn't think so. There will be absolutely no running in the house. Got it?"

Lindsey whispered something to Sam, her blond curls appearing white against his silky black hair. Then both children did a comical tiptoe up the stairs.

Millie turned, intending to remark on the kids' antics, but lost her train of thought when her face nearly grazed Jeff's chest. She hadn't realized he was standing so close.

She blinked. Swallowed hard. Took a step back. One of them was radiating some pretty potent vibes.

"You were very good with my son just now," he said thoughtfully.

She shrugged, still feeling off balance. "Running in the house is a pretty easy thing to fix."

"I meant before. You easily distracted Sam, and soothed his emotions. You were honest about your reasons for sending the children to play."

"No sense lying to them." She wasn't quite sure what he was getting at and wished she could read the thoughts behind the intense look in his eyes. "Sam's a neat kid, Mr., uh, Sheikh…"

She stopped and impatiently scooped a handful of curls off her face.

"Okay, this feels really stupid. I don't know what to call you or how to address you, so why don't you tell me up front so I won't goof up again. I don't want to insult you."

"Just call me Jeff."

"That works for me. And I'm just Millie. Now that we've gotten that out of the way, do you want to interview me or something?" She thought she saw his lips twitch, but wasn't sure. What in the world could he find amusing about a perfectly logical…

Oh, good gosh! *Or something?* He probably thought she was propositioning him!

A flash of heat scalded her face and she opened her mouth to explain, but he simply turned and walked away as though he hadn't noticed that her cheeks were suddenly flushed with telling color. Color that clearly wasn't a result of her drugstore-brand powder blush.

The curse of blond hair and fair skin.

She supposed she was expected to follow, so she did. He led the way into an office that was decorated in deep tones of burgundy with accents of gold, black wrought iron and dark wood. The ceilings were stamped copper, and the decorator had gone hog-wild with the ornate carvings. It seemed a bit busy in Millie's opinion, yet had a museum beauty to it.

"Please sit down."

She perched on the edge of the button-tufted leather chair facing Jeff's desk, too nervous to actually lean back. He was watching her like a hawk watches a field mouse— patiently, intently, waiting for the right moment to make his move.

Used to facing things head-on, she squared her shoulders. "So? Did you want to ask me any questions? I'm sure Katherine told you about me. You know about Lindsey—by the way, I'm curious. Why was it a requirement for the job that the nanny be a single parent?"

He lowered his brows. "I was under the impression *I* was conducting this interview."

"Oh. Of course." Wait a minute. That didn't feel right. He barked and she caved in. After the ordeal Aunt Flo had put her through, trying to take Lindsey away, Millie had sworn she wouldn't bow to intimidation. "In all fairness, I'm interviewing you, as well. Despite the generous salary you're offering, if I'm uncomfortable with you, I have every right to refuse the position."

He nodded, though he clearly didn't like her turning the table. "As I told Katherine, I wanted Sam to have a companion close to his age."

"So, if the applicant wasn't a single parent, it would be a deal breaker?"

"I am not sure why we are engaging in this line of questioning, Ms. Gallagher. Are you trying to tell me you are married?"

"Oh, no."

"And Lindsey's father? Where is he?"

"He died." It was the absolute truth. She just didn't mention that Lindsey's father had been her father, too. She wasn't sure why she kept that information to herself.

She just didn't want to risk anything that might make him send her packing. She desperately needed this money.

"I am sorry for your loss. And the deal breaker, Ms. Gallagher, would be the lack of a child the appropriate age, since I specifically requested a playmate for my son. Does that explanation meet with your approval?"

She wasn't sure if he was mocking her or trying to be helpful. She decided to hope for the best. "Yes, thank you. And it's Millie, remember?"

"I forget very little," he said softly, his gaze locked onto hers.

In a staring contest, he'd win hands down. Her heart thudded and her palms grew damp. He truly was the most gorgeous man she'd ever seen. And the oddest thing was happening. Each time their eyes met—accidentally or by design—the air between them came alive with something…something exciting, and frightening, as well. She had no idea how to describe it. A pull of attraction, yes, but she felt as if she could actually touch the transparent energy between them, as though it had substance.

And maybe she was hallucinating from lack of sleep. She shrugged out of her coat, using the action to break eye contact without letting it appear as though he'd won the round. For some reason, she figured that's exactly what he'd intended. To win.

"As for Sam's needs," he continued, "they are quite simple. I employ a staff, so you will not be required to prepare meals or do housework. Your only responsibility will be to the children—mine and your own."

Butterflies took wing in her stomach again. He was talking as though she had the job. "Actually, I love to cook. I'd be happy to help out in that area."

"I cannot see how that would be of benefit to Sam." He dismissed her suggestion without hesitation. "I have taken Sam out of school for this trip to Washington. The woman I brought from Balriyad was to have spent part of each day keeping up with his studies. I was displeased with her performance, and Sam was unhappy with her, as well—"

"It was the fishy hands that clinched it."

His brows slammed down again and he glared.

Uh-oh. Perhaps you weren't supposed to interrupt a sheikh. "Sorry."

He took a long breath, blew it out, then simply stared across the room. Millie turned around to see what he was looking at. When she didn't find anything out of place, she swiveled back, her gaze slamming directly into his. Her heart jumped into her throat.

"What?" she asked. "You were staring like there was someone behind me. Did you lose your train of thought?"

Jeff nearly fell out of his chair. That's exactly what had happened. He didn't know how she did it, but every time he was around this woman—which had been only twice, and briefly at that—she had him so confused and tied in knots, he didn't know which way was up.

Her casualness caught him off guard. He was used to formality and reserve—people following his orders without question, even fearing him at times.

He wondered if this petite woman in front of him feared anything. She was young and fresh faced. Bubbly. The kind of woman, he imagined, who would have a thirst for adventure and fun. He had an idea she wouldn't back down from a fight easily.

That might be a problem. Because Jeff was a man who was used to having complete control in his household.

She intrigued him, though. In the foyer, she'd reacted to him on a personal level. He'd felt it—the chemistry between them and seen it in the blush of her fair skin.

For that reason alone, he should send her right back to Seattle. He didn't want another woman in his life.

Then he remembered Sam's excitement when he'd seen Millie and her little girl. Sam hadn't been this animated since before Rana died. That had been over a year.

"Okay, now you're really freaking me out."

Startled, Jeff met Millie's gray-blue eyes. "Excuse me?"

"That should probably be my line. Didn't your mother ever teach you that it's impolite to stare?"

"Was I staring at you?"

She bit her bottom lip, then actually laughed. "Well, *that* was great for my ego. A man gazes into my eyes for a full three minutes, and I come to find out he's looking right through me."

She was definitely bold. He wasn't used to a woman speaking her mind so freely. During what he'd thought were the good years of his marriage, he had talked openly with his wife about everything. But Rana had been more reserved—at least that's what he'd thought.

Millie Gallagher had enthusiasm, energy and fire. And Jeff was determined not to get burned by that fire.

"I am not looking for a relationship, Ms. Gallagher. Just a caregiver for my son."

She cocked a brow at him. "Funny, just yesterday, I said very similar words to Katherine Kinard."

"And they were?"

"Let's just say I don't have room in my life for a relationship, either. I don't have designs on you, Jeff. But I adore your son, and I'd really like this job. I really *need* this job."

Oddly enough, her declaration that she wasn't interested in him felt like a direct hit to his ego. Never mind that staying uninvolved was exactly what he'd told himself he wanted. He'd also told himself he would never hire this woman if she were a nanny. The irony of fate.

"Since my son apparently feels the same about you and your daughter, you have the job." Her eyes filled with distress. Well, hell. "Is something wrong?"

Millie took a deep breath, folded her hands in her lap and looked him square in the eyes. Technically he hadn't given her a solid yes or no answer to her single-parent question, and she knew she wouldn't sleep until she laid all the facts on the table. She prided herself on honesty. When all was said and done, even omission didn't sit well with her.

"Lindsey is actually my sister." After four years, it wasn't any easier to talk about. "Our parents were killed in a car accident when she was barely a year old and I was awarded full custody."

"Which makes you a parent, does it not?"

"Yes."

"Katherine assured me you were qualified for this position. Are you having second thoughts about your abilities?"

"Good grief, no. I'm great with kids. Half the time I have more fun playing than they do. That's not a bad thing," she hurried to explain. "I'm not a pushover, either."

"I witnessed that myself with the running episode." His leather chair creaked as he shifted. "I am truly sorry for your loss."

"Thank you." He'd said similar words a few moments ago, but this was the first hint of true emotion in his voice. The very gentleness of it wrapped around her like a warm hug. "Some people offer those words simply because they don't know what else to say. But I know you understand. Sam told me about his mom. Your wife."

A muscle tensed in his jaw, and his head barely tipped in a nod. "I am told you work at Forrester Square Day Care."

Evidently the subject of his wife was off limits. Millie wasn't offended. She knew about the aching chasm of grief, the need to hide from it, the fear of emotions swelling out of control and rendering one unable to do even the simplest tasks of everyday living.

"Part-time," she said. "I also work at Caffeine Hy's—which is an excellent coffeehouse if you're ever in the city—and in the evenings, I baby-sit for various people in the community."

His dark brows drew together, creasing his forehead. "If you enjoy children, why do you not work full-time at the day-care center?"

"Because I make more money at Hy's than I can working full-time at Forrester Square. It works out better for me to fill in the extra hours with a part-time position."

"And Lindsey? Who watches her while you work the hours required for three jobs?"

"I do. I've chosen work environments that allow me to keep her with me as much as possible. It's important to me."

He studied her as though he could see into her soul. It made her nervous when he did that, but she tried not to squirm. If he *could* actually look into her soul, he certainly wouldn't see anything fancy.

"Why?"

Now it was her turn to frown. "What do you mean, why?"

"It is a simple question. Answer it."

She nearly laughed at the demand. Then she realized he was serious. Good grief. This guy was so used to commanding his subjects he did it without thinking.

"Why is it important to you, Millie?"

She had her mouth open to tell him she didn't do well with demands, but his soft tone sneaked right past the sensible part of her to the vulnerable layers beneath.

"Because that's what I had," she answered before she thought. "My parents had careers that were flexible, so I wasn't raised by sitters. Ours was the kind of house where all the neighborhood kids came to play, and friends stopped by because the coffeepot was always on, something just baked from the oven scented the air and everyone felt welcome and safe. I thought I was the luckiest kid in Seattle. If I wasn't with my mom in the kitchen or on one of her catering jobs, I was at Pop's side on a fishing boat. Lindsey was cheated out of what I experienced by our parents' premature deaths. She deserves the same advantages and happiness I had."

"You feel guilty?"

"Yes…and no. That's a hard question to answer. I mostly feel sad that she'll never know two really great people. But I can't change what happened yesterday or any time in the past. I can only do something about today and the future. And that, I *will* do." She had a lump in her throat the size of a boulder and energy to burn. If she was going to work here, she'd just as soon get started.

"So, am I staying on as Sam's nanny or not?"

"I thought we'd already established that you were."

She tried to keep her pleasant, the-boss-is-always-right expression in place. The facial muscles were a snap. The brain and tongue signals were another matter.

"That was before we cleared up the parental issue. You know, this is just a suggestion, but we might want to lay down some ground rules on communication. I've always told Lindsey that 'yes' and 'no' are the most efficient answers. They leave less room for misinterpretation. Do you agree with that?''

His obsidian eyes narrowed. She wasn't sure if he was appalled or stunned. Too late to take it back now. Besides, this was an important issue. How was she supposed to do her job if he didn't make himself clear?

''Yes, I agree it would be most efficient. Yes, you have the job. Yes, we need ground rules. And no, *we* will not be 'laying them down.' I will. Is that clear?''

''Absolutely.''

His brow arched.

She waited. ''Oh! Yes. Yes, it's clear.'' Good grief. The man was going to split hairs. She thought back on Katherine's words. *Jeff's gotten a little stuffy lately. I think you'd be just the one to shake up his household a bit.* Maybe that wouldn't be such a bad idea after all. For Sam's sake, at least.

She was anxious to get out of this office, check on the kids, and get to work, but she had one small problem. She wasn't quite sure what her duties entailed or where to begin. She hated to ask, especially since she couldn't read his present mood—he was doing the mannequin-mode thing. But she hated making mistakes more than she did asking stupid questions.

Slowly, she raised her hand cheek-height, palm out in case he was in another one of his trances and was looking through her. Evidently he wasn't. His features went from plasterlike to putty in a heartbeat.

''Mostly clear,'' she said, tucking her hair behind her ear. ''About the job part. I'm generally an excellent self-starter in a new position, but I'm feeling a little out of step with you being a sheikh and all. Would you mind giving me a little clarification? Is there anything special I should be doing? Or not doing? I mean, do you want me to just go upstairs and start watching the kids?'' She stood and started pacing the floor as her mind whirled with questions.

''The most important part of your job will be adhering to strict security rules. Sadiq, my minister of security, who met you outside, will explain the alarm system to you.''

A twinge of unease halted her pacing. ''Is there a reason you're overly security conscious?'' If hanging around this guy would put Lindsey in any kind of jeopardy, Millie wanted to know now so she could call a halt to the deal.

''It is a part of our lifestyle—similar to your president and his family, who are guarded day and night by Secret Service agents.''

''Oh. That makes sense. Alarms aren't my favorite gadgets, but I'll adapt. So, where will you be while I'm with the kids? Are you going to hang out with us at all? Will you want to take Sam off alone? That's always nice, you know. Lindsey and I do that every chance we get. We call them our special days. And—'' She stopped. Her hands were doing their typical maestro gig, and Jeff was staring again.

She crossed her arms at her waist, tucking her hands away so they couldn't butt into the conversation again. It was the Irish blood in her.

''Did you want to say something?'' she asked.

The corner of his lips twitched, but his expression remained utterly bland. ''If I may.''

''It's your house.''

''I am glad one of us remembers that. As for the time I spend with my son, I cannot give you specific schedules. I have business to conduct—''

''But I thought you brought him on a vacation?''

The pencil in his hand snapped.

Millie's gaze darted from the fragments of slivered wood and lead to Jeff's unblinking gaze.

"Rule number two." His voice was utterly calm, pleasant even. "The party speaking will finish his sentence before the second party commences speaking."

"Sorry. Katherine said you were a visiting businessman here for a couple of weeks. I assumed vacation." She shrugged. "That, plus the things Sam said the other day at the Space Needle."

"Perhaps you should tell me about these subjects my son discussed—besides the revelation of Amala's odorous hands."

The barest twinkle of amusement in his dark eyes coupled with his oh-so-slight, exotic accent was a potent combination. One she liked just fine.

"I believe he said they smelled like fish," she corrected, "although I can't imagine Sam not liking someone based on an odor. In my experience, kids are pretty candid about those things They'll usually tell the person right to their face that they stink and that's that."

In the midst of tipping back his chair, he jerked to a halt. The chair rocked forward again and his feet hit the floor.

"And the only other things Sam told me that day," she continued, "were that his mom was gone, his father was rich—actually, he told that to Lindsey, but I was standing right there—and that you talked on the telephone all the time. Oh, and that you wouldn't care if he rode the elevator by himself—which is the kind of fib kids tell when they want to get their way."

"But you knew it was a fib?"

"Of course. When it comes to kids, I'm good."

"I could use you in my company. I am always looking

for people who have a strong self-image. That is three-quarters of the game in success.''

She smiled. ''Thanks for the offer, but I plan to be the boss of my own company. My mom was a caterer and I'm going to rebuild her business. I still have most of her equipment and she taught me all about the industry from the ground up. Now that my finances are looking up, I'll be dipping my toe into the entrepreneur pool once Lindsey starts kindergarten.''

''So that's why you offered to help Zaki in the kitchen.''

''Yes, and I'm dying to get a look at the one in this place.''

He stood and came around the desk. ''Then please allow me to fulfill your wish. We cannot have the new nanny expiring before she even begins.''

''See there? You *can* joke around.''

He touched the small of her back, a simple gesture indicating she should precede him out of the room. Heat shot up her spine, spreading over her chest and neck. For a moment she stood frozen, unable to move.

She didn't have a lot of experience with this sort of thing, but for a bare instant, he looked as stunned as she felt.

He dropped his hand at the same time she took a step to the side. Neither one commented on the synchronous movement.

Wouldn't you just know it, she thought. For the first time in years, she actually had a little breathing room to contemplate a relationship, but the man who made her heart skip was so far out of her league she felt ridiculous even thinking about it.

CHAPTER FOUR

JEFF FISTED HIS HAND, his palm still tingling. What the hell was happening here? Millie Gallagher was beautiful, yes, but a woman's looks had never given him a punch of desire straight in the solar plexus.

"I, uh…I should check on the kids before we fulfill any…um, wishes." She took a breath and tugged at the hem of her sweater, then smiled. "I probably shouldn't have left Lindsey alone right off the bat like this. There's no telling what she'll talk Sam into doing."

"The children are not alone. Sadiq is with them."

"How do you know? He was outside when I came in and I've been with you ever since. Do you have a pair of eyes I don't?"

About to urge her forward once more, Jeff stopped. At this rate it would be dinnertime before they made it across the foyer.

"Sadiq has been assigned to Sam since the previous nanny was sent home. And since Sadiq has a sweet tooth, chances are very good that we will encounter them in the kitchen. Despite your unfortunate first impression of me the other day at the Space Needle, I do regard my son as precious cargo and I make every effort humanly possible to keep him safe."

"I realize that now. You can bend over to tie your shoe and kids will flit off somewhere. It's terrifying. Especially in today's climate of child abductions. That's part of what prompted my reaction to you—that and your lack of gratitude.''

Honest to a fault, and chastising his manners in the bargain. He understood, but damn it, he'd had good reason for his actions.

''I was frightened out of my mind,'' he said in his own defense. ''My telephone rang while I was paying for sodas at the café. When I looked up, Sam was gone. Evidently, I headed the wrong way on the circle deck, and by the time I saw my son, he was on the elevator and a strange woman had her arms around him. Under those circumstances, what conclusion would you draw?''

''Probably the same one you did...at first.'' She stressed the last two words.

''I am not an emotional man, Millie. But I do owe you my gratitude. Sam told me you insisted on finding me. He thought I was still at the café, so he was not worried about making his way back to me. At times, he is more independent than I like. I am glad it was you who watched over him.''

''Thank you for telling me. The image I carried in my mind of you holding Sam in your arms so protectively just didn't seem to gel with that of a negligent father.''

''You have been thinking about me?''

''Don't read too much into it. I was pretty disturbed. Lindsey thought you'd get a time-out for sure.''

He frowned. ''Are we discussing sports now?''

''No. Attitude adjustment. When kids misbehave or aren't playing well with others, they're sent to their room or somewhere by themselves for a designated length of time to think about their actions. It's called a time-out. The fidgety kids can't stand it. The daydreamers don't mind a bit. Personally, there are days when I wish somebody would give *me* a time-out and send me to *my* room.''

"You are welcome to retire upstairs and rest if you like."

She laughed. "No. I was kidding."

He noticed that she did nothing in half measures. Including laughing. There was a joy that seemed to radiate from her, and made him want to bask in it and absorb some for himself. Yet from the moment he'd laid eyes on Millie Gallagher, he'd felt as though every shred of normalcy had spun out of his control. He couldn't figure her out, nor did he trust his usually sharp instincts in reading a woman's thoughts and signals.

By damn, this spunky little blonde made him feel as though he was standing on a sheet of slippery marbles.

They finally made it out of the office door and headed across the foyer—this time with a respectable two feet between them. He didn't want to chance another of those electrical jolts he'd felt moments ago.

"What was it that prompted my son to volunteer information on my wealth at the Space Needle?" Jeff asked.

"They wanted to buy 1,320 candy bars."

He glanced down at her, shook his head and kept walking.

Millie counted each step her tennis shoes took on the stone floor. She didn't think she'd get much farther than five. Heel-toe-one, heel-toe-two, heel-toe-three, heel—

"All right, I will bite. Why would two six-year-old children want exactly one thousand and something candy bars?"

Millie grinned. "I knew the curiosity would get to you. Lindsey's only five, by the way. And if you'd played the trivia games on the observation deck with your son, you would know that's how many candy bars stacked end to end it would take to equal the Space Needle's height. Lindsey decided they couldn't conduct their own experiment because her pocketbook wasn't quite flush enough to buy that much candy, but Sam assured her that you were the man for the job.''

"And what did you think?''

"That they were just being imaginative kids.''

"I meant about Sam's comment. Weren't you curious to find the wealthy man who could purchase thirteen hundred chocolate bars?''

"Jeff, *I* could buy that much candy—if the store stocked that amount, and if I was crazy. Which I'm not.'' She knew darn well he was asking a much deeper question, but she wouldn't be led there.

They didn't know each other well enough, nor was theirs a relationship where he should be concerned whether or not she was a gold digger. Despite the fact that he was paying her an obscene amount of money for two weeks' employment, *he'd* been the one to set the price, and neither of them had known they actually had a nodding acquaintance with each other.

"And at the time,'' she continued, "it was best for your sake that I *didn't* try to find you. I can be pretty fierce when it comes to kids.''

"In my country, it is against the law to threaten a powerful leader.''

"It is here, too, but under the same circumstances, I'd be just as steamed at the president.''

Amazingly, he smiled. Lips only, no teeth showing. But it was a smile. It transformed his face, softening his eyes to a velvety French-roast-coffee brown and easing the masklike tension in his features. He was even more handsome—if that was possible.

"What are you—about five feet?''

She straightened her spine. "Five-one-and-a-half.''

"I think your president is safe.''

He skirted a grouping of overstuffed chairs and she followed behind him. "Go ahead and mock me. But keep in mind, explosives are often disguised in little packages, and that's not something—or someone—the average person wants to mess with."

He stopped so fast she plowed right into his chest. She had no idea how *that* happened. One minute she was talking to his broad back, and the next thing her lip gloss was smeared on his white shirtfront and her hands were clinging to his biceps. Nice ones, too.

No smile this time, she noted. Just a look hot enough to smoke a skillet. And so were the hands cupping her elbows to steady her.

"I am *not* the average person, Ms. Gallagher. That, you will want to remember." His eyes dipped to her mouth. "Do you understand?"

No. Maybe... "Yes. Um, of course." She felt as though she'd been put on notice. A warning of sorts. She might be inexperienced, but she knew sexual sparks when she felt them. And they were arcing pretty darn fiercely.

The part she wasn't sure about was, did he think she was coming on to him and he was warning her to knock it off? Or was he intimating that he was attracted to her and she should tread carefully lest he lose control?

Frankly she didn't care for either possibility. And why the heck should *she* shoulder the responsibility for *his* libido?

If that's even what he meant. Good grief. Two brief encounters with the man and every thought in her head managed to slide right to sex.

"I am glad we understand each other," Jeff said.

Speak for yourself, Millie thought.

Releasing her elbows, he stepped back.

She shouldn't speak. A truly prudent woman would call

it a day and regroup. She'd been hired for a dream job on a paradise island that paid a king's ransom. It wouldn't scar her for life to keep her opinions and curiosity to herself for a mere two weeks.

Besides, this was a man she had no business fooling around with—likely more man than she could handle.

Millie sighed. It was a crying shame she hadn't been more attentive to Mom's lectures on prudence. "Are house rules different from the ground rules we discussed in your office?"

"Yes. The ground rules are between us. And I am making them up as I go."

"Technically, *I* was the one who established the first rule. The clarification thing."

He uncrossed his arms, then didn't seem to know what to do with them for a moment. Finally he perched his hands on his hips and stared at her with an utterly bewildered expression on his face.

"Have you had difficulty with any of your other employers? Anything along the lines of, say, chain of command issues?" Jeff asked.

"No."

"No struggles over who is supervising whom?"

She shook her head. For the life of her, she wasn't following this conversational minefield. "You know, sometimes it's best to just dive right in and say what's on your mind."

"Fine. In plain English—I am the employer, you are the employee. I give the orders and you follow them."

Jeff crossed his arms over his chest again. A defensive gesture, he knew. He'd never had trouble commanding his staff, but those were hard words to get out. Millie Gallagher was a tiny thing, and strangely enough, he didn't want to hurt her feelings. It just felt…wrong, some-how, to pull rank.

Obviously, he needn't have worried. She was staring at him with those wide, blue-gray eyes as though waiting patiently for the punch line of a stupid joke.

Damn it, that *was* the punch line.

"Well?" he asked when she didn't fire back any verbal missiles.

"That's it?" She frowned, pushing springy blond curls away from her face. They fell forward again and his arm actually flinched with the need to touch, to brush away that single strand that stubbornly clung to her eyelashes.

"Jeff, I'm very grateful for this job," she said softly. "You can't know what this means to Lindsey and me. I honestly wasn't aware I'd disobeyed any direct orders. Especially since I haven't actually started the job."

Hell, now he felt like he'd stepped on a kitten. "I chose the wrong wording. I meant, I am not accustomed to hav-ing my every word challenged."

"So you say frog, and somebody leaps."

He had to think about that for a minute. Okay, it fit. "I lead, and those who work for me follow without question, yes."

"Doesn't that bore you? To have everyone agree with you, never express a contradictory opinion? I rarely think twice about sharing my opinions, and my bosses don't feel threatened by that. They welcome debates and sug-gestions."

"I am *not* threatened by your opinions."

"Frustrated, then."

"Somewhat. Not used to it is perhaps a better descrip-tion."

"Do you want to reconsider your decision to hire me?"

He studied her for several moments. On the one hand,

her candor continued to give him a jolt. On the other, it was refreshing. Now that he thought about it, he realized that most of the people he associated with were like puppets waiting for him to pull the strings. Lately, he'd blindly expected it.

There had been a time when he *hadn't* expected it, though. A time when laughter filled his heart and life flowed through his veins. A time when he'd traveled the world, had close friends all over the globe…married the woman he'd been engaged to since he was ten years old.

That had all ended over a year ago in the waters of the Mediterranean sea.

These days, only his son could spark embers of those emotions…and now, oddly enough, Millie Gallagher.

"No. I need a nanny for my son. And Sam appears quite taken with you."

Millie let out a relieved breath. "Will it be horribly painful to get used to my…opinions?"

"Not quite as high up on the scale as *horribly*."

"Fingernails on the chalkboard?"

He shuddered. "That's worse than horrible."

"Matter of opinion, I suppose."

"You mean you actually allow others to have their own?"

"Eventually."

Her smile hit him right in the gut, and her blond curls danced around a face he realized he'd seen in his dreams last night.

If he had an ounce of sense, he'd send her right back to Seattle. He didn't know what to expect from her, and while that intrigued him, the unwelcome attraction he felt for her distracted him.

He couldn't afford distractions. Not until he got Samco Oil established and running smoothly.

"Now, as promised, the kitchen awaits." He turned and led the way through the dining room, past a twelve-place, Gothic Revival table dressed in burgundy silk taffeta.

Opening the door to the serving room—an enclosed area separating the dining room and kitchen—he sketched a slight bow and waved her through.

She grinned and slipped beneath his raised arm. "I like a man who's a gentleman. They're a dying breed, you know."

If she'd substituted "a man who knows his *place*" instead of "gentleman," they'd have had a big problem. Why the hell had he expected her to say that? He definitely needed to regain the upper hand.

Closing the door behind him, he allowed his shoulder and chest to brush against her back, and she felt the tickle of her soft curls against his chin.

"No," he said softly. "I did not know we were on an endangered list."

Her chest rose on a deep breath, her sweater molding her breasts and hinting at the outline of her bra. She executed a slight pivot, breaking contact.

Pretty smooth. He knew he made her nervous, yet she hardly missed a beat. Cool under fire. Steady. Nice trait for the woman responsible for his child.

Not so great for his ego when he was trying to prove something to himself.

What he found most interesting—and most frustrating—about Millie Gallagher was that she did not answer a question or comment simply. He could say one word, and an instant later find himself swept up in a verbal typhoon, disheveled, dazed and amazed at the twists and turns the subjects took.

"You're staring again," she commented, taking a moment to caress the warming ovens, her gaze feasting on the wall of refrigeration boxes. He'd never seen anyone lust after appliances.

He swallowed and shoved his hands in his pockets. "I am debating whether to ask you a personal question."

"Go ahead. Chances are fifty-fifty that I'll answer."

"Fair enough. Do you always win debates in relationships?"

Millie rolled her eyes. "I'm too busy for relationships."

"On a date, then. With friends. Whatever. Do you have to have the last word?"

"Somebody's got to have it. I can't very well help it if the person I'm talking to doesn't have anything else to say."

"Maybe they are worn out," he muttered.

Millie felt a sting of surprise. Normally she would have laughed at his remark, but holding her own against this powerful man was beginning to take its toll. For some odd reason, every look or word between them seemed to spark a challenge. Two weeks of this, and spontaneous combustion was a given. Since that thought scared the very devil out of her, she decided a little less togetherness might be in order.

"I'll make you a deal. You introduce me to your staff, and I'll take care of myself from there. Just let me know when you're leaving the room, and I'll zip my lips and you'll get to have the last word. In fact, I don't have a problem handling introductions on my own, so you can go on back to work now if you want."

Faster than she could blink, his features melted into what was becoming a familiar mold of hardened detachment.

"The last time I checked, my name was still on the

deed to the house and island. I will decide when to dismiss myself.''

Said the cobra to the mouse, she thought. But Millie was no mouse. She had a pretty even temper, but certain attitudes and tones could make it flare into an uncomfortable, momentary sizzle. This was one of those moments.

She shrugged, then saluted for the hell of it. She'd be damned if she'd bow. Or admit to herself that she'd been stupidly deluding herself by thinking they were on the road to building a friendship. A combustible one at that.

And she would not, by so much as a twitch of an eyelash, admit that the foolishly naive misassumption hurt.

She held his gaze, knowing he expected her to look away. He was in for a good long wait. She might let him have the last word, and she would hold her conversation to the minimum, but she would not be intimidated.

Maybe she did talk too much. He just made her so nervous. Cocky behavior aside, this man's innate sexuality overwhelmed her. She'd never experienced anything like it, never been in the presence of someone who radiated pheromones that twined with hers like two curls of steam blending in the pull of a cooktop fan.

She'd been friendly ever since she was a child, but after Mom and Pop died, the tendency to run on at the mouth when she was nervous had blossomed. It came, she suspected, from the days and nights when she'd felt so alone and scared. A terrified, grieving eighteen-year-old suddenly responsible for a year-old baby, a house and an income—responsibilities she'd thought she would have plenty of time to ease into like the rest of her friends.

Three seconds on Interstate 5 had changed that.

Three seconds to grow up. And it had scared her to death.

So she talked. To herself, the baby, the walls, the washing machine when it peed water all over the kitchen floor. The van when it refused to start in the middle of Seattle's worst rain storm. The telephone when it wouldn't stop ringing because she'd accidentally bounced checks all over town. Teddy bears, leaves, ants marching in the house, a cricket in the heater vent—conversing with them created noise in a too-quiet house. It was a calming technique.

And if she talked out her problems long enough, she usually came up with the right answer to them. Mom always told her that deep inside each person was a treasure chest of knowledge that could validate what you already knew was the right thing to do.

Sometimes it took a while to find it, but Millie absolutely trusted that she would.

And what that knowledge told her right now was: To heck with Jeffri al-Kareem. He could take his too-sexy self back to his office and play king of the oil wells. She'd stay clear over in another wing of the house with the kids. Less chance of them butting heads.

Besides, this kind of annoyance wasn't worth the effort it would take to overcome. Mr. I'll-dismiss-myself oil tycoon lived halfway around the world and would only be here a couple of weeks.

A surge of pride leaped in victory when he looked away first. He tried to seem casual, but Millie knew different. He'd buckled under pressure, as she'd known he would. She'd had plenty of practice in stare-downs with Lindsey. A five-year-old in a snit could be quite stubborn.

"The kitchen is through here," he said, and turned toward an oversize set of glass-topped, swinging doors.

Like a perfectly sweet, malleable nanny, she followed

him into the kitchen without a word. And stopped dead in her tracks.

Oh! It was an absolute dream. Top of the line appliances, a grill, four ovens, four dishwashers, a commercial mixer sprouting right out of a granite countertop that shone like a reflection of lush pines swirled with ebony ribbons.

The room was at least thirty-by-thirty, maybe larger, and featured several work islands. She wanted to touch the mahogany, trace the incredible stained glass inserts in the cupboards, poke around in the cabinets and play with all the gadgets.

But just then, a man rose up from behind one of the work islands, a cookie sheet in his hand. He looked to be in his late fifties, and his once dark hair was shot through with gray. Shorter than Jeff—she liked him already—he had the round belly of a man who obviously enjoyed his own cooking, and his warm smile was very refreshing after spending nearly an hour in the moody sheikh's presence.

"Zaki," Jeff said. "This is Millie Gallagher. She will be Sam's nanny for the rest of our stay. Millie, this is Zaki—though he will be happy to have you call him Zac. He has been part of my family since I was a boy. If you have any questions, he is the man with the answers."

Zac grinned and came forward to shake Millie's hand. "It is nice to meet you, Ms. Gallagher. I have already met the little miss and she is quite the energetic one."

Millie smiled warmly. Zac's accent was much heavier than Deke's or Jeff's. "Please call me Millie. I hope Lindsey didn't give you any trouble."

"No, of course not. Sam has needed a playmate. She will challenge him. They have informed me, however, that Sadiq has a life-and-death craving for chocolate chip cookies with smiling faces on them. And no nuts," he added dramatically, holding one hand up in surrender, the other clutching the shiny cookie sheet. "Nuts will do scary things to Sadiq."

Millie grinned and relaxed for the first time today. She and Zac were going to get along splendidly.

"Sadiq likes nuts," Jeff said. "He eats them all the time."

Both Millie and Zac glanced at him to see if he was joking. Nope. She could explain that Lindsey was the one who didn't like nuts, but that would start a conversation, and she'd promised him he could have the last word between them.

He shifted on his feet and glanced around. "I have work to do still. Millie, I will expect daily reports from you on Sam. Evenings after he is in bed will work best. If anything arises, of course, you may come to me anytime. My door is open and I am available to my son and everyone in this household. So, do you have any other questions for me?"

She shook her head.

His brows drew together. "Millie?"

Damn. "No."

He studied her for a long moment, then turned and walked away.

Damn, damn! Hadn't she just given him a gaping wide opportunity to have the last word? This competitiveness they seemed to fuel in each other was ridiculous. But right now, it was bigger than she was.

"Jeff?" she called just as he reached the entrance to the serving corridor.

He turned. "Yes, Millie?"

She shook her head and waved him away in a "never

mind'' gesture. Without a word, scowl in place, he disappeared through the doorway.

When she turned back, Zac's sagacious eyes were watching her. Nonthreatening, gentle in fact, but the eyes of a man who knew loyalty and love.

"I have known Jeffri since he was ten years old. He can be, how shall I put it, difficult at times. But he has a good and decent heart."

"I'm just the nanny, Zac."

"Did I imagine it, or did I detect a bit of tension in the air?"

Millie desperately needed a few minutes' respite. She'd been on guard since the moment Jeff had opened the front door, and felt as though she'd been whirled in the blender, squeezed through the rollers of a pastry press, blasted in the oven, pried out of the pan, and splattered on the floor. Although she'd made it through in one piece, thank heaven, and had the job that would secure her and Lindsey's future, she needed a short break from thinking about her new employer.

"I'll tell you what, Zac. You give me the nickel tour of this place, starting with the kids' rooms, then we'll come down and I'll show you how to make those smiley faces on the cookies. By that time, if you can't figure out a possible reason for tension, then we'll talk."

CHAPTER FIVE

THE NEXT MORNING, Millie was up and dressed early enough to watch the sunrise through her window. It seemed odd that as Sam's nanny, she hadn't been assigned the room next to his.

Jeff had wanted a woman with a child so Sam would have a playmate. Then he'd put them half a mile apart.

What if Sam needed her in the night? And even now, she had to run down the hall to see if he was awake, then haul herself back to check on Lindsey.

Okay, this setup definitely had some bugs in it that she'd need to alter. Two perfectly good Murphy beds tucked discreetly in the walls of the sitting room were going to waste. The room was a combination playroom, media room and guest suite, connected to Sam's bedroom by a set of oversize double doors that were kept open, creating an eight-foot passage and a clear view from one room to the other.

It didn't make sense for her and Lindsey to mess up two additional bedrooms on the opposite side of the house. She'd been so busy yesterday just trying to figure out everyone's routine that the strange setup hadn't even dawned on her until she'd climbed in bed.

Well, she'd get it straightened out today. She left Lindsey sleeping as she went from the east wing of the house to the west wing, where Sam's room was located. It had taken the better part of yesterday to get her bearings.

Twice, she'd gotten lost merely going from the kitchen to the kids' rooms.

She trailed her hand along the banister of the open balcony landing, glancing down at the massive stone foyer and the separate stairways that swept in dramatic curves toward the opposite wings of the house. The interior reminded her of a castle with its tall, echoing ceilings, ornate carvings, heavy furniture and gilded accents everywhere. The decor might not be to her taste, but the architecture was truly stunning.

As she rounded the corner toward the last leg of the hallway leading to Sam's room, she passed a set of open double doors and glanced inside. The sheer size of the suite made her pause. Stone floors were softened by a rug in muted shades of burgundy, ivory and gold. A king-size bed upholstered in button-tufted fabric was elevated on a stone platform and flanked by heavy, dark wood cabinets. Satin sheets trailed on the floor as though the occupant had slept fitfully and just crawled out of them...

She realized the significance too late. Amid a billow of steam, Jeff stepped out of the bathroom.

Millie's heart jumped into her throat. She wanted to run, but her legs weren't going to obey.

Casually, as though women invaded his privacy on a daily basis when he was wearing nothing but a jet-black bath towel, he said, "Did you need something, Millie?"

She could have died. Her cheeks were on fire. "I am *so* sorry, Mr. al-Kareem. Truly." She knew her voice rang with sincerity, because she felt it. Deeply.

Focusing her gaze on the chaise by the marble fireplace rather than on Jeff's near nakedness, she attempted to explain. "I had no idea this was your room. I didn't mean to—I was on my way to see about Sam and...the doors have always been closed. At least, every time I've passed by they've been closed.'' Since she'd been there only one day, that excuse didn't justify gawking in someone's private room—whether they were there or not. On the other hand, why was she being so hard on herself? This time, she did look at him.

"What kind of person closes the door when they're *not* in the room, and opens it when they *are* in it?"

He gaped at her with a jaw-dropping expression, except of course he was too dignified to actually allow his mouth to fall open.

Well, Millie thought, feeling a slight tug of unease, this was not the finest way to start the day.

His features relaxed and he shook his head. "Millie, Millie. You were doing so well. I accept your apology."

On his tongue, her name sounded softly exotic. His voice could mesmerize, his body…oh, she wasn't going to torture herself with those images. Thankfully, she was too embarrassed to actually take a good look at him. The basic overview was potent enough.

"When I am in a room, I leave the door open so Sam knows where I am and feels free to come in. If the door is closed, he knows to look for me elsewhere."

"So…this is, like, an established routine?"

"Yes."

"Did you do it when the other nanny was here?"

"Amala's room adjoined Sam's. I didn't worry so much about him wandering."

"That's exactly what I want to talk to you about." Intent on her subject, she stepped into his room. "I don't understand why you hired me as Sam's nanny, then put me clear over in Timbuktu when—" She stopped, realized where she was standing, and clapped a hand to her forehead, her eyes trained on the floor.

"When what, Millie?"

"We shouldn't be having this conversation like…like this." My gosh, she couldn't *believe* she'd walked into the man's room! "I'll just step outside and—and let you get dressed in peace. We can talk when everyone has a shirt on and a certain party has boned up on her privacy manners. I do apologize again." Mortified, she backed toward the door.

"I did not put you in the room Amala was using because it also adjoins mine," Jeff said, causing her steps to halt at the threshold. "The sitting room connects to both Sam's room and this suite."

She lowered her hand and frowned. "Did it bother Amala to have three doors in her room?"

"She never mentioned it, no."

"Then why did you think it would make a difference to me?"

"Amala was an old woman."

Millie blinked. Was he inferring that she was a temptation to him? That he couldn't trust himself unless she was clear down the hall? Or was she projecting those thoughts on to him?

She didn't quite know how to handle the sizzling chemistry that reached out and zapped her every time she came within sight of this man. Even when she was annoyed with him, she could swear she smelled sulfur lingering from the sparks. The experience was both foreign and overwhelming.

But to allow a sophisticated man like Jeff to see that vulnerability was out of the question.

"So, you're saying that an old woman wouldn't open the connecting door to your room, but a younger woman would?" she demanded, folding her arms across her chest.

He arched a dark brow, and gestured to her foot, which was still halfway inside his room.

She snatched it all the way back into the hall. "That's different. These doors were open. And you've gotten two apologies out of me, which is my quota for the day, so don't expect another. Really, Jeff. Lindsey and I would be perfectly happy to switch rooms. I promise I have no designs on your person, I'm not going to jump your bones in the middle of the night, and I don't think you're going to come sneaking into my bed with Lindsey there."

He fisted his hands against the black towel. "The arrangements have been made, and they will stand. Sadiq is sleeping in the adjoining room when he is not on duty. You and Lindsey will remain in the suites assigned to you. They are larger and more comfortable anyway."

"I came here to do a job, not to be impressed by the five-star accommodations."

"I have given my decision."

Taking a breath, she counted to ten, then to fifteen, just to be safe. "As you wish."

With sheer determination, she clamped her teeth together. She wasn't going to say another word. Wasn't going to tell him how to run his household, even though he needed a total overhaul with an instruction manual in large print.

But like a scream that batters at your throat until you have no choice but to let it out, Millie's words came tumbling out.

"I understand that you're set in your ways when it comes to running your household," she said, her tone surprisingly nonconfrontational and her voice steady. "Being on the other side of the castle makes my job a bit more difficult, but I can adjust. However—"

"Somehow I knew there was going to be one of those."

He folded his arms across his bare chest, his brown eyes clearly filled with amusement. For a moment, she forgot what she'd intended to say. Her gaze skimmed from his arresting face to the towel tucked below his waist. With his arms crossed, his reflexes would have to be pretty fast to catch that towel if it slipped. She'd get a lot more of a show than she'd bargained for.

"However," she repeated, trying to ignore his laughing eyes, "for common decency's sake, you can't just parade around in here half-naked, or all the way naked for that matter, with the doors wide open. I have to walk by this room to get to and from Sam's room."

A smile actually curved his lips. It was amazing, made her knees weak.

"Do you not trust yourself to walk the hallway without looking into my room?"

"Honestly? No. And not because you're in it or because it's your room, so don't get a swelled head. It's human nature. If a door's open, you just look. If you know you're not supposed to look, well, then give it up. There's no way on earth you'll stop yourself."

"You have no self-discipline."

"I have plenty of self-discipline. But now that this is an issue, I'll end up having a panic attack just arguing with myself over whether to run this leg of the hall, or walk, or cover my eyes and sing 'Yankee Doodle.'"

Something hit his funny bone, because he laughed. Not a polite little chuckle. A full-scale laugh.

Well. Wasn't that something. A smile *and* laughter in one morning.

She felt her own lips curve. "You laugh. I dare you to walk past an open door, especially one that's usually shut, and not look in."

"If I accepted that dare, you'd have to follow me around twenty-four hours a day to find out, wouldn't you?"

"Not necessarily. Want to put a wager on it?"

He moved toward her with the unhurried grace of a jaguar. "Maybe."

Okay. *That* was a look she understood and didn't know what to do with. Sensual. Typically masculine. *Let me show you paradise. And then you can show me.* She was game for the first part. Way over her head for the second.

She could smell the soap from his shower, see a bead of moisture clinging to his collarbone. Since she was in the hallway, he really didn't have any business coming all the way out here to crowd her...to torment her.

Just when her heart was lodged firmly in her throat, her palms sweating, he leaned forward, his breath warm against her cheek.

For so long she'd dedicated her life to raising Lindsey. She didn't regret it. But it didn't leave any time for herself. In those early-morning girl-talk sessions in the daycare kitchen, hadn't she told her friends that when a man finally came into her life who made her yearn, she'd go for it?

His gaze was steady on hers, as though he could read her thoughts. His eyes appeared black, but were actually the most beautiful shade of dark chocolate brown.

She moistened her lips, her heart pounding in her ears. If he kissed her, there was no question about it—she would kiss him back. Or she might pass out.

"I accept the dare. I'll let you know what I decide to wager."

His words were a puff of warm breath against her lips, and with that, he stepped back and gently shut the double doors, leaving her trembling in the hallway with a single thought racing through her mind.

Jeffri al-Kareem scared the hell out of her.

"Mimi?"

Millie jolted and looked around. Lindsey was standing in the hallway, dressed in a shocking pink flowered top, paired with bright red striped pants. These particular tones of red and pink did not complement each other. Her blond hair was a halo of Shirley Temple curls that frizzed as though they'd barely survived an overprocessed bleach job.

"I waked up and got dressed," Lindsey said brightly.

"Well, you certainly did." Today would be an excellent day to explore close to the estate, Millie decided. "You're getting to be such a big girl. Pretty soon, you'll be off to college and married. Here, let me tie those shoes before you hang yourself."

"I'm too little to get married."

"Now you are. But someday you won't be."

"How come you don't get married."

Millie was keenly aware that they were directly outside Jeff's doorway, and that she was still shaken by what she'd thought was a near kiss. Fool. Fool.

"I'm not getting married for a *long* time, pet. I've got places to go, things to do."

"Make your business?"

"Yes, ma'am. All set?" She patted Lindsey's blue tennis shoes. "Come, my colorful peacock. Let's see if Mr. Sam's awake."

Lindsey skipped down the hall and waited impatiently outside Sam's door. Millie caught up, knocked softly, then poked her head in. "Do I see any sunshiny faces in here?" Sam's dark head peeped out from around the private bathroom door. "Are you decent?" she asked.

"Yes."

"Good, because we're coming in." She walked across the room, stepped over a plastic F-14 giving a ride to a muscle-bound action figure, and opened the brocade curtains. A heavy mist shrouded the island, and the sky was a swollen mushroom of gray, but Millie wasn't daunted. The sun would burn through in a few hours.

"It's going to be a beautiful day, and I have a plan. First we eat—that's always important, then we need an indoor activity until these yucky clouds go away. Since *I* apparently have the directional skills of a goose when it comes to finding my way around this castle, I'm electing you, Sam, as our tour guide. It'll be your job to show us the layout. And I mean the whole thing. Any secret trapdoors, or passages behind the walls—stuff like that, okay?"

Sam grinned. "I know some places. I do not think Father knows about them."

Uh-oh. She hated to rat the kid out, but trapdoors would probably be included in her daily report to the sheikh.

"Cool. Let's go eat—" She stopped, looked at Sam and frowned. "You know, kiddo. This tour guide job requires a different type of uniform." The boy was wearing beige trousers with a permanent crease, a light brown button-down shirt, and leather loafers. Fine for church or a wedding. Not for playing. "May I have a look at your clothes?"

"Sure." Sam charged over to the walk-in closet. A light automatically came on when he opened the door.

On one side were neatly organized rows of dress clothes—perfectly pressed pants, shirts, vests and jackets. Opposite were casual sweats, jeans and T-shirts. Exactly the kind of little boy stuff she was looking for.

She snagged the pair of jeans that looked the most worn, paired them with a long-sleeved T-shirt and tennis shoes, and plopped the ensemble in Sam's arms.

"This is perfect. Then when we go outside later, we won't worry about ruining your nice clothes. In fact, while

I'm here, we'll be doing a lot of outside exploring, so your blue jeans and tennies will be fine most any day.''

"Okay," Sam said, holding the clothes to his chest.

"How come you're always dressed up?" Lindsey asked.

He shrugged. "My father is an important man. I want to make a good impression."

Millie took him by the shoulders and turned him toward the bathroom. "You, my handsome little man, would make a good impression if you were wearing feathers."

"Feathers!" Lindsey shrieked and fell to the floor in a fit of dramatics. Sam giggled all the way into the bathroom. When he came out several minutes later, his hair was damp and clinging to his forehead from hurrying.

The shedding of the oh so-proper clothes seemed to transform his personality, as well. He tossed the pants and shirt over a hanger in the closet and raced over to a wall of shelves that held every toy imaginable. He began stuffing tiny neon balls in his pockets, passing more to Lindsey to shove into hers.

Millie straightened the discarded clothes on the hanger, then met the kids by the door. "What's in the pockets?"

"Super Balls," Sam said, pushing hair off his sweaty forehead.

"And what do they do?"

"They bounce really high. Do you want to see?"

Before she could say yea or nay, both kids whipped out a tiny rubber ball and fired it at the stone floor. Flashes of neon pink and green ricocheted from ceiling to floor to the walls and back, whizzing and slamming all over the place like Wiley Coyote and the Roadrunner on a sugar high.

Millie ducked twice before the bouncy balls finally lost

enough momentum that she could catch them before they wreaked havoc on an irreplaceable antique.

Thank the Lord Lindsey hadn't been a twin. This was what Meg Bassett-Taylor, Forrester Square's music teacher, and her husband, Brody, dealt with on a daily basis with their twins, Kevin and Kelly. She'd have to remember to offer them baby-sitting services more often.

She held out her hand, palm up. "Hand 'em over."

"Aw, Mimi. How come?" Even as Lindsey complained, both kids fished inside their pants and emptied their pockets of Super Balls.

"You'll get them back when we're outside. There's too much stuff in this house to have one of these missiles boinking all over the place. You could break five windows and ten priceless pieces of art in one swoop."

Sam stuck his hands into his back pocket and rolled his feet outward, standing on the sides of his shoes. Lindsey perched her hands on her hips, the braver of the two. "You don't got any pockets. How are you gonna hold 'em?"

"I don't *have* any pockets," she corrected. Which was a problem she hadn't considered. She didn't intend to carry a purse just to haul around psychotic little balls that would be better off bouncing themselves right into the ocean. Her jeans were fairly snug, so she couldn't slip the little menaces in her waistband.

She glanced at her blouse. Long-sleeved, it had a scooped, gathered neckline similar in style to the old peasant blouses of the seventies. It wasn't clingy, so it wouldn't show any weird bulges.

Turning her back to the kids, she slipped one ball into each cup of her bra, then set the extras on the shelf where she'd seen Sam get them.

"We're only taking two," she announced.

"Where did you put them?" Sam frowned, checking her out from head to toe.

"That's not for you to worry about. When we get outside, I promise to hand over the Super Balls. Now, let's go eat so we don't faint dead away on our tour."

As she opened the bedroom door, she heard Lindsey's none-too-subtle whisper, "She put 'em in her boobs."

Millie just smiled and shook her head. Little Sam was going to be good and loose by the time their two weeks were up.

In a way, Sam and Lindsey were very much alike. Both were limited by their circumstances, unable to be as adventurous and carefree as most children. Lindsey was obligated to go where Millie went, though she never complained. Her imagination was limitless and she had the spunk to carry out plenty of mischief.

Sam seemed to try so hard to be a proper little man, befitting his family's heritage, yet his longing to simply cut loose was clearly evident. Millie wanted to see the little boy emerge. Not only for Sam's benefit, but for Jeff's, as well.

She had an idea Jeff had closed himself off since his wife's death, even to his son. If he saw Sam coming to life, perhaps he, too, would let go of whatever chains were binding him. Maybe Sam's growth would release Jeff so he could once more become the gentle, happy man Katherine claimed he had been.

With this job, Jeff was giving Millie the opportunity to seize her future. To realize a dream she'd thought would take her years. If she could give him something in return, it would mean a lot to her. Even if it was simply teaching him the joys of laughter and play, reminding him how good it was to have fun in life.

She rounded the corner at the bottom of the stairs and

slammed into the solid wall of Jeff's chest. His hands shot out to steady her. The kids giggled and danced around them as though they were a May pole.

Frowning, Jeff glanced down at her breasts, then away, as if he'd seen something he wasn't supposed to.

She looked down to make sure nothing was exposed. Then she realized what he was so gallantly trying to pretend he hadn't felt. A bubble of laughter spilled out. "They're balls."

His frown turned to bewilderment.

"She put balls in her *bra*," Sam said with emphasis on the last word.

"Samaal!" Jeff admonished.

"Well, she did!" Lindsey was primed to fight Sam's battle. When Jeff's gaze snapped to her, she bobbed her shoulders and made a quick retreat back to Sam's side.

Millie laughed. "Oh, lighten up, Jeff. I didn't have anywhere else to put the darn things. Sam was merely being helpful by passing along information that Lindsey had given him."

"He should not be *shouting* about women's intimate clothing in the foyer." Jeff still wore a look of confusion. "Why don't you kids go on into the kitchen. Zac is waiting to start your breakfast."

"Are you coming to eat with us?" Sam asked.

He reached down and caressed his son's hair. "Absolutely. I am starved."

The kids didn't waste any time hanging around. Millie shook her head. "Shame on you, Jeffri. You just lied to your son." She brushed toast crumbs off his sweater.

"I only ate enough to take the edge off my hunger, since the three of you were so long coming downstairs. Evidently you were playing ball. What I'd like to know,

now that the children aren't present and I feel free to speak, is why you have balls stuffed in your bra?"

"Obviously you've never played with one of these fun things." Since he was looking at her breast, she knew immediately the leap his mind had made. "I'm talking about the balls, Jeff. I felt it would be in everyone's best interest if I kept possession of the toys until we'd made it outdoors."

She glanced around. The ceilings in the foyer were high, and there wasn't too much damage he could do. The chandelier was a little iffy. She turned her back to him, fished out one of the balls—neon green—then lifted Jeff's hand and put it in his palm. "Give it a try."

Lindsey poked her head around the corner. "But you said not in the house." Sam's head was right next to hers.

"I thought you guys were going to start breakfast."

"We wanted to wait for Father," Sam said.

Jeff seemed to puff up over his popularity—and the fact that he had an audience. He gave the little ball a bounce as though practicing a basketball dribble. The green devil shot up, binged off the arched opening, hit the tile floor, and was on a return path when Jeff reached out and snagged it.

Millie couldn't decide if he had excellent reflexes or pure luck. The startled expression on his face, however, was priceless. Sam and Lindsey clapped and cheered.

His lips canted in a half smile. "I see." Pointing his finger at the kids, he said, "Go. I am right behind you."

This time they obeyed. She heard the slap of their feet against the tile floor of the dining room.

He set the ball in her hand. "Excellent decision. You may put it back where you found it."

"Actually, I think *you* found it." She had no idea what prompted her to say that. He went absolutely still. Except for his eyes. They locked onto hers, and darkened. If they'd been capable of speech, Millie was fairly certain she'd get an entire course in sex education merely in that one long look.

"Shall I put it back for you, then?"

His voice was so deep, so quiet, so mesmerizing that she forgot to answer. He took a step forward. She shook away her trance and quickly stepped back, then laughed as though she was used to playing this teasing game.

"I'll manage, thanks. Go ahead and join the kids. I'll be right there." *Right after I analyze my brain and find out what the devil is going on up there.*

CHAPTER SIX

WHEN THE FRONT DOOR alarm bells screamed and clanged for the second time in one day, Jeff's nerves only suffered a slight jangle. At least her average was improving. The previous three days had been worse.

Casually, he got up from his desk, snagged his cell phone and strolled to the office door, which was a stone's throw across the foyer from all the commotion.

Sadiq rushed in from outside, Zaki circled from the kitchen, Millie stood glaring at the code box, while Lindsey and Sam covered their ears with their hands and rolled their eyes.

"Damn it!"

Even over the earsplitting noise, Millie's frustrated curse rang loud and clear. Strong words coming from the little spitfire. Not her usual prissy cursing.

Since he'd already punched the speed dial button for the security company, he lifted the phone to his ear. A good deal of aircraft fuel had been wasted today—and yesterday and two days before—because when the alarms at this estate sounded, a fleet of armed helicopters were immediately started up, ready to set off.

"Still training the new employee," he said into the phone. "I do apologize for the false alarms."

Disconnecting, he leaned his shoulder against the doorjamb. No sense traumatizing the nanny further with a swarm of guards brandishing assault rifles.

The shrill bells could be heard for miles. Inside the walls of an estate with copper ceilings, the sound was ear-numbing. A bottle of aspirin added to tonight's dinner menu would likely be welcome.

Millie was talking to the box as though it had the capability to understand, casting aspersions on anybody or anything that had to do with security devices. Jeff heard the word "idiot" several times. He noticed that Sadiq hesitated, as did Zaki. Hell, she barely topped five feet. What was the problem here? They were all going deaf.

Jeff took a step forward. Someone had to turn off that infernal noise. Afterward, he and the nanny were going to have an alarm operations seminar. Otherwise, she and the kids would just have to stay in the house until someone let her in or out.

As though she could feel him closing in, she whirled around, her gray eyes spitting fire, hands outstretched like a cornered suspect determined not to be taken alive.

"Don't! Just leave me alone and let me *do* this!" She punctuated her words by glaring at everyone in the room, her voice rising above the shrieking alarm.

"I can't think with everybody hovering like a pack of superior poodles who've forgotten they peed on the rug more than once before they got the hang of squatting on the newspaper. So go away and let me concentrate!"

Sadiq and Zaki stared at Jeff. He knew they were stunned to hear an employee speak to him in such a manner and were gauging his reaction. Interesting thing was, instead of feeling outrage, he found himself in the grip of a strange, enlivened sensation.

Millie Gallagher had spunk. And she had an excellent point. The poodle comparison, however, didn't sit too well. She could have at least chosen a Great Dane or shepherd, something more masculine and powerful, befitting his self-image.

He backed up, indicating that Sadiq and Zaki should do the same, and watched as Millie concentrated on her task.

Determined to show the alarm who was boss, she took a breath, then spread out the fingers on her left hand. A new approach, he thought, but he waited to see where she'd go with it.

He didn't normally have the patience for this kind of thing. Half-deaf from the bells, he was willing to stand here as long as it took.

The alarm code was Samco spelled backward. It was the name of the new company he'd recently opened in Seattle. One day it would be Sam's company, thus the name.

He could see Millie spelling the name out loud, figuring the letters backward, then hunting the corresponding keys on the code pad, slowly punching them as though she was disarming a pressure sensitive bomb.

Jeff glanced at his watch. By now an intruder could have had the run of the whole place, stopped in the kitchen and helped himself to a beer, hopped in a seaplane and been across the Canadian border. Assuming, of course, that the Balriyad security helicopters were grounded.

With his ears still ringing, it took a good three seconds before he realized the din had stopped. At last. Blessed silence. The inside of his head didn't sound all that quiet. His ears still throbbed, reminding him of the night he'd paid for front-row seats at a Bon Jovi concert and ended up in a screaming crowd next to the amps.

Now that Millie had accomplished her task, he expected her to turn and flash a triumphant smile. She turned, but the smile was nowhere in sight, and if eyes could spit fire, he'd be nothing more than a skeleton of charred bones.

Damnedest woman to figure out.

He crooked his finger, indicating she should join him in his office. She spoke to Sadiq, left the kids in the bodyguard's care and marched over to the office, brushing past him in the doorway as though she owned the place. She got as far as his desk before the serious pacing began.

Jeff considered closing the door. A glance into the foyer told him the two men were herding the kids toward the kitchen. He and Millie should be safe with the door open.

Provided neither one of them actually shouted.

He didn't consider that a danger—at least for himself. He couldn't remember ever having raised his voice in a common shouting match—except for once, with his brother.

He went to his desk and started to sit.

"What kind of an *idiot* rigs an alarm that you have to turn off to get yourself out the door, then race over to another hidden box and turn the fool thing back on right quick in case an I-don't-know-what slips by when you blink. Then to get back *in,* you have to turn it off again outside, *then* have the sense to stop and turn it back *on* once you get inside. It's ridiculous. What if your arms are full of groceries?"

"We have them delivered."

"What if you have to go to the bathroom?" She perched her hands on her hips. "Really bad. Can't stop to think. And you're a woman," she added, lifting her chin, "who can't slip off and find a handy bush?"

Jeff decided he wasn't going to touch that one.

"Do you know how many times children run in and out of the house?" she asked. "Don't you remember your own mother ever saying, 'Jeff, either come in or stay out—make up your mind'?''

She shoved her hair out of her face. He started to sit down again.

"Well, do you?" she demanded.

He straightened. It didn't seem wise to sit when she was pacing and in this…state. "I do not believe she said that, no."

"Well, maybe—no, *probably*—your house was bigger than mine. I was in and out of the kitchen door, so the screen slapped constantly. Mom got tired of swatting the flies and hearing the door bang. I don't know." She brushed the air with a flutter of hands. "Kids change their minds every two seconds. They want what's outside, then they want what's inside, then out, then, oops, somebody has to go to the bathroom, or they forgot the frog or the pet rock or their underwear."

"Children forget their underwear?" Surely she was exaggerating.

"Of course they do. You're lucky if they remember while you're still in the driveway rather than in the middle of church or the family reunion. One time Lindsey forgot hers. There we were, sitting in the third pew of the church singing 'Glory Hallelujah.' She stood up on the bench, bent over to grab for the pew in front, and flashed the whole Sunday morning service."

Jeff didn't dare crack a smile. She was obviously still on a tear. He was starting to get used to her anecdotal side trips, and realized she had no idea how extraordinary and amusing they sounded to him.

Just for the pure pleasure of watching her, he said, "So what did you do?"

Distracted, her mind apparently back on the original track, she frowned.

"Oh, the underpants. I snatched her up and took her home. I figured we'd all been quite blessed for the day. I can't totally blame the naked behind on Lindsey. We were in the potty-training stages, and I thought we had it licked, but she had a slipup just before we walked out the door. I was in a rush, quickly took off the wet panties, I think the phone rang about that time, then we got halfway to the car and she'd forgotten her little purse that matched her shoes." She gestured with her hands as though she expected him to know that missing accessories could cause a national crisis.

"So, I went back for the purse, and I admit I was a little testy at this point, especially since the phone call had been Aunt Flo, and Aunt Flo still thinks I'm ten. Plus, she's not my favorite person because she tried to screw up what should have been a simple custody legalization after my parents died. Anyway, during all this, I forgot I hadn't put dry underwear on Lindsey. She was either reluctant to mention it after the purse incident, or she forgot, as well."

"Must have been quite a morning." From the brief description, Jeff didn't like Aunt Flo, either.

"That's a perfect example of what I'm talking about," she said. "This all happened in the front hall. In and out. Can you imagine if I'd had one of those evil boxes to contend with?" She pointed an accusing finger in the direction of the alarm code box in the foyer.

"I'm not saying you shouldn't have an alarm system," she went on, "although we *are* way out here on a private island that looks pretty darn peaceful to me. But can't you just be like a normal person and set the silly thing at night after everyone's inside? You've got cameras up the ying-yang, and if someone can get through Deke, well then,

God bless 'em. That man is built like a tank. The island is protected, Jeff. Can't you lighten up?''

"No."

She stopped dead in her tracks. "No? Just like that?"

"Please sit down, Millie."

Her tense shoulders sagged and she slid into the chair in front of his desk. She didn't look defeated, just accepting. That surprised him. He'd thought they would go through a minor war—one which he would win.

"I am not deliberately trying to antagonize you," he explained. "As I told you the day you arrived, security is a natural part of my world—and Sam's. My wealth and my family's name will always make us a target of greedy or unbalanced people. I know you have heard many stories of children from wealthy families being kidnapped and held for ransom." He saw her eyes widen with instant understanding and compassion.

"You don't think someone wants to kidnap Sam, do you?"

"No. But just because it is broad daylight doesn't mean I should leave my Ferrari outside with the top down and the key in the ignition, either. We did not intend to stay on the island this trip, but we had a security incident at my penthouse in Seattle, and Sadiq insisted we relocate."

"Were you robbed?"

"No. A few items were moved, but nothing was taken."

"I guess it's a good thing you had this place."

"Yes. I bought this property last year. It was a whim actually. Then Sadiq came in and rigged the estate to a degree even *I* considered overkill. As it turns out, that was a good thing. I know Sam is safe here, and that is what matters to me."

"A whim? You bought a whole island on a *whim?*

Were all the car dealerships out of Lamborghinis that day or something?'' She rubbed her temples. ''Going overboard on alarm systems is one thing, but…that just boggles my mind. It's nuts. I tell you what, if you have those kinds of whims often, someone needs to take away your checkbook before you do yourself some real damage.''

Since he'd been wealthy all of his life, spending money wasn't something Jeff gave much thought to. He'd never deliberately set out to impress anyone. He simply did as he pleased. It never occurred to him to wonder what others might think.

Oddly enough, right now he was feeling pretty good that he could impress Millie Gallagher with his bank account. Craziest thought he'd ever had, but there it was.

''It's sweet of you to worry about my finances, but it is not necessary.''

''To heck with your finances, I'd be more worried about your common sense.'' She shrugged. ''But then, that's just me.''

He suppressed a smile. That didn't stop it from flooding his insides, though. This slip of a woman truly energized him. Even when she was annoyed, she made him think of fun. *That* was damned near a miracle.

''Tripping the alarm is what is endangering my common sense and sanity at the moment.'' He saw the fire leap back into her eyes at the reminder and held up his hand in a gesture of calm. ''I might be able to help you out—''

''You could shoot it. That would be helpful.''

His lips twitched. ''As you reminded us—using a reference to poodles, I believe—mastering certain tasks can take a bit more practice. Or maybe a new learning approach. When the alarm trips, you become flustered and you forget the code, or you spend too much time entering the code because you are thinking Samco first, then trying to reverse the letters correctly. Am I right?''

She wiped at a smudge on his desktop. "You might be a little warm."

He wasn't sure he understood that but took it as a yes. After writing the letters on a memo pad, he slid it across the desk. "So, why not try word association? Do not think Samco. Think o-c-m-a-s. Or, 'Oh, cee, M, as.'''

He could tell by the way her head bobbed that she was silently testing out his concept. Five dips, then four dips. Her gaze snapped up to his. Blue dominated the gray as her eyes lit up.

"I get it! 'Oh see my ass.' O-c-m-a-s. Why didn't you say this in the first place instead of confusing me with the backward thing?"

Jeff *felt* his entire hairline lift. He swallowed. "There is no *Y* or extra *S.*"

"So…it makes sense. When I turn off the alarm, you'll see my butt going in or out."

"Now you've just changed the association. There is no *B* in the code. Aren't you going to confuse yourself?"

She gave him a look that suggested he had the IQ of a dim camel. "That's the clean version. With my track record so far, and the kids' sharp minds, they're going to ask how I suddenly became so quick fingered. It's also an excellent lead in to an educational subject and they won't even know they're doing lessons. Sam will learn the trick to help him remember the names of important people he meets. Word association. Satisfied?"

Not hardly. The thought echoed through his mind like a gunshot. Do not go there, he cautioned himself. "I could use some of those lessons."

"So come hang out with us. Sam misses you."

Jeff's gut tightened. The one thing that could make his

heart bleed was his son. More than anything, he wanted to shut out the world and give Sam all he had to give, but what if it turned out that he didn't have enough of the right stuff left? Although the emptiness inside him didn't echo as loudly, he still felt like a new shoe that hadn't quite been broken in yet and was raising blisters. He didn't have Millie's knack for pulling fun out of thin air.

Then there was business. The fax machine was stacked with land proposals, lease agreements and drilling reports on the test wells he'd charted. His cell phone showed eight phone calls that had been fielded by the answering service just in the short space of time since the alarm fiasco. He had a conference call scheduled in twenty minutes between his headquarters in Balriyad and the CFO at Samco in Seattle. The EPA was scrutinizing one of their Alaskan rigs and his pilots were readying the jet now to fly him up there. Any possible leaks or hazards, Jeff dealt with personally.

"I can't," he said. "I will be leaving within the hour."

She reached out and placed a hand on his arm. "Is everything all right?"

The genuine concern caught him off guard. "A small business problem. The Environmental Protection Agency people are losing sleep over one of our oil rigs that seems to have developed a nasty habit of breaking drill bits."

Twin creases formed between her brows. "That's not good."

He smiled. "No. I have a spotless reputation for maintaining my equipment and adhering to the strictest EPA rules. I have parts replaced before they become worn. This rig, however, is new. It should not be problematic. Yet this is the second bit we've lost this month. Either we're doing something wrong or—"

"You just said the equipment's new. Have you changed parts suppliers or your regular crew?"

"No."

"Well, I don't know anything about the type of machinery you use or how it works, but it sounds to me like quality control fell asleep when it was their turn to watch the assembly line." She laughed at herself. "Listen to me going on as if you haven't already thought of all this." As she stood up, she reached across the desk and squeezed his arm. "It'll work out fine, you'll see."

He was rendered speechless. She didn't know a thing about him or his business, yet she championed him without batting an eye, gave him encouragement in case he needed it. He didn't need it. But it was nice. Damned nice.

She argued his case quite well, too. If it turned out the drill bits were defective, the supplier's CEO would not last more than five minutes against her.

He rose and came around the desk, stopping in front of her. "If you ever find yourself in need of a job, I want you to call me." He looked directly into her eyes, making sure she understood he was serious. "I would hire you in a minute, Millie Gallagher."

For brief seconds, emotions registered on her face so openly he could have been watching movie clips with all the subtitles. She was surprised, skeptical, flattered, disconcerted, honored, and all those reactions coalesced into the sweetest smile he'd ever seen.

"Thanks," she said softly. "I can't imagine that I'd ever take you up on the offer, but…" Her voice faltered. She bit her bottom lip and glanced quickly toward the ceiling as though she was fighting a battle with tears. Before he could panic over that prospect, she looked back to him.

"I believe you're serious, and that gives me more peace

than you'll ever know. From now on, when I reassure Lindsey that I'll always take care of her—'' her tone lowered to a heartfelt, gentle caress ''—I won't have any doubt. I'll know my promise is solid.''

Jeff didn't know how to respond, so he just inclined his head, acknowledging her gratitude. She humbled him. She didn't need proof—no signed contracts, no up-front money in the bank. She found peace and security merely by trusting. He wanted to tell her that was foolish, that she'd never survive the big bad world with that attitude.

But how could he? His offer was sincere. It would stand twenty years from now. His word was his bond.

''Well,'' she said. ''I'd better get out of here so you can finish whatever you need to before you leave. Do you know how long you'll be gone? And do you want me to keep Sam close so you can say goodbye before you go?''

''It should only be an overnight trip. And yes, please bring Sam to me in about forty-five minutes. If I am finished with my conference call sooner, I will come find him.''

''Okay. We'll either be in the kitchen or the television room. Amazing that neither one of those kids wears a watch—or tells time—yet they seem to know the exact moment it's midmorning snack time. Then, evidently the satellite dish is programmed to entertain us with children who attend wizard school.''

She glanced at the stainless steel watch on her wrist, and when she looked up, she wore the most enchantingly sheepish smile. It hit him like a sucker punch and he nearly reached for the desk to steady himself.

''Actually, the satellite thing was my doing. I've read all the Harry Potter books to Lindsey, but we never saw the movie. I'm dying to see it. And so are the kids,'' she added. ''Really.''

"I am very glad we are able to provide this wizard movie. Viewing kitchens, watching missed films—I had no idea there were so many desires that could put a person on the verge of expiring."

She grinned. "See what you miss when you don't ease up and take time to enjoy life?" Stepping back, she placed her hand on the doorjamb. "The movie's playing again tomorrow if you're interested. Watch it for yourself and see what all the fuss is about—we'll even watch it again with you. Then you'll be up to speed and can come listen to our bedtime stories. I'm going to start reading the second book in the series to Sam. Hopefully we'll get it finished before you guys have to go home. If not, it'll be your job to pick it up, and you'll need to know how to do the voices. That's important."

"Voices?"

"Surely you don't think all wizards talk alike? You have to get into it, make it fun. You'll especially enjoy how their competitive sports are played on flying broomsticks."

She wiggled her fingers and strolled away, arms swinging, her body vibrating with energy, enthusiasm and joy, as though she hadn't a care in the world. Which he knew was far from true.

Millie had more responsibilities than some women twice her age. She'd suffered through tragedy, adversity and God knows what else, but she didn't hang her head and bemoan the cards life had dealt, or wait around for someone to show up and take care of her.

No, she took care of herself—and everyone around her, as well. And she did it with trust and enthusiasm and laughter. Genuine, deep-in-the-heart joy.

And damned if she didn't manage to sweep innocent bystanders along with her. A man could be minding his own business, know exactly where he was going, a place he'd gone every day of his life, then suddenly find himself snatched by the hair into a revolving door, spun around until he was pretty sure he'd lost his mind, then spit out onto the sidewalk, wondering why the hell he hadn't realized that's where he'd meant to be in the first place.

He had no business noticing her fresh apple scent or dwelling on her personal life and traits—he had enough on his plate. The oil companies weren't the only responsibilities sitting heavily on his shoulders. His father's poor health was a concern he had to make peace with, as well.

He still felt such ambivalence about that part of his future. It had been Kasim's desire to succeed their father, not Jeffri's.

But Kasim was dead, and Jeff had mixed feelings about that, too. They'd been twins, uncannily alike in appearance, but polar opposites in personality. When they were dressed alike and stood side-by-side, not speaking, there'd been only one person who could accurately tell them apart at a glance—their mother. She'd never told anyone how she knew—and plenty of people had asked. She just said, ''Am I not a mother? Did I not give birth to them? Of course I know!''

So, when Jeff had walked in on his wife kissing his brother, Rana's shock had convinced him she was merely an innocent victim, that she'd *thought* she was kissing her husband.

Kasim, well known for his cocky attitude, hadn't offered an excuse or an apology for his part. Jeff hadn't cared. He'd washed his hands of his brother and hadn't seen him until eight months later, the day of the boat accident.

Meanwhile, Jeff's marriage had gone on as before—he had experienced these identity mix-ups too often in his life to doubt Rana's word. Deep down, though, it had bothered him that his wife, the woman who should have known him body and soul, couldn't even distinguish the slightest nuance that would separate him from Kasim.

He wondered if Millie would have made the same mistake as his wife had. The minute the thought surfaced, he swore. He was not going to compare Millie to Rana. The only thing the two women had in common was the ability to make him feel too much, to shake his control.

In only five days, Millie's guileless disregard for authority and her ability to turn his entire household upside down had put him through a full range of emotional reactions. But when her unique eyes darkened to the color of the sea, and that intriguing pulse fluttered just above her collarbone, she could damn near name the stakes and he'd meet them. Way too dangerous.

He stomped over to his desk and stabbed the button to open the line for the conference call, leaving the other five numbers forwarded to the service.

All he needed was a few hours away. To clear his senses of that enticing apple scent...

He lifted his arm and sniffed the sleeve of his sweater where she'd touched him. She'd really been interested in his business concerns, he thought. Not just asking to be polite then zoning out and thinking about a hair or nail appointment. She'd held his gaze, listened with intent, *interrupted* with vehemence and—

"Damn it, man." He jerked his arm down and shoved his sleeve to his elbow.

He desperately needed a break here. The confounded woman had him thinking things to death.

Aw, hell.

He threw up his hands and let them drop on the mahogany surface of the desk.

Now she had *him* doing the dying drama.

CHAPTER SEVEN

MILLIE SCRAPED the last bit of frosting out of the bowl and swirled elaborate curls over the top of her freshly baked banana layer cake while the kids sat at the bar having a snack before bedtime.

Jeff had called this morning to let her know his overnight trip had turned into two nights, and she shouldn't expect him before tomorrow. The sound of his voice on the telephone had made her feel like a giddy teenager on a first date.

When she'd passed the phone to Sam so he could talk to his dad, she'd practically hovered over him in case Jeff asked to speak with her again before they disconnected. Of course Sam hung up the phone immediately after he'd said goodbye.

Remembering her disappointment made her feel foolish all over again. She rinsed her hands, then Millie punched out Alexandra's number on the phone, making one last attempt to get through. She'd been worried about Alexandra, especially since the strange flashback her friend had tried to make light of the night of Hannah's shower. This time, the line barely rang before it was picked up.

"When are you going to get call waiting?" Millie asked. "Do you know how frustrating it is to get a busy signal for a solid thirty minutes?"

"Well, hello to you, too," Alexandra said. "And I can

only talk to one person at a time, so why should I pay hard-earned money for a service I wouldn't use anyway?''

"Good point." Millie snapped her fingers at Lindsey and covered the receiver with her palm. "Lindsey, stop dipping your banana in Sam's milk." Turning, she spoke into the phone. "Sorry about that."

"How's the job working out?" Alexandra asked.

"Fine. The island is beautiful, the kids are a dream and the *sheikh*," she stressed, "is away on business."

"Don't waste a good snit on me. He's Katherine's friend. I heard he's a hottie, though. Is he?"

"Yes, and that's all I'm saying because the kids are sitting right here." She smiled at Alexandra's dramatic groan. "Now, tell me what's up with you."

Her friend hesitated. "What are you talking about?"

"You know—the nightmares, the homeless man you seem to have adopted."

"Hannah and Katherine think I'm spending too much time with Gary." She sighed. "They think it's an un-healthy obsession."

"They're just worried about you," Millie knew that Alexandra was convinced that Gary Devlin, a homeless man who'd been hanging around the day-care center for months, was somehow linked to her late father. "Has any-thing changed?"

"Not really. It's just that he has these periods of con-fusion, and he seems to know things about Seattle, Millie. And about *me*."

Millie didn't like the sound of this. "Like what?"

"Oh, things like my favorite foods—and that I'll only eat an apple if it's cut into quarters and smeared with peanut butter. I've done that ever since I was a kid."

"Alexandra, doesn't any of this scare you? Is there any way he could have gotten a hold of your personal information? Did you lose a diary? Or can you remember writing any of these things down somewhere?''

"No. And I'm not afraid of him. I feel as though we've known each other before, and that we were very close. But I can't pinpoint it. There's something about his eyes." Her voice trembled. "They remind me so much of my dad's—or at least, what I remember."

"Oh, Alexandra," Millie said softly, her heart aching for her friend. She knew only too well what it was like to lose your parents, and Alexandra had been such a little girl. But she was worried that her friend's attachment to this man could lead to more heartache, or even endanger her. "Please be careful." She wanted to say more but kept her thoughts to herself. Alexandra counted on Millie to provide a supportive shoulder to lean on, and that's all she would offer for now.

"Thanks for not telling me I'm nuts," Alexandra said.

"Do you think this paradise island has made me go soft in the head or something? You should know I always save my insults for face-to-face delivery."

Her friend laughed. "Yeah, well, don't get too cozy in paradise and decide not to come home. Katherine and Hannah are no challenge. I could use a down and dirty debate with a worthy opponent."

"It's a date," Millie said. "Meanwhile, I'd better get these children to bed. Call if you need me." She hung up and turned back toward the kids.

"You got milk on your mustache." Lindsey grinned at Sam and licked her own upper lip. She propped her arms on the granite breakfast bar and leaned closer, her face nearly touching Sam's cheek. A serious case of hero worship was going on here, Millie realized.

"I do not have a mustache."

"Uh huh. A white one." Lindsey's bare legs and feet

swung in a crazy figure eight, her heels bumping the bar stool's brace.

"I have a *milk* mustache on my *lip,*" he told her, arching his brow in a perfect imitation of his father.

"That's what I said, silly." Lindsey giggled. "I drinked mine already."

"Drank," Millie corrected, tossing a banana peel in the trash compactor.

Sam gulped the rest of his milk, scooted the glass across the counter, then lifted his arm toward his mouth.

"Use your napkin," Millie said before he could take a swipe with the back of his sleeve.

For an instant, it appeared as though he had no idea how his arm had ended up so close to his face. Then, with his twinkling gaze darting away, he grabbed the napkin, scrunched it in his hand, swiped his mouth and politely handed her the soiled remains.

Millie suppressed a smile. The determined-to-please child with impeccable manners rarely wore his little-man hat these days, slipping instead into typical six-year-old behavior. *Good for you, Sam.*

She covered the cake with a crystal dome, then put the dirty dishes in the dishwasher and wiped the counters, restoring the kitchen to its spotless condition.

"It's bedtime for you two." Lifting Sam, she gave him a smacking kiss on the cheek, set him down, and then did the same to Lindsey.

"But we're not sleepy yet," Lindsey said.

"Ah, but you will be by the time you get up to the bed, because milk has magic sleepy sparkles in it. I can see your eyes getting heavy already. Lead the way, Mr. Tour Guide," she said to Sam.

"*I* didn't see any sparkles." Lindsey whipped around and glared at the refrigerator as though daring any magic twinkles to escape the milk carton inside, her round eyes indicating she was secretly hoping they would.

Sam flashed Millie a dimpled smile, letting her know his six-year-old wisdom was much superior to Lindsey's, but they wouldn't make an issue of her gullibility. What a cutie.

As he'd been on their first morning here, he was tickled with the leadership assignment. Puffing out his chest, he marched ahead, the bottoms of his blue cotton pajama pants dragging on the tile floor.

Lindsey, milk sparkles forgotten, scrambled to fall in line behind Sam. In her exuberance, she tripped on the ruffle of her gown and both kids went down on the hard floor in a tangled heap.

In two steps Millie was on her knees beside them, her heart pounding.

Both kids were in a fit of giggles.

Millie blinked. They'd scared her into early gray hair and premature wrinkles, and they were *giggling*. She'd have been absolutely devastated if one of these precious kids was injured.

Plus, she was responsible for the safety of another person's child. How would it look if Jeff came home to find that the first time he'd left his son alone overnight in her care, she'd let him get hurt? Not that she could have foreseen the mishap. Accidents could happen right before your eyes and you couldn't do a thing to stop them.

Crisis over, she released the tension in her shoulders and spine, gazed down at the giggling duo, and smiled. There was simply nothing more soul stirring than the sound of children's laughter.

Checking for bumps or injuries, she brushed the fingers of one hand through blond, baby-fine curls, and the other through midnight strands so utterly soft and silky they poured over her skin like feathery satin threads.

As though her touch had thrown an off switch, their silliness hushed in midsqueak. Amazing.

"I'm too young to have a heart attack, but if you guys keep scaring me to death like this, I might end up with my name in the medical books," she said softly, her fingers caressing more for her own pleasure now than for examination.

Lindsey gazed at Sam, grinning, waiting for an excuse for more silliness. But Sam's brown eyes clung to Millie's, so serious, a combination of adoration, yearning and awe. Oh, she wanted to snatch him to her and fill him up with all the motherly love he so obviously longed for.

Somehow, this little boy had slipped firmly and completely into her heart when she wasn't looking.

That hadn't been part of the deal.

When she'd accepted the job, she'd known she would care about the child, and would miss him when the assignment was over. That was natural.

With Sam, it wasn't going to be that simple. She wouldn't just miss him. She had an idea her heart would bleed. If she was smart, she'd pull back for both their sake.

But, she couldn't do that to Sam. Even if it was only two weeks, he needed this extra attention and love. He needed to rediscover his childhood joy.

"Okay, you giggle monkeys. I didn't feel any goose eggs on your heads, there's no blood flowing and everyone seems to have their teeth. Hopefully you didn't break the floor. I'm not too great with that kind of repair work."

"You would not have to fix it," Sam assured her, clearly appalled that she would fear such a thing. "My father would hire a company to do it."

"Yes, but then we'd have to tell him how hardheaded you two are. Running in the house and all."

Sam and Lindsey jackknifed to a sitting position and inspected the floor.

"It's not broke!" Lindsey patted the square of tile as though it was a whimpering puppy in need of love.

"Good thing. Now, do either of you have any hurts that need doctoring or a kiss?"

Lindsey poked out her elbow. Not a red mark in sight.

Millie cupped the little arm and showered the elbow with gentle kisses. "There. All better."

She turned to Sam, who was watching in what appeared to be a near trance. "Sam? Do you have any hurts?"

A brief hesitation as he took a quick inventory. He pointed to his knee, then quickly jerked back. "No. That's wrong." He thrust out his wrist. "This one."

Millie managed to remain absolutely solemn. She cradled his hand and arm, pushed up the sleeve of his pajama shirt. "Poor wrist." Gently, she rained kisses over every inch of the small joint, then looked up and smiled. "Did that make it better?"

He waggled his hand, his cheeks dimpling with a shy smile. "The hurt's all gone."

"I should hope so. My kisses are very powerful!" She stood up. "Let's hop along to bed now."

Lindsey popped up. Millie realized her mistake. She should never have said hop. Lindsey bounced out of the kitchen, curls flopping around her head. Sam glanced back at Millie.

She smiled. "I'm right behind you. Go on and hop. But we are *quiet* bunnies," she added.

As the kids made a game of hopping on each of the tile squares, trying not to let their toes touch the grout lines, Millie followed behind turning off the lights.

The house felt empty without Jeff. Zac had already gone to bed, and Deke—well, Deke was a mystery. He somehow stayed hidden until he was needed, and then he simply appeared. For such a big guy, she didn't know how he pulled it off.

Taking advantage of the extra freedom, Millie had indulged herself and changed into her pajamas after she'd bathed the kids. The cotton pj's were faded from many washings, as old as Lindsey and as roomy and modest as a pair of sweats, but now she felt a slight prickle of unease...of impropriety. If Jeff was home, she wouldn't be wandering through his house in her nightclothes.

But it felt nice. She trailed her fingers over furnishings and fabrics as they passed through the enormous dining room decorated in burgundy silk, then made their way toward the foyer, where dual staircases created a dramatic welcome that put Tara to shame.

The wood gleamed, the floors were spotless and every book, tasseled throw pillow, fresh floral arrangement and antique accent piece was in the right place—thanks to a team of housecleaners who slipped in and out like elves three times a week.

She glanced over at Jeff's office door. It was closed, as she knew it would be, since he was off taking care of misbehaving oil wells. A sense of disappointment and longing washed over her, which was crazy. She had to keep reminding herself that he was her employer. He wasn't hers to miss.

''Mimi, what's all those ladies?''

Lindsey's voice jerked Millie out of her semitrance. She realized that the kids had bunny hopped past the east staircase, and she'd followed right along like a goose in a duck parade.

She looked at the gilt-framed tapestry hanging above

an ornate mahogany console in the foyer. "Do you mean *who are* all those ladies?"

Lindsey rolled her eyes. "Sam doesn't know, either."

"Well, if I remember my Greek mythology correctly, I believe this is Apollo and the Nine Muses."

"What's a muse?" Sam and Lindsey asked at the same time.

She glanced at the tapestry. "The muses were nine Greek goddesses, daughters of the god Zeus. He was the king of the gods, and very powerful."

"Like my father," Sam said.

"Yes." Thank goodness the man wasn't here to listen in. His ego would puff up like a soufflé. "Their mom was the goddess of memory, so she was very smart, and because they came from such excellent parents, artists believed that the muses were like good-luck charms."

"Tell us their names," Lindsey said.

"Oh, that's tricky. I'm not sure I remember them all. Let's see—Erato was love, Thalia was the comic, Urania handled the stars in the sky…. How many is that?"

"Three," Sam said. Lindsey echoed the answer, her eyes wide and earnest as though she hadn't simply mimicked Sam.

"Hmm. And I said there were nine? Erato, Thalia, Urania. Love, laughter, stars. I know there's a dancing girl, and a flute girl—" She snapped her fingers and grinned. "Euterpe! Lyric poetry."

"What about the flute girl?" Sam asked.

"That was Euterpe."

"Then why did you call her the lyric girl?"

"Because she's the muse of lyric poetry, which is sung while someone plays the flute. It was the flute that reminded me of her."

"Can Euterpe play the flute?" Lindsey asked.

I have no idea. "Need you ask, child? She's a goddess."

Lindsey fanned her nightgown and swished it back and forth, obviously trying to mimic the flowing scarves in the tapestry. "I could be a goddess."

Sam giggled. "She's too funny. Who else, Millie?"

"You mean I don't have them all yet?"

Two heads shook back and forth. In the middle of the head shaking, the kids suddenly gasped, then darted past her. Short attention span—

"Father!" Sam shouted. "You're home early!"

Millie's stomach lurched and she whirled around as Lindsey's voice chimed in with an exuberant, "Jeff, Jeff, Jeff!"

A pure shot of adrenaline sang through her veins, causing her to reach for the support of the antique console table. Their backs had been to the door, and she hadn't heard him come in, nor had she expected him tonight.

Trying to act as though it was perfectly acceptable to wander through someone else's home in her pajamas, she let go of the table and pasted a welcoming smile on her face.

Oh, he looked even better than she remembered. His midnight blue cashmere sweater skimmed his torso, emphasizing the breadth of his shoulders, the taper of his waist and the flat plane of his stomach. Dress pants tailored in a rich fabric that seemed to defy wrinkles draped over his hips and legs with a sexy elegance few men could pull off. Somehow, it felt as though she was seeing him through new eyes. And darn it, she *had* to get those crazy notions out of her head.

She watched as he bent down to hug Sam, including

Lindsey in the embrace, which made her sister beam from ear to ear.

Lighting from the overhead chandelier glinted off his raven hair as he stood.

"Millie is teaching us about the muses," Sam said, clearly excited to have his father home. "They are goddesses—"

"Like me," Lindsey interrupted.

Jeff's lips quirked as he looked from Lindsey to Millie. She imagined he was thinking, *I bet I know where she gets that trait from.*

Millie ignored him and turned back to the tapestry.

"She told us four of the ladies, but she cannot remember the others."

Thanks so much, Sam.

She didn't realize Jeff had come up behind her until he rested a hand on her shoulder. Unprepared, especially for his touch, she jolted. Then she stood as still as Apollo's nine muses in the framed art before her.

"Interesting that you remembered most of the happy muses," he said close to her ear. "The girl of song and dance, I believe, would be Terpsichore."

Her head whipped around. "How long have you been home? And how did you get in here without me hearing you?"

His lips curved in a half smile. "I came in through the garage entrance. And I did not check the time, but I recall seeing two small persons...hopping."

His warm palm branded her shoulder, and the clean smell of his ocean-scented skin wreaked havoc on her nervous system. Was he deliberately invading her personal space to get a reaction out of her?

She was fairly confident she could handle him in most situations. Except when he got this close. These were the times she found herself in trouble. Her brain went stupid and her senses became sheep—they'd follow his lead blindly.

Since she wasn't quite ready to be a lamb chop, she stepped out of his hold.

"You know your Greek mythology, do you?" she asked.

"Evidently better than you do."

She tsked. "In the interest of the children's education, please *do* refresh my memory on the final three."

"Four," Sam corrected.

She glanced down at the boy, who looked so much like his father. "Are you sure?"

"You did love, laughing, stars and the flute girl." He counted them off on his fingers. "Father did the song and dance girl, remember?"

"Very good, Sam." She reached out and caressed his hair.

Jeff watched how she touched and praised the kids. He realized that she most likely knew all the names of the muses. Her way of teaching was by drawing it out. Telling a story. Making it a fun game where everyone participated.

She put herself on the kids' level so they felt equal, and understood that she was human and didn't know everything.

He, on the other hand, just tossed out an answer whenever Sam asked for clarification on school assignments. Or else he'd turn the question back on his son and ask what Sam thought the answer was, then merely tell him if he was correct or not. Quick and tidy. Dealt with and done.

Realization struck him with the force of a geyser. By

damn, he was using his business's time management system to handle his own son.

It was important to raise Sam in the manner of a leader, but he'd sworn to accomplish that with love, affection and patience. Damn it. Each time he started to pat himself on the back, thinking he had the single-father syndrome licked, something jumped up to show him he was an idiot.

"Jeff?"

Millie's voice jerked him out of his trance. His heart was pounding against his ribs and a lump formed in his throat. He loved his boy more than life. What the hell had he been thinking this past year? Obviously he *hadn't* been thinking. But he was damned well going to change that.

He scooped Sam up and easily perched him on his forearm, bringing him eye level with the tapestry. Sam was getting too big to carry, but right now, Jeff needed the contact.

His need, though, left Lindsey out. She stood by his side, accepting Sam's right to special treatment, her wide, gray-blue eyes fixed on the tapestry. A tough one, Jeff thought. Like her big sister.

He bent his knees and hooked his other arm around her bottom. "Up, little one. If I am to give lessons, I insist my pupils have an excellent vantage point to see the study subject."

Lindsey curled her arm around his neck, her stubby fingers grazing his ear. She pressed her cheek against his, and he understood in an instant why people claimed little girls could wrap their fathers around their pinkies.

But he wasn't her father.

"How come that one with the wings doesn't have no clothes on?" she asked.

Maybe they were standing a bit too close to the study subject. At least Apollo wasn't exposing any sensitive male parts. Still, Jeff was passing this hot potato without an ounce of shame. "Millie? Why doesn't that one wear clothes?"

Her jaw literally dropped open. He waited patiently, along with the kids. He was only prepared to name the muses, not explain naked people to a five-year-old girl.

She collected herself, gave him an I'll-deal-with-you-later look, then turned her attention to the kids.

"Because the artist is painting what it was supposed to have been like during that time period. What would you think if someone painted Scooby-Doo wearing a pink dress and a sun bonnet?"

Lindsey scrunched up her face. "Eeeew. That's silly. He doesn't wear dresses."

"Usually not. And some of the Greek gods don't wear clothes."

"Oh. Okay."

Lindsey seem perfectly happy with the explanation, but Jeff was still back at the part about the dog in the dress and hat. He'd seen the cartoon—crazy dog, scared of its own shadow, always getting into mischief. You couldn't help but laugh. But dressing it up in a—

"Jeff?"

"Yes?"

"The floor is yours."

"So it is." He shifted the kids in his arms. "You two are heavy. What do you eat? A whole cow at each meal?"

"No, we had P. B. and J. with tater chips and pickles on it," Lindsey announced.

"I didn't have pickles on mine," Sam said. "Just chips."

"I am not familiar with this P.B.J. dish."

"You don't know peanut butter and jelly?" Lindsey stared at him as though he'd landed from another planet.

Millie stepped back and watched the confusion filter across Jeff's face. His brows shot up when his brain finally wrapped around the complete image.

"You put pickles and potato chips on peanut butter and jelly sandwiches?" His voice was as horrified as Lindsey's expression.

Millie covered her mouth to keep from laughing.

"'Course you do! And Mimi says you should never turn up your nose at something if you never tried it."

Jeff looked at Millie. "You actually eat this delicacy, as well?"

"No. I prefer mine with bananas and honey." She licked her lips. "I'm a sweet sugar girl."

His gaze stalled at her lips, then dipped down her body. He looked like a man under a deep hypnotic suggestion. Slowly, he lowered the kids to the floor. She didn't think he even realized it.

What in the world? She'd licked her lips, likened herself to sugar...

And rendered this sexy sheikh momentarily helpless.

A sense of feminine power filled her. She'd never experienced anything like it before, and it was a heady feeling. A slow, sensual smile started deep inside her.

It broke his odd trance, and his eyes snapped to meet hers.

She'd caught him at a vulnerable moment and she could tell by the tightening of his jaw that he didn't like it. He looked away, ruffling the kids' hair.

Millie's smile grew even wider.

Go ahead and slip back behind your scowling sheikh mask. We both know I won that round. My point.

CHAPTER EIGHT

JEFF CLEARED his throat and avoided Millie's seductive smile, willing his body to settle down.

He felt like a fool. Control had never been an issue in his life, so what the hell was wrong with him? No woman had ever made his mind go blank or driven him into a near stupor like Millie just had—and with nothing more than an innocent comment and a perfectly normal human gesture.

He didn't like it. Not a bit. The only justification for drooling over his son's nanny was exhaustion. That's all it was, he told himself. After two days of tense meetings, a potential financial loss that could reach billions, too much coffee and too little sleep, who could blame him for a moment's insanity?

All he needed was rest and he'd be back in top form.

If seduction was on the agenda—which it was *not*—then he would plan it. No surprises. Eyes wide open. In control. It had to be that way.

Otherwise, a man could lose his soul. He knew that from experience.

He'd already made the mistake of surrendering his power to the sweet enchantment of a woman, and the emotional pain from that folly had stripped away his spirit.

But Jeff had been lucky. Somehow, during the nights he'd watched his son sleep or held him close, he had managed to salvage a shrivelled portion of the soul he had feared he'd lost.

And by damn, it might be a sorry excuse for a soul, but it was all he had left and he wasn't giving it up.

"I think it is bedtime." He presented the statement so that it encompassed Lindsey, too, then glanced at Millie to see if she would object. Daring her.

She winked and flashed him a gesture of approval.

"We can't go to bed yet," Sam wailed. "You did not tell us the names of the other muses!"

Under normal circumstances, Jeff would not have tolerated Sam's raised voice, but he no longer understood the meaning of normal. For the first time in his life, he was actually swallowing back a wail of his own. Emotions he couldn't name roiled in his chest, the pressure building, begging for release. He tasted frustration at the back of his throat, astonishment, a tickle of madness, the total, utter loss of reason.

Was it too much to ask, for a man's peace of mind, that he be allowed control of his own household?

He'd told *both* kids to go to bed, regardless that only one of them belonged to him. Then he'd glanced at Millie to make sure she understood that in his home he could still make the decisions.

And what had she done? She'd circled her fingers in an okay sign—given him permission. *Permission!*

He'd been attempting to return his environment to the way it should be, and she'd upstaged him without even saying a single word.

Fine. It was a stupid, petty issue to get worked up about, an asinine bone to fight over in the first place.

But *damn* it! Couldn't he at least have the last say?

The kids were still gazing up at him with hopeful,

puppy dog eyes, awaiting his reaction to Sam's demand. Neither one appeared particularly concerned or nervous.

Well, hell. No sense putting a bucket over a geyser when it was already spewing out of control.

He strode to the tapestry and pointed to one of the females. "This is Calliope, the muse of epic poetry. Clio—" He shifted his finger as he snapped out the name, and caught sight of the two, round-cheeked little kids staring up at him with rapt attention.

Inhaling deeply, he dropped his hand. Even a jackass had to look at himself in the mirror sometimes—and give a swift kick to the idiot looking back. Jeff gave himself that mental boot and felt some of the tension drain out of his shoulders.

"Clio," he continued, "is the lady of history—"

"Mimi said they're girl goddesses, not ladies."

His mouth was still open. He snapped it shut. Now he was being corrected by a five-year-old with big blue-gray eyes. He drew in another deep breath. Much more of this and he'd be hyperventilating into a bag.

"Thank you, Lindsey. It can become quite tedious knowing when to use politically correct terminology." His words went right over her head, but she seemed happy to have made her point.

"The last two girls are Melpomene, the tragic one, and Polyhymnia, the girl of sacred song. That is nine. And it is officially bedtime."

"Okay," Sam said before Lindsey could complain. "Can Lindsey sleep in my bedroom? Millie said no because we didn't have your permission. But you are here now. Please, Father? Please, please, please?"

Millie folded her arms and waited to see how this would play out.

Jeff's mood had gone through so many shifts in the

short space of time he'd been home, it was hard to keep up. But Millie felt she was doing a fairly good job.

Right now, his expression reminded her of a stunned elk who desperately wished he could *not* read the license plate numbers on a semi. Millie decided it wouldn't be fair to laugh. Decisions about sleeping arrangements could be scary, she reasoned. Not for little kids, but...despite her brave actions to the contrary, if someone asked her to share a room with Jeff, *she'd* probably resemble the wide-eyed doe hugging the semi's hood ornament.

Oh, now this was good. Hands on his lean hips, a lock of dark hair falling over his forehead, he was frowning. Slightly distrustful. A confused warrior, she decided, who didn't have a clue about kids or how to read their behavior signals. Likely, that was because they were doing the jumping, cross-the-legs potty dance.

Still scowling, he glanced back and forth between Millie and the kids.

Then he pointed a finger between Sam and Lindsey. "Do either of you need to use the bathroom? No? Then please be still and stay right there."

She was fairly certain the man could use a hug right about now, but she resisted.

He stopped in front of her and leaned close so his voice wouldn't carry. "Is this...you know...the boy and the girl...?"

"Good grief, Jeff." Despite his sudden inability to complete a sentence, the helpless-guy look provided the interpretation. "They're five and six. It's perfectly acceptable for them to share a room. But I wasn't about to give my permission without knowing your feelings."

That actually seemed to surprise him. Pleasantly. He nodded, turned and walked back to the kids.

Strutted, actually. Pretty wild, Millie thought. A simple

common courtesy, withholding permission until he approved, as well, and the man literally preened.

She nearly laughed. He was standing over those kids, trying to look menacing, and he couldn't even pull that off because he was so happy with himself.

"Did you intend this slumber party to be for one night, or are we discussing an entire reorganization of the previously assigned accommodations?" he asked Sam.

"For the whole time. Millie does not want us wandering the halls, but if I wake up early, Lindsey is way over on the other side of the house and I cannot go see if she is awake so we can play." His velvety brown eyes pleaded. "I have two beds in my room."

Jeff looked at Lindsey. One of her bare feet was resting on top of the other. He wasn't sure how she kept her balance. Her fingers were tangled in the skirt of her white cotton gown, and with an innocent lack of modesty, she swished it around like a dancehall girl.

"I suppose you would like to abandon your present room and move in with Sam?"

She nodded her head vigorously.

Jeff sighed. He was a sucker for pleading faces. "Well then, I guess we better get you decamped and relocated before we all miss our bedtime and fall asleep in our breakfast."

The kids shrieked and raced up the stairs.

"Walk, please."

Even though Millie hardly raised her voice, Jeff gave a slight jolt. The kids obeyed in midstep.

He shook his head. "My mother used to do that. She never yelled but I was scared to death of her. Do you realize I deliberately towered over those kids just now, trying to make them think I was intimidating? It didn't faze them."

"That's because you were pretending."

"And you weren't." With that acknowledgment, he swept a hand in a gallant gesture, indicating that she should precede him up the stairs. She rolled her eyes and hooked an arm through his, tugging him along until they were side by side.

"You've spoiled my demonstration of gentlemanly behavior," he complained.

"Give it up, sheikh, you're digging your own grave. Maneuvering me in front so that my butt is at your eye level doesn't have a thing to do with chivalry."

He put a hand over his heart. "You wound me."

She laughed. "Obviously I don't *scare* you."

"Actually, you do." More than he wanted to admit.

Now that they were moving Lindsey in with Sam, leaving Millie alone in the east wing, he didn't hold out much hope for his ability to get a decent night's sleep. Knowing a child occupied the room next to hers had created boundaries he knew he wouldn't cross. He was going to have some problems with these new arrangements.

"So, you don't raise your voice and the kids know you mean business. What are the consequences for disobedience?" The stairway curved to the left onto the landing.

"Depends. Most likely they'd get a time-out."

"Ah, yes. I remember. The one that does not involve sports strategy, or team captains conferring with the coach."

She laughed. "That description's not half-bad. Just consider me the coach who's determining the rules of play."

"There is a flaw."

"Time-outs are against the law in Balriyad?"

He grinned, briefly touching the small of her back as

they made the partial Z-turn in the hallway. "The flaw is, if you are the coach, *you* cannot be sent on a time-out."

"If that's your polite way of saying I need an attitude adjustment, I'm afraid you're too late. My mom decided I was a hopeless cause years ago. And it's just as well I keep my coach title. A time-out wouldn't do me a bit of good. I'd enjoy it too much."

She breezed into Lindsey's room, retrieved the small, soft-sided Scooby-Doo suitcase and laid it on the bed. Sam already had an armload of pants and shirts he'd scooped from one of the open dresser drawers. That mess wouldn't pack as nicely, but they were only going down the hall.

"You can carry those, Sam, or dump them in the suitcase."

"I will carry them. They are not heavy." He sat on the bed, hugging the wadded outfits to his chest. As she scooped a fuzzy duck off the pillow and retrieved a stray sock, she patted Sam's leg to let him know she appreciated his muscles. His chest puffed out in pride. Then he giggled and flapped his elbow, using it to point since his hands were occupied.

Millie turned around in time to see Lindsey struggling to reach into the deep bottom drawer. Her head was *in* the drawer, as was most of her nightgown. They all had a very nice view of her pink cotton panties.

"Lindsey, you're going to fa—" Millie dropped the duck and nearly crashed into Jeff as he raced across the room, catching Lindsey just as her bare legs flew up like the weightless end of a seesaw.

"We are gathering clothing, little one. Not diving for pearls." He set her on her feet.

"Thanks," Lindsey said, adjusting her nightie. "Those

drawers are pretty deep for kids. You should tell the furniture man to whack 'em down a little bit.''

Millie lightly squeezed Sam's shoulder. "Are you sure you want her camping in your room?" she whispered.

He gave her that cute, just-between-us grin. "Yeah." He shrugged, his smile wide and happy. "She's *too* funny.''

"That, she is.''

"Well?" Lindsey said to Jeff.

"Uh, drawer whacking…" Jeff hesitated a moment. "When I bought this house, the furniture was already in it, so I did not have an opportunity to speak to anyone about the dangers of very large furnishings in a little girl's room.''

"Oh. Okay. But how come you didn't bring your own furniture?"

"There was no room for any more.''

She scrunched up her face as though she'd gotten a whiff of rotten eggs. "Some of the junk is kinda ugly. I didn't think you picked it out.''

"Lindsey!" Definitely bedtime, Millie thought. "That's not a nice thing to say.''

Her eyes widened. She quickly looked at Jeff. "I'm sorry." Tears were already brimming. "I didn't mean to hurt your feelings. Only some things are sort of…not pretty. But *most* of it is pretty.''

He squatted in front of her and ran his palm over her curls. Millie sat on the bed beside Sam and slipped her arm around him, her eyes on Jeff and Lindsey.

The tenderness he displayed brought a lump to her throat. Lindsey never complained, but Millie knew her sister longed for a dad.

She'd seen the way Lindsey watched her friends' fathers pick them up from day care. She would wrap her arms around her knees and pull them to her chest, her gaze taking in every hug and kiss, a smile on her lips at the happy display. And Millie could tell she was lost in her own world for those few moments, casting herself in a starring role where she was the little girl whose daddy picked her up when Mom worked late.

She saw a hint of that yearning now, the adoration in the wide eyes of a little curly blond cherub gazing up at a dark-haired hero. Even though Jeff was kneeling, Lindsey looked so tiny next to him, and that made his gentleness all the more touching.

This man had a soft spot in his heart for children. And not just his own.

"I will tell you a secret, little one." With his thumb, he wiped a tear from Lindsey's cheek. "I think some of this junk is downright ugly, too. So do not worry that my feelings are hurt. I am as tough as an alligator."

She gave him a skeptical look. "No, you're not."

He stood slowly, widening his eyes and raising his arms overhead. With his hands bent like arthritic claws, he hunched slightly, contorted his face into a darn good impression of a scary monster and let out a roar.

Lindsey gave a piercing squeal and took off. Sam flung clothes in every direction and shot off the bed. The kids crashed into each other, then popped back up like coiled springs almost before their bottoms touched the floor. Chaos ensued.

Millie considered calling a halt to the fright-night escapades, but seeing Jeff skulking around the room, imitating a scary alligator monster was just too good. Here was the boy that was inside every man, the goofy side that girlfriends and wives rolled their eyes at but secretly thought was cute.

She'd be willing to bet Jeff hadn't chucked his stuffy dignity like this in a good long while.

The kids were wound up, running around like crazed mice, their squeals ear piercing. Lindsey had the hiccups. She and Sam had conked heads twice.

Millie opened her mouth to put an end to the romp but she never got a chance.

A deep voice from the hallway cracked like the report of a pistol. ''Do not move!''

Squeals turned into instant gasps of silence. Everyone froze exactly where they were, which turned out to be in a short of cluster. Jeff had his back to the door, his arms still raised above his head and his fingers spread in pretend claws.

Millie was facing the door, as were the kids. She started to reach for their shoulders, to pull them in closer to her, but Jeff's eyes snapped out a warning. Her knees turned to pudding. He was dead serious. She'd never seen a person's eyes speak so clearly. She heeded that silent warning without question and with complete trust.

The way his body was positioned, Millie could only see below his armpit.

Her knees shook. Sweetly scented air stung her eyes as she gaped in horror at the gun.

Her gaze whipped back to Jeff's. *Gun. Do something.*

In the dead silence, Lindsey hiccuped.

Jeff's lips quirked. ''May I put my hands down now, Sadiq?''

''Deke!'' Millie automatically moved to step around Jeff, to count her chicks and make sure she was the only one traumatized by having a gun pointed at them.

Swifter than lightning, her body was lifted flat against Jeff's, her feet inches off the floor. From knees to chest, not even a butter knife could have fit between them. The adrenaline surge pumping her heart into a frenzy rushed into other sensitive nerve endings, pulsing, robbing her of speech.

His dark eyes were filled with the frightening intensity of a very dangerous man. And he was aroused.

Through the smooth, lightweight fabric of his dress pants, she felt the hot, steel-hard length of him pressed firmly, solidly against her. Her arms were trapped at her sides by his hold. The position of their bodies—whether accidental or designed—aligned them in a manner that made it nearly impossible not to give in to the throbbing urge to undulate against him.

Yet neither one of them moved. With her heart thundering, she held his gaze, couldn't look away. Even if she'd thought her vocal cords would work, she wouldn't have spoken. As she had moments ago, she heeded his vehement, silent message to let him lead.

Everything that had happened within the last few minutes had scared the devil out of her. A gun aimed at her head. Now another type of...*equipment* was pressing against the front of her pajama pants, and though her body's natural reaction flashed a bright neon green light to pursue this in private when the pandemonium settled, she had enough sense left to realize it wasn't a good idea to make rash decisions in a state of near shock.

On top of that, she was confused as to why they were locked together like boa constrictors in the first place.

"The green file is okay, Sadiq," Jeff said.

Millie frowned. Her feet touched the floor and his arms loosened, but he didn't totally release her.

"Do not *ever* move in a situation like that until I tell you it is safe." His voice was dangerously soft, his expression hardened in an intensely serious mask he would let no one see past.

"But it was Deke," she whispered. "And the kids—"
She looked around. Sam and Lindsey were gone!

"He could see the kids. He could not see you. Sadiq
is responsible for lives, Millie. That is his job. He will
protect my son and me at any cost. Do you understand
what I am saying?"

Her nerves were shot. She wasn't sure if she was going
to lose her temper or cry. "I need to see about the kids.
Can I go now?"

He stepped back so she didn't feel so crowded, but he
didn't let her go. "They are with Sadiq."

"How do you know? Do you have eyes in the back of
your head? And how the hell did you know it was him at
the door?"

"I know he took the kids because he would have seen
us talking. Sadiq does not need instructions, Millie. We
have known each other since we were Sam's age. Since
the alarm has not gone off, and Zaki and Sadiq are the
only two besides us in the house, I was ninety-nine percent certain it was him at the door. Mostly it was the smell
of peppermint that tipped me off. Sadiq carries a pump
bottle and sprays the scent ahead of himself if he has any
reason to believe I might need a means to identify him
by."

"Well." She crossed her arms, uncrossed them, then
tucked her hair behind her ear. "I hope he doesn't still
have that gun out around the kids. I just don't like that,
Jeff. Sam and Lindsey don't need to be traumatized any
more. They don't need to be glamorizing guns, either—"

"Millie."

He pronounced her name like the softest caress, stroked
the backs of his fingers over her cheek with little more
pressure than a feather, and whispered his thumb across
her lips.

"He will not show his weapon like a toy, even if the kids ask to see it. There are no guns lying around in this house where curious children might put their hands on them and come to harm." His fingers skimmed the tip of her ear, sending chills over her arms, as he gently untucked the clump of curls she'd just anchored.

"If Sam and Lindsey were traumatized, they would be in here clinging to our legs, would they not? I know Sam would. And you are avoiding my question. Do you understand what I am telling you about Sadiq's job, about our lifestyle? It is important."

She shook her head. "I guess not. I can't understand how squealing kids and a family game of monster could make a smart, sweet guy like Deke think we had an intruder or that someone was being hurt. I can't understand how people live with bodyguards, or put so many alarms on the house a person with a weaker constitution than mine might end up becoming a hermit or go deaf. And I guess I *don't* understand why you felt the need to flex your muscles—" she paused a beat, and dipped her gaze without actually looking "—when all I had to do was step out and Deke would know me."

"First off, the additional muscle flexing is called a hard-on, and I would apologize, but I cannot. You are an exciting, beautiful woman. If your body is pressed against mine, that will happen. I do not do well with apologies, and I am certainly not going to parrot them twenty times a day."

Her jaw dropped open.

His finger under her chin snapped it shut. "Secondly, I could apologize for having your body against mine to begin with, but I *will* not." He shook his head when she opened her mouth to speak. "Sadiq is one of the nicest men you will ever meet, yes. But he is trained to kill,

Millie. Do you understand that?'' His voice was strained yet somehow gentle.

"We have a code," he continued. "Sadiq does not stand down until he is absolutely certain all is well, that I am not being coerced into sending him away. When he is at his job, he is a different man." He raked a hand through his hair. "This was my fault. The situation, the silliness—I was imagining the look on his face when he realized *I* was the one playing the monster. I relaxed my guard. It was not until you moved that I realized I had not given him the all clear."

The green file, she thought. That was their code.

He looked toward the ceiling, took a breath. "I have never felt the depth of fear and dread that I felt at that moment. It consumed me until I could not see. Millie, you have not been here long. Sadiq does not really know you. He has never seen me romp in the house. He has never heard Sam squeal like a pig. The commotion was foreign and suspicious to him. And there I stood, with my back to him. At this point, he most likely had an idea it was you standing in front of me, but he could not see you and he could not be sure. My error could have cost you your life."

Some of the fear he'd spoken about flashed in his eyes before he went on.

"Because even if he knew it was you, had seen you with his own eyes, if I remain deliberately silent...then that means you are an enemy."

Millie needed to sit down.

CHAPTER NINE

"I WILL UNDERSTAND if you feel you must leave," Jeff said, quietly.

Millie glanced up. He was leaning against the heavy mahogany post of Lindsey's bed—or rather, Lindsey's former bed—watching her for a reaction, yet keeping his own hidden.

What kind of family were they that a friend or an employee could suddenly become a suspected enemy?

"Forrester Square Day Care conducts a thorough background check on all of their employees, and I'm pretty certain Katherine faxed mine over to you." She paused while he nodded. "Based on what I saw tonight, am I also right in assuming that overly cautious folks such as yourself and Deke wouldn't take someone else's word, and that you would do your own research, as well?" He nodded again.

"Then how in the devil could anyone possibly even *think* I could be an enemy?" Frustration underlined each of her words.

"Records can be altered."

"What the heck kind of people do you hang out with?" A shadow of something that resembled pain flashed in his eyes, but it was gone so quickly she couldn't be sure. She picked up Lindsey's fuzzy duck and held it in her lap. "Jeff, are you in danger?"

"No."

His answer was too resolute. "Look, I know you don't like to get into the touchy-feely personal stuff, but can't you give me a hint here? You're primarily an oil baron, yet you're also an heir to rule an entire country, a very peaceful country—don't frown, I haven't pried into your life. I've just had some basic conversations with Zac and pieced some things together from Sam and Lindsey's chatter. What I'm asking is, do either one of these occupations, or titles, or whatever they are, make you and your family the equivalent to ducks in a carnival booth?"

He shook his head. "It shouldn't. I have no enemies that I know of. I am heir to the throne in Balriyad but there is no one opposing me. The only person who would have vied for the position was my brother, Kasim, and he died on a boat with my wife."

"Oh, Jeff…" She didn't reach out to him because his body language clearly stated he didn't want sympathy.

"I told you about the intruder at the penthouse in Seattle, but we may never know who it was or what he intended other than to flaunt his skill at breaking and entering. The note was probably nothing more than a foolish prank."

"What note? You didn't tell me about a note. What did it say?" Great. Now she sounded like an overwrought wife. Thankfully, he didn't seem to notice.

"Just the words, 'I will be you.' Which makes no sense. As I said, I do not know of any enemies. But since the deaths of my brother and my wife, I have become much more cautious. I have insisted on what you might consider extreme security. Mostly for Sam's sake." He glanced toward the ceiling, the tendons in his hand straining as his grip on the bedpost tightened. "I could not bear to lose him, Millie."

There it was, she realized. He had lost so much, and

the one precious thing he had left in life, his son, he would protect with every means at his disposal. She doubted Jeff would admit that the fear was mostly for himself.

"I was," she said, "and still *am* somewhat the same way with Lindsey—overprotective. When my grandma Liz died, I was prepared. She'd lived a full, happy life and was ready to hang up her apron and rest. I didn't get this awful, scared feeling inside." She put her hand over her heart.

"But when Mom and Pop were killed, they were too young, with too much to look forward to. I held Lindsey on my hip and waved to them from the door. It took them forever just to back out of the driveway because Mom kept stopping Pop so she could shout out the car window and remind me of one last thing. I remember hollering back, 'would you just go, already. I know what to do, I'm practically this kid's mother.' I never dreamed those words would come back to haunt me within a few days." She swallowed the emotion that swelled in her throat.

"All I had left was Lindsey, and I was scared to death to let her out of my sight. That's what happens, Jeff. You hold on tight to what you have left because you can't bear the thought of losing them, as well. But alarms and an entire army of bodyguards can't always keep a child from getting hurt. Tonight, I was three steps behind the kids when they both fell. They could have seriously injured themselves and I was right there watching, helpless to stop it. It's impossible to control everything."

He nodded, but she didn't know if that meant he agreed or disagreed. He hadn't spoken, yet she knew he'd absorbed everything she'd said. He was still in that watchful state, waiting to see if she intended to go or to stay. Right at this moment, he looked utterly alone in the world, though she couldn't pinpoint what it was that gave her the strong impression.

She wondered if he suffered some sort of guilt over the deaths of his wife and brother, maybe felt he was responsible or that he might have somehow been able to prevent whatever tragedy that had occurred. She wondered if that guilt had been resurrected tonight when he'd been beating himself up over putting her in jeopardy. She didn't know those answers.

What she *did* know was that she wasn't a quitter, and that life didn't come with a guarantee. Forty thousand dollars, her dream and Lindsey's future were only a week away. Deke was skilled at his job. She liked him, trusted him, instinctively knew he would not have harmed her. He might have detained her until he was satisfied that she was on the up-and-up, but he would never make a fatal judgment error if he had even a shred of doubt.

That gut-level belief gave Millie the reassurance she needed for Lindsey's safety and well-being. If she thought for one minute that staying here would put her little sister in danger, she'd be out of here in a flash. Staying on a private island, with Deke as a watchdog, was actually safer than going to confession at Our Lady of Mercy.

She also knew that Jeff wouldn't make the same mistake again. She'd seen the genuine fear in his eyes. Fear for her. It hadn't been overreaction.

But she wasn't the type to go screaming into the night, and she didn't intend to change her stripes now. Sam needed her, and so did Jeff—to pick up the slack while he took care of business, she clarified to herself.

Idly stroking the fuzzy duck, she glanced at him from the corner of her eye. Judging from his body's intriguing reaction when they'd been pressed together like flypaper, she had a pretty good idea he liked her. That knowledge made her fantasies not seem so foolish after all. Logically she knew it had only been a short time, but it felt as though she'd known Jeff and Sam for so much longer.

Her biggest problem was that she wanted to know Jeffri al-Kareem on a much deeper level—which was an incredibly foolish desire for a relationship that was a mere two-week interlude.

She stood and began folding clothes, arranging them in Lindsey's suitcase. As though he'd been holding his breath, Jeff let his shoulders fall. For one telling instant, his shield lowered and he dropped his chin toward his chest.

Millie realized that he'd misinterpreted her actions. He thought she'd decided to leave.

"Are there rules against a sheikh packing a little girl's suitcase?" His head jerked up. Her voice was casual as she continued, "I mean, if it's going to cause some sort of royal uproar for you to snatch a few hangers off a rail or pick up a pair of shoes, then forget it. Otherwise, make yourself useful and grab the stuff in the closet. I'm a lot more pleasant at breakfast if I've had a little sleep the night before."

It took him a moment to grasp what she was saying. Then, his features relaxed and he did the most amazing thing. He smiled. Not with his mouth. Only with his eyes.

Amusement with a healthy dose of gratitude spanned the distance between them. What power did this man possess that he could literally speak to her with his eyes? And what gift did she embrace that she could understand him?

If eyes were truly the windows to a person's soul, Jeff's core was a darn good one. He just needed a little help dusting off the cobwebs.

As he started across the room, he brought his hand up

in a sharp salute, and said, "Absolutely, madam coach. 'Grabbing stuff' is one of my top skills."

"Oh, don't start. *You* wouldn't like a time-out."

He plucked hangers off the closet rail. "Why would you say that?"

"Because you can't have your computer, or your electronic scheduling thingy, or your cell phone, or talk to your secretary, or catch up on your files and reports, or have anybody in the room with you, or—"

"I get the picture. You are torturing our children."

She knew he meant "our" children in the generic sense, but it felt very intimate and familial. After what she'd just been through, why was it that she could clearly visualize the four of them as a family?

"Millie? I was only kidding."

She glanced up and saw the worried expression on his face. The items from Lindsey's closet hardly filled both of his hands. She wasn't about to tell him the real reason she'd gone mute.

And she wasn't about to let him go on blaming himself and feeling horrible about tonight, either.

"Okay, listen up." She tossed the fuzzy duck on the bed and turned to fully face him. "I'm tough, but I can still get spooked. But then I'm tough again—"

"This is a similar thing as the 'I am good' conversation that I admired during your employment interview, right?"

"Maybe. I'm not sure. I haven't gotten that far yet. And you broke the interrupting rule. I don't know why we have a rule in the first place because we have no consequences. We're going to have to think about that. Or maybe you will because that was your rule. Anyway—" She lifted her hands, then let them drop. "I forgot what I was saying."

He laid Lindsey's clothes on the bed. "You are tough, you get spooked, then you are tough again."

"Thank you. You're a very good listener for a man." She frowned when he held up a finger. "Yes?"

"I only wanted to object to the sexism. Now proceed. You are tough again."

The whole ridiculous thing struck her as funny and she started to laugh. The real, tickle-your-tummy kind of laugh. It lifted her spirits and made her feel as though she glowed.

"Are you laughing at me?" Amusement still lurked in his eyes, yet there was reserve, as well.

She shook her head. "I'm laughing at us. It's amazing what laughter can do for your mood. You should try it. Then maybe you'd stop moping around on this guilt trip— a guilt trip, by the way, that you didn't buy a ticket for and have no business taking."

"I am not on a guilt trip."

"Yes, you are!" Frustration twisted in her stomach. The man could be so muleheaded. Hands on her hips, she marched right up to him. "You think you accidentally told your bodyguard to off me. Well, give the man some credit, why don't you. Not everyone leaps when you say frog. I'm here, I'm staying, you are *not* getting rid of me, so you might as well—" His mouth swallowed the rest of her words.

In one single move, he hauled her close, his hands gripping her upper arms, his lips waging a gentle onslaught on her senses.

Accept it was what she'd been going to say. After the first astonished moment, she took her own advice.

And accepted him.

With the tension radiating from him in nearly palpable waves, she would have expected aggression. Yet his lips contradicted. He kissed her with a tenderness she would never have believed him capable of, his mouth slightly open, lips to lips. He didn't try to dominate or rush.

She flattened her palms on his chest, noted the fine tremor in her hands as she tentatively stroked the soft cashmere that molded his torso. Whatever demon that had pushed him so close to the edge seemed to retreat with her touch. His grip on her arms eased, slid upward.

His fingers toyed with the underside of her hair, sending exquisite chills over her arms, her face, the tips of her ears.

He angled his head, changing the pressure of his lips, and somehow she knew he was going to stop. She wanted to cling, wanted to taste. She wanted to feel each new and exciting sensation, sensations she'd never felt before, ones she didn't know if she'd feel again.

But when his head lifted and he looked down at her, his eyes black with desire, she didn't cling. The last thing she wanted was for this larger than life, sensual man to realize she wasn't exactly an expert in this particular arena.

A few more of these sessions and she would be.

"Well," she said, stepping back and tugging at her pajama top. She crossed her arms beneath her breasts, uncrossed them. "Did that come under the heading of an interruption? No. Wait." She held up her hand like a traffic cop. "Don't answer that. If we have to assign consequences for ground rule violations, I don't want that one in there."

His teeth raked across his bottom lip as though he could still taste her. "Why?"

"Because interruptions are rude—but that was very nice."

He shook his head. "I have never known another woman who speaks her mind so boldly and so honestly."

"I hope that was a compliment. Because if it's a criticism, you're out of luck. We made a deal, you and I, and I'm holding you to it. I've got seven days left and I always honor my commitments."

She lifted her chin, wishing she had a pair of platform shoes to give her a little more stature. Because when he towered over her in just that way, with his head bent and his gaze straying to her mouth, she wanted to melt right there on the spot and admit flat out that she was in over her head.

In high school she'd been the goalie on the water polo team. She could certainly tread water better than this.

"I intend to start my catering business. So you can stop watching me like a hawk to see if I'm going to fall apart or walk out on you. I can't have you slinking around the house feeling all guilty and bending over backward to be nice."

His brows shot up. "I'm not—by damn you *do* like to argue."

"Who said anything about arguing? I'd just like everyone to be normal again."

"Sweetheart, I'm not sure if normal exists."

Sweetheart.

Okay. Her heart was tripping; lungs were having major struggles. Acting normal was difficult... She wasn't going to look at his mouth, would *not* put any significance on the fact that he'd kissed her and used an endearment.

The rest of his statement filtered back through her mind. She narrowed her eyes. "You were dying to add two more words, weren't you? '*Around you,* I'm not sure if normal exists,'" she rephrased for him.

He laughed, scooped up Lindsey's duck and flipped the

suitcase closed. "You will always keep a man on his toes, won't you? You love to argue, you want to be in control, you make up your own rules, you want the flexibility to change these made-up rules at will *and* you would like to add words and thoughts to other's statements."

"I don't know why you keep insisting I like to argue. Arguing is when you're yelling and screaming and hurting someone's feelings."

"That is fighting," he said.

"Now look who's calling the kettle black. You're as bad as I am. We don't argue. We contradict."

"Then let us contradict as we finish packing Lindsey's belongings."

"We're done."

"What do you mean we are done?" He looked around the room. "Are you telling me that baby only has what is in this small suitcase and on those meager clothes hangers?"

"She's not a baby. She's five. And how much does she need for two weeks, especially since you've got a perfectly good washer and dryer?"

"Toys? Games?"

"The duck. I've got a game and a book in my duffel, but she hasn't even asked for them. Sam has enough to keep an entire day-care group busy. Are you ready?"

"Yes." Scooping up the hangers, he followed her to the door. "She has toys at home, though?"

Millie chuckled. "Yes, Jeff. I take very good care of my sister. If she tells you she's a poor waif and lives in a shack, don't believe her."

"Would she tell me that?"

"I wouldn't put it past her. She's a drama queen." As they passed Millie's room, she caught Jeff looking in the open door. She held her smile and her tongue until they were almost at Sam's room.

"In case you were wondering, you're as human as any other mortal. I just caught you, fair and square, looking in my bedroom." With a cheeky grin, she left him standing in the hall, slightly bemused, and breezed into Sam's room.

Deke sat in a leather chair at the game table, his gaze shifting from the two giggling streaks who had just disappeared under the covers to Millie's. In his eyes, she saw both apology and affection.

"You're a pushover, you know." She tipped her head toward the trundle bed pushed up against the sleigh bed and the two lumps burrowed under the blankets.

"Not always."

She nodded to let him know she wasn't going to dissolve into tears or smash one of Sam's action figures over his head. Stepping over to the mahogany sleigh bed, she gave the trundle a push in the opposite direction.

Lindsey flipped the covers off her face. "Hey! I can't be far away. I have to be close to Sam so we won't see the spiders under his bed."

Sam's head popped from beneath the quilt and he rose up on an elbow to peer over the side of his bed—presumably to check out any escaping eight-legged creatures and the ruination of their redecorating scheme.

"There aren't any spiders under the bed." Millie tucked the blankets snugly around Lindsey and kissed her soft, warm cheek. "But we don't want Jeff to step on you or fall and break his neck when he kisses Sam good-night. We'll push you back before we turn out the lights."

"Is Jeff gonna kiss me good-night, too?"

Well, this was awkward. He was standing less than ten

feet away, and Lindsey's voice had two volumes—medium loud, and really loud. "I'm sure he will."

Jeff glanced up from his quiet conversation with Deke. "I always save the pretty ladies for last."

The joyous expression on Lindsey's face was priceless. Blinking back a sudden sting of tears, Millie pecked another kiss on Lindsey's forehead. "Night, pet." A slew of "love you's" and more kisses followed, and it took a minute before she managed to unwrap herself from Lindsey long enough to stand.

Maneuvering between the trundle and the sleigh bed, Millie smoothed the blankets over Sam and tucked them under his chin.

"You guys aren't going to stay up all night giggling, are you?" she whispered. His head shifted back and forth against the pillow. "Good, because we've got a busy morning planned. Remember what I told you about those early birds finding the best worms?"

His dark eyes grew round. "I remember," he whispered.

"Okay. Sleep tight, sweetie." She kissed his forehead, then hesitated. The words that nearly spilled out grew right from her heart.

Solemn brown eyes gazed up at her with awe, adoration and the same hopeful anticipation she so often saw in Lindsey's. She knew Sam had been listening to the exchange between her and Lindsey.

Even though she'd made a firm decision not to shield her emotions around Sam, that didn't stop her from worrying whether she truly had the *right* to speak her heart, since she was so temporary in his life.

Yet how could the truth ever be wrong? Especially for a little boy who'd lost so much and desperately needed to hear it.

She dropped her forehead to his and let her heart lead as she usually did. "I love you, Sam, my man. Sweet dreams."

"I love you, too, Millie."

Oh, yes. When she boarded the boat to go home, she would definitely bleed.

She smacked a kiss on his cheek to cover her emotions, and sat up.

Jeff was standing at the foot of the bed.

Her gaze collided with his and her heart jumped into her throat. She felt as though she'd been caught gossiping—by the very person she'd been gossiping about.

His features utterly stoic, his body as rigid as a carving knife, she didn't need special mind-reading abilities to know he'd heard every word. And he wasn't happy about it.

CHAPTER TEN

MILLIE WASN'T GOING to apologize for her relationship with Sam. He was a smart boy. He understood she was a temporary employee—not a future mother.

Hopefully Jeff wasn't going to say something upsetting. As she eased by him, she gave his arm a squeeze, not quite sure what she intended the touch to accomplish. To soothe, perhaps. Or to just make him stop and think for an extra second before he plunged into his "I'm the authority around here and I know best" mode.

Lindsey was fighting to keep her eyes open, determined to be awake for Jeff's kiss. Millie didn't think she'd make it.

While Jeff spoke quietly with Sam, Millie looked around the room to see where he'd put Lindsey's suitcase. She spied it lying on the round game table by Deke.

He was watching her, and she realized that the two of them needed to clear the air. She could tease and laugh about tonight's drama, but truthfully, she would harbor a tiny seed of doubt unless she talked to Deke straight out. He would be honest. That much she was sure about.

She moved next to him. Although he was sitting, his head was nearly level with hers. She bent slightly, the softness of her voice carrying no farther than the two of them.

"If I'd stepped out from behind Jeff tonight, would we be here discussing it?"

He reached for her hand and carefully pressed it between his own huge palms. Utter sincerity radiated from his gentle touch and steady, unwavering gaze. It seeped from the pores of his skin, emanated from the unfeigned kindness in his eyes. As though linked by kinetic energy, she could literally feel this man's emotions and his truth.

Millie wondered if Balriyad men were born with these unsettling nonverbal skills, or if it was part of their required curriculum in school. Because, like Jeff and Sam, Deke's eyes and touch could speak as clearly as his words.

"I knew the truth the moment you spoke my name with such annoyance," he said quietly, releasing her hand. "Personally I was glad I was the one holding the weapon, and not you."

She dipped her head and gave him a mock scowl that, surprisingly, didn't take too much effort. "Well, you scared me to death."

"Guarding the al-Kareem family is scary and serious business."

"I know. And I'm glad they have you." She squeezed his massive shoulder and turned just as Jeff was tucking Lindsey's duck beneath her chin.

He brushed the curls from her forehead and tenderly pressed a kiss there, fulfilling his promise, even though Lindsey was already asleep. His gentleness with the children moved her. It was a side of him only a select few were privileged to witness.

Millie walked across the room and pushed the trundle back against Sam's bed as she'd promised. "I still need to put away Lindsey's clothes," she said quietly to Jeff. "You don't have to wait."

It didn't take her long to empty the suitcase and tidy the dresser drawers. The clothes they'd carried on hangers were already hung in the closet—evidently by Jeff.

Who would ever have believed she'd have a sheikh helping out with the chores? She was smiling over the thought when she shut the closet door behind her and realized he was still waiting for her.

"Oh," she whispered, glancing at the kids. "I thought you'd gone to bed."

He shook his head, arched his brows. Her ability to intuit expressions and body language was starting to give her the heebie-jeebies. Head shake translation: *Not a chance.* Arched brows: *I believe we have something to discuss.*

She didn't blame him. In his situation, she'd be just as wary if she believed a guy was blindly allowing Lindsey to build hopes that would crush her when she learned he had no intention of delivering. Oh, she still worried plenty about Lindsey's daddy radar. But they communicated.

"Night, Deke," she said softly as she headed toward the door. As soon as he had some privacy, the bodyguard would pull one of the Murphy beds from its hidden wall panel and rest. A human night-light, surrounding the children in a warm glow of safety.

Once they were in the hall, Sam's bedroom door shut behind them, Millie walked ahead a few steps so their conversation wouldn't be overheard. Her first instinct was to jump to her own defense, explain her reasoning for what she'd said to Sam, but this wasn't about her or Jeff. This was about Sam.

Comfortable with the distance, she stopped and leaned her back against the wall, facing Jeff. For several minutes, they stood in silence. Then Jeff raked a hand through his hair.

"I think you already know what is bothering me," he said. "Sam has been through so much in his young life. It worries me that you are encouraging him with affectionate words. He is hungry for that special bond all children wish for. I do not want my son hurt.''

''I know, Jeff. And I agree with you.''

''Then I do not understand.''

The evening had taken an emotional toll on her, and now that she was standing still, it caught up with her. She slid her back along the wall until she was sitting on the floor, her knees drawn to her chest.

''Sam is an easy kid to love. He just wiggled his way into my heart before I could stop him. The oh-so-proper little man striving for perfection to honor his family's name and make his father proud. The lonely child who's limited to watching life from the inside of a beautiful glass ball called royalty. The curious little boy with the impish sparkle in his eyes who wants to race with the wind, bounce Super Balls off the walls and ceilings and giggle until he can't catch his breath. The boy who's too young to really understand the full impact of grief. Oh, he feels the loss, and he has memories, but he'll lose them if someone doesn't keep them alive.'' She looked directly at Jeff. ''Do you keep those memories of his mother alive for him?''

For a moment, he seemed unaware that a response was required, then his spine snapped rigid. He loomed over her, insulted that she would question the way he handled a personal matter that was basically none of her business.

''If he asked me, I would talk to him. But I do not make it a point to bring up a subject that will only make the sadness greater.''

She ignored his pomposity. ''That's what I was wrestling with earlier. If Sam asked me directly how I felt about him, should I answer him honestly, or push him away with an easy, acceptable platitude that might be safer? I told myself it wasn't *right* to form a bond with

Sam. I came here to do a job. This one shouldn't have been any different from my others.'' She was truly at a loss to explain how or why his son was different.

''Believe me, getting my heart tangled up wasn't part of the deal when I signed on for this gig. It won't be easy…leaving Sam is going to be painful for me.'' She gave a flippant shrug. ''I usually make it a point to avoid pain.''

With the fluid grace of a jaguar, he hitched his dress pants, crossed his ankles and folded his legs beneath him as he sat down facing her on the floor. The hallway was unusually wide, yet he positioned himself where they were nearly touching. Resting his elbows on his knees, he leaned forward as though he'd heard the sadness in her voice and needed to get closer to offer comfort.

''And here we find ourselves,'' he said softly, ''between the proverbial rock and hard place.''

The quiet understanding in his tone seriously tested her shaky emotions. ''Seems like it. I'll promise you one thing right now. Sam won't come away with bruises. I'll do my best to make sure of that.'' Pressure built in her chest as she tried to find the right words.

''It's just that…we're playing or doing something together nearly every waking moment. I'm an open book when it comes to children. How could I hold him at arm's length when he's clearly seen that's not my personality? Those big brown eyes were so accepting, Jeff, yet so desperately longing….''

She swallowed, widened her eyes and looked toward the ceiling to stanch the burning moisture. She nearly lost the battle when Jeff touched the top of her bare foot, his fingers tentative, as though he wasn't quite sure how to handle this particular situation.

That made her smile. He probably hadn't thought about

offering comfort, he was just scared silly she was going to cry.

Under control now, she looked back at him and shrugged. "I had to weigh one choice against the other. I'm sure it's the same for you. If you hold back the memories of Sam's mother, that part of him will die. He'll think it's wrong to talk about her, or that it hurts you, or that he is somehow lacking—children take these things on themselves."

"Sam doesn't."

"I don't know the circumstances, Jeff. And I'm not asking for them. But I know kids. And my biggest worry with Sam's attachment to me—and mine to him—is that it would hurt him *more* if I held back. That if I went through all the motions, yet deliberately ignored his emotional needs, it would make him feel abandoned. So I chose honesty."

Jeff watched her for a long moment. She was wise for a woman so young. And unless she was a damned good actress, her honesty was deeply ingrained and genuine. That alone made her special. He wanted to believe she was exactly as she appeared, but he'd learned firsthand he could be a poor judge of character.

His own father had pointed that out at Rana's funeral when he'd refused to look upon the casket. Faruq al-Kareem had spat on the ground and turned his back. "Good riddance to her. She was unworthy, a disgrace, an adulteress. With your own brother. She and Kasim should rot in the desert and let the vultures pluck their flesh."

Jeff had been distraught over the loss of his wife, and livid that his father would care so little about his feelings. He had tried to salvage the day, even though he'd wanted to plow his fist into his father's face.

He'd reminded Faruq that even *he,* their own father,

could not tell the two brothers apart by appearance alone, and that the kiss incident between Rana and Kasim was months past and forgotten.

That's when his father had shattered Jeff's illusions of love and taught him the folly of blindly trusting with his heart.

"I did not raise an imbecile, Jeffri. You are heir to this throne, and must be protected. I have had your cheating wife under constant surveillance. You are so soft you go away on business and do not believe your wife will betray you. She thinks she is smart because her lover looks exactly like her husband. Your brother eats at your table, sleeps in your bed and makes love to your wife. They do not have to sneak. But then you begin to stay home more, because you are so in *love*. At least you had enough sense left to step off that boat when you saw Kasim. The only reason she wanted to mend the bad feelings between you as brothers was so Kasim could come and go freely in your home once more, and they could laugh in your face. I could not allow that to continue."

That's when Jeff had realized the unthinkable.

"Jeff?"

He blinked, then focused on Millie's earnest gray-blue eyes. "My wife's and my brother's deaths were not an accident." He hadn't planned to talk about this, but the words came spilling out.

"Rana and I went boating most Sunday afternoons, but that day I was finishing up some calculations on test wells. She said she wanted to go early to lie in the sun, so I told her I would meet her at the marina. When I got there, Kasim was on the boat with her. I had not spoken to my brother in eight months, and Rana decided it was time we repair our brotherly relationship. I was angry that she would try to manipulate me that way, and I refused to stay anywhere near Kasim.'' He idly traced the pattern of the Aubusson rug beneath him.

''The captain already had the engines running. I turned around and got off the boat as he was maneuvering her out of the slip. I halfway expected Rana to call off the afternoon trip, but she didn't. Ten miles out in the Mediterranean the boat exploded.''

Millie sucked in a breath and reached for his hand.

''The explosion ejected Rana from the boat. Kasim was in the cabin below deck—where the fire was centered. His body was never recovered.''

''Oh, Jeff, that could have been you in the boat.''

''No. If I had been on board, no one would have died that day. Rana and Kasim were lovers. I did not know that my father had Rana under surveillance. Evidently she did very little to hide the affair. Anyone who saw them together thought she was with me. And when I continued to blindly trust her, my father hired someone to kill them.''

''Oh, my God, Jeff! His own son? Why didn't someone arrest him?''

''It is difficult to arrest the man who makes the laws. Not impossible, but a person would have to care in order to initiate that battle. I did not care. I had been betrayed by my three closest family members. I was numb, to everything and everyone except Sam—and even that I botched up.''

''No, you didn't. And you're getting back on the right track now, anyway.''

''The memories I have of Rana—everything I believed about her—were a lie. That is why it is difficult to talk about her with Sam. How do you tell a boy of six that his mother was dishonest and an adulteress?''

''Was she a good mother?''

"Yes." He didn't hesitate over that answer. "She did love Sam."

"Then those are the memories you keep alive in his heart. You remind him that he was and is loved—by both of you. You have to separate your Rana from Sam's Rana. This isn't about you, Jeff. It's about Sam. I'm doing my part. I want you to promise me you'll do yours."

He stared at her for several long moments. "Did you attend a special school that taught you the secret to wearing a man down to get your way?"

She smiled because his tone was filled with both teasing and genuine admiration. "I watched how Mom handled Pop. He was so crazy about her he would have fallen in line anyway, but he let her *think* she was running the show."

Chuckling, he pushed himself up from the floor and stood. "Smart man, your Pop. As for running the show, should Sadiq step out the door and catch us socializing on the floor of the hallway, he will feel well justified in questioning my sanity and leadership abilities." He held his hand down to her, palm up. "Especially after my excellent impersonation of the alligator monster."

Millie grinned and placed her hand in his, letting him pull her up. Her smile faltered as a stunning jolt of sensation zapped every nerve ending in her body to life. She used the forward momentum to neatly side step him and quickly dropped his hand. Either she was ultrasensitive or this man was exuding enough sexual energy to jump-start a corpse.

"Do all guys think they have to look macho in front of other guys?"

He walked beside her. "Sure. Well, not necessarily macho. Self-assured."

"You never want to get caught looking like you don't know what you're doing, right?"

"Exactly." His lips canted as he glanced down at her.

"So, that's why you won't ask for directions when you're lost, or read instructions when something needs assembling."

"There you go, faulting my fellow man. However, I do not believe I am guilty of these traits."

She laughed, lightly smacked her head as though her brain had gone to sleep. "Of course not. You have a driver to deal with maps, and you pay people to put things together...." They'd reached his bedroom and she paused outside the closed door. "What about Sam's toys? Do you help him with those?"

"Yes."

"A lot of them come with instructions. Don't you have to read up on them?"

"They are toys!" His tone was incredulous, as though he couldn't believe she could possibly question his ability to figure out how a kid's toy worked.

Well, she thought. The mighty ego wasn't so mighty after all. Who'd have imagined it could be bested by a child's toy? She patted his arm to soothe.

Jeff looked down at her and saw the sparkle in her eyes. His lips twitched with the need to smile. He didn't know how she did it, but she could drag him right into the craziest conversations, and before he knew it, he'd lost all perspective and his dignity was shot to hell.

Like a moth too stupid to stop butting against the same lightbulb, he kept going back for more. He *wanted* more. There was something about Millie that gave him a sense of peace. Hell, maybe he'd gone mad after all.

This little spitfire could run circles around a platoon of well-conditioned soldiers. She talked faster than a door-to-door salesman with his foot wedged in the door, switched subjects with the reckless abandon of a race car driver turned loose in a labyrinth, and accompanied these amazing feats with pantomiming hands that somehow managed to leave the person she was conversing with unscathed. Mostly unscathed. There had been a couple of times—and he suspected it had been deliberate—when she'd flung her hands a bit more wildly and whacked him.

Full of energy, she hardly stopped from sunup to sundown. She'd practically taken over the running of his house and even told *him* what to do.

So how the hell did all that translate into peace?

"I think this is your stop on the guided tour of al-Kareem castle," she said, sweeping her arm with a flourish toward his room.

"This feels very wrong—a lady leaving me at my door." With a hand at the small of her back, he urged her down the hallway.

"Jeff!" She shook her head and laughed. "We're not on a date, and I don't need an escort to my room."

"Indulge my gentlemanly traits—which you cannot impugn, since there are no stairs that I am attempting to maneuver you onto. Besides, we need to discuss that dare—"

"Oh no you don't. You looked, buddy, and you lost."

"I feel I must point out in my defense that I merely turned my head. I did not stand in the hallway and gawk like you did."

"That's because you had me herding you along."

He merely shrugged. "We never did define a wager. What do you get for winning?"

"Satisfaction. That's all I need—well, almost. Open doors let Sam know you're home, and I don't want to mess with that. It would be nice, though, if you'd at least shut your bedroom door partway instead of leaving it flung back against the wall for all and sundry to happen by and catch you in your altogether or something.''

''My altogether?''

''Naked. Do we have a deal here?''

''For growing up most of your life as an only child, you are quite competitive.''

She laughed. ''I think what you mean to say is that I'm bossy and I like to win. *That's* what comes from being the only child. No competition, so we're used to having it our way.''

He shook his head. ''You have an answer for everything, even when it does not present you in the best light.''

They were in front of her bedroom door now. He put a hand on her shoulder.

''What makes you so strong, Millie? So different. Most people visibly change when they find themselves in the presence of dignitaries, or royalty, or wealthy, powerful people. Yet you do not.''

''Why should I? I'm sure wealthy, royal dignitaries slouch on the sofa, eat pizza, drink beer and watch Monday night football like everyone else. They laugh, cry, joke and make rude noises. They get blisters on their heels, or scrapes on their knuckles…and they look in open doors.'' She shrugged. ''I'm a hundred percent sure on the last one. How'd I do on the rest?''

''I am debating on the rude noises and crying.''

She socked him lightly in the arm.

''You see? If anyone dared do that to me, Sadiq would have him wrestled to the ground in nothing flat.''

She rolled her eyes. ''Despite the two of you trying to scare me half out of my mind this evening, Deke's crazy about me. And he knows I wouldn't hurt a flea. But, Jeff, how do you feel when people gush and fall all over themselves to please you?''

"That they simply respect the rudiments of protocol."

"Oh, pul-leeze. What's wrong with treating you like a normal man?"

"I think we might have covered that earlier."

"I'm not talking about sex—or kissing," she added, in case kissing wasn't considered sex and he thought she was confused.

"I am your employer."

"Yes, but that wasn't what you were asking me about. You wanted to know why I didn't bow and scrape and lick your boots."

"I said nothing about bootlicking."

She shrugged. "I admit I was surprised and nervous when you dropped the sheikh bombshell on me, but now I'm just curious. What else can I say? I respect you as a man, and I respect you as an employer. I adore Sam, and I would guard him with my life—not because he's your son, or just a job. The biggest difference between you and me is that you're programmed to bark orders. I'm programmed to bite back when someone barks. So what do you think? Can this marriage be saved?"

The minute the teasing words escaped her lips, she wanted to snatch them back. But she wouldn't, even though she could feel the heat flushing her neck and cheeks. To backpedal would only make it look as though she had marriage on her mind and was trying to pretend she didn't.

He'd think she'd really read something into that kiss.

So she stuck out her hand instead, praying her knees wouldn't melt under the steady gaze of his deep chocolate eyes. "Friends?"

He pulled his right hand out of his pocket and wrapped

it around hers. When he cupped his left hand around it, too, her heart skittered.

Still holding her gaze, he slowly lifted her hand to his mouth and gently pressed his lips to her knuckles. The air in her lungs froze in midbreath.

This was no dry peck on the hand. Although she couldn't actually *see* his lips open, she felt moist flesh against hers. Incredibly warm, velvet-smooth, his slightly parted lips sipped at her hand as gently as a butterfly's wings.

He lifted his head, still holding her hand. "You can breathe now, Millie."

She'd forgotten to breathe? When she exhaled, tiny white specks flashed around her head like baby fireflies. Wouldn't that be sophisticated as all get out—to pass out over a kiss on the hand. God help her if she ever decided to go for *all* the bases.

"Well. If that's how you greet a friend, I'd like to know what the custom is for a lover." Oh, this nervous tongue was going to get her in trouble. She saw his eyes darken and held up her hands. "Forget I said that. I can figure out that answer on my own, thank you very much. I'm probably dingy from an overload of wizards and mythological muses, and here I am standing in the hall in my pajamas and—" His fingers against her mouth stopped the chatter."

"Millie?"

She answered with a lift of her eyebrows, given that his fingers were still covering her lips.

"You talk more than any woman I have ever met."

She narrowed her eyes and he smiled. A smile that showed his teeth and went all the way to his eyes.

"This is still my house," he reminded her.

Smart man, he kept his fingers over her lips, and his

smile slid into a grin. He obviously knew she'd love to toss out a rebuttal.

"I will work on the friendship concept," he continued, "and I'm willing to compromise—on some things. Not all. I have my reasons, and you will simply have to trust that I know what is best." He paused. "I can see in your eyes that you are wanting to tell me my reasons could be wrong and your argument might be stronger. No need, spitfire. I have no doubt we will butt heads. But I am better prepared for the game now." He removed his fingers from her mouth.

"I'm not playing a game," she said. And perhaps she'd let him off his guilt trip too easily.

"Figure of speech, poorly chosen. Now, I think I should retire. No sense keeping you standing in the hallway in your nightclothes…unless you are interested in a good-night kiss."

It took a great effort not to climb right up his body and let him give her another taste of bliss. "Um, I don't think that will be necessary."

He grinned and stepped closer. With his fingertip, he traced a pattern on her pajama top, right over her heart. She sucked in another breath, aware that he was watching for a reaction. She couldn't do a thing about the tremors running rampant inside her, but she could at least remember to exhale.

She had no idea what his fingertip sketched so lazily, unable to let go of his seductive gaze long enough to look down.

She'd played this game countless times in school with her girlfriends, writing words or drawing pictures on one another's backs, then trying to guess what they were.

Well, this drawing wasn't anywhere near her back. Instead it was straying to the upper swell of her breast. Was it any wonder she couldn't summon a speck of competitive spirit? A vague resemblance to a heart shape, she guessed, oval, tapering, two humps and dips.

His deep brown eyes flared as the last segment of his imaginary art took his finger down the upper slope of her breast, until the lapel of her pajamas created a blockade. He glanced down as though he could see his invisible masterpiece, then slowly, oh so slowly, looked up, stunning her with the intensity of his gaze.

Anticipation tripped over fear. Was he going to kiss her after all?

This was a powerfully sexual man, a man who could consume a woman. Oh, Lord, she wondered if he could see her shaking. Feel her heart knocking against her ribs.

His gaze dipped to her lips and her heart nearly stopped beating. To have a man focus on her mouth in a blatant show of desire, of intent, had been a fantasy she'd scripted a thousand times during the lonely hours at night.

His eyes slowly lifted. He was so close, his breath warm against her cheek, his skin still carrying a hint of sea air.

Everything within her screamed for action, urging her to drag him those last few inches and end this intoxicating torture, yet she kept her arms at her sides, her short nails digging half moons in her palms. She shouldn't start something she wasn't entirely certain she was ready to finish.

But the cheering committee in her brain wouldn't let up. He'd kissed her hand. She could indulge herself and kiss him good-night. They'd already broken the ice earlier. Why was she even more nervous now?

She'd gotten as far as uncurling her fingers when he straightened, tapped her chest—closer to her collarbone this time—and stepped back. His smile was enigmatic.

"I like you, Millie Gallagher. A lot."

CHAPTER ELEVEN

BEFORE MILLIE could form a coherent thought or response, Jeff simply turned and walked down the hall, leaving her to contend with legs that were more unstable than a stack of gelatin blocks.

Shoving her hair out of her face, she watched his trim backside, noted the way his slacks molded without pulling, defining his assets just enough to make any woman with a speck of hormones drool.

I like you. A lot.

Well, she thought. What do you know about that. A smile bathed her insides, stretched her mouth and lifted her cheeks.

The world had shifted on its axis while she stood right here in the hall wearing her Tweety Bird pajamas.

Her… Oh, God.

Grabbing the hem of her shirt, she stared numbly at the cute yellow birds with oversize heads and wide innocent eyes stamped on the front panels of her pajama top.

Not once the entire night had she given a thought to the print on her pajamas. She'd had them so long, they were like the heirloom rattan-back chair that sat in the corner of her living room. She rarely noticed the details of the rattan, she just knew it was a chair and it was there.

Granted, there were only four faded birds on the pajama top—the bottoms, thankfully, wcrc solid gray. But faded or not, in Millie's mind, the cartoon pj's might just as well scream out, "Virgin!"

She was such an idiot. He hadn't been drawing a heart. He'd been tracing the wide-eyed canary. She slipped into her bedroom, shut the door and leaned against it. Her insides were jumping like frog legs in a hot skillet.

Letting her head fall back against the hard surface of the door, she gave in to the bubble of laughter tickling the back of her throat.

Wouldn't you just know it, she thought. Her first *real* adult kiss, and the first time in her life a man had kissed her hand…and she'd been wearing Tweety Bird pajamas!

JEFF SEARCHED the house from top to bottom and didn't see or hear any sign of Millie and the kids. It was only 8:00 a.m. The kids had been up late last night with all the commotion and room switching, and he'd have thought they might want to sleep late. Hell, *he* would like to sleep late. Or sleep period.

Big, *big* mistake kissing Millie.

He'd sworn he would resist temptation, yet he hadn't even lasted until Lindsey was completely moved out of her bedroom. He felt as though he'd been cast under a spell, and his will was no longer his own. That was insane.

So what if she wore soft oversize pajamas that shot his concentration to hell, turned him into a raging mass of testosterone, tortured him with their loose-fitting style that guaranteed he could have her naked in two seconds flat. And just because the erotic tilt of her mouth, or sassy toss of her head, or the sweet shape of her butt in a tight pair of jeans could shoot his body from zip to hard in two seconds, there was no reason to think he would relinquish his emotional control or the control of his household. No reason to overreact.

He'd never been a slave to his sexual urges, only to his heart. And since that organ was well insulated, he was a damned fool for wasting hours of sleep worrying about the other one—which was merely fulfilling its male duty as nature intended.

He opened a false set of books on the shelves in the library and pressed the button, impatiently waiting for the hidden section of the rich mahogany bookcase to pivot, opening the way to a tunnel that led beneath the house and eventually ended up on the beach.

Damn it, why couldn't she stay put indoors? He should not have coached her on operating the alarm. The bells were annoying, yes, and the security people were weary of false alarms, but at least he knew when she was indoors or out.

Stepping inside the musty passageway, he listened. Voices would echo in here. Dust and sand covered the concrete floor. Imprints of adult male shoes tracked in both directions, but no impressions of kid-size prints. The footprints could belong to Sadiq, or to one of the service men who'd done work on the house during the title transfer after he'd bought the island last year. The fact that he wasn't sure made him edgy.

He knew Sadiq would be with Sam and Millie and Lindsey. He wasn't so much worried as he was annoyed. A man liked to know about the comings and goings in his own house.

Once the false wall of the bookcase was back in place, Jeff headed out of the library and toward the kitchen. Slapping open the swinging door, he strode across the stone tiles.

''Zaki!''

''Yes, Your Highness?''

Jeff whirled around, scowling at the man who had practically raised him. Zaki, arms folded across his chest, leaned lazily against the wall by the cellar door.

"I would accuse you of spending too much time in the company of Sam's nanny," Jeff said, "if I was not already aware of your deliberate delight for irreverence."

Zaki grinned, pushed his shoulder from the cellar door and stepped forward, hands clasped at waist level as though in prayer. "What may I do for you, Sheikh Jeffri?"

"You can cut the crap before I belt you."

Zaki threw back his head and laughed. Jeff simply stared. They both knew he'd never lay a finger on any of his friends, employees or not. But damn it, had the whole world gone mad? Last week he did not have to search half the morning to find his son, he did not have to make sure his bedroom door wasn't standing wide open, he did not have to explain naked muses. In fact, he did not have to explain *anything*. He made a decision, and it was done. Period.

Now, his man of service mocked him, his minister of security trusted his gut instinct—thank God for that—and his son had raised his voice and gotten his way because Jeff had been too dumbstruck by an impertinent tongue and voluptuous lips. And worse, the tiny, energetic woman who possessed those enticing lips was leaving a set of size six tennis shoe tracks up one side of him and down the other.

That was a hell of a lot for one man to put up with in his own household. He had every right to own this foul mood, and by damn, he would.

He waited until Zaki finished his solo laugh festival. "Do you know where Millie and the kids are?"

"Fishing."

"Fishing?" He wasn't sure he'd heard right. "On the yacht?"

"No. In a tin boat."

"A tin boat?"

"Did you sleep with your stereo headphones on again, Jeffri? I have told you that will ruin your hearing. Shall I speak louder?"

"Just speak." *Smart aleck.* When Zaki resorted to absurdity and sarcasm—which had become a habit since the deaths of Rana and Kasim—it was his way of saying that Jeffri might be the Crown Prince, but Zaki was the man who'd practically raised him, and he'd better step back and think about that for a minute.

At times Jeff had felt comforted that Zaki knew his secrets and was available to talk as his own father had never been. Other times, his raw emotions could not bear it, and to prevent himself from disrespecting his friend, he would merely grit his teeth and walk away.

Right now, Zaki had him over a barrel. Jeff leaned his hip against the kitchen island and waited.

"It began very early this morning," Zaki said. "The children reported to the kitchen with bright eyes and tails of bushes, and after a small bit of coaxing, they dined on oats to tickle their tummies and glue to their ribs, and keep their pigs and ears toasty."

Jeff blinked. "Have you been drinking?"

Zaki held up his hands as though swearing an oath. "I am only repeating and reporting back to you what I witnessed and heard. Although, I do not think I got the bushes on the tails correct, and the pigs…" He frowned, clearly bothered. "I have taken inventory of my own body and I cannot find a pig."

Laughter shot straight up from Jeff's gut, erupting in a howl that turned into a side-splitting guffaw. He grabbed the countertop to keep himself upright. There went the foul mood he'd been so determined to nurse. He would laugh it away and it would be all Millie's fault for telling stories about pigs and squirrels.

Zaki wasn't sharing the amusement. Shoulders stiff, he folded his arms, looking annoyed because this time *he* was the one being serious. Jeff tried to get himself under control, he really did, but every time he looked at Zaki, it just started him off again. All he could picture in his mind was this man, late fifties, graying hair, trying to figure out which one of his body parts resembled a pig.

"It was not that funny," Zaki said, a smile pulling at his lips.

"I know. It just hit me that way." Jeff took a few deep breaths and wiped his eyes. "I suspect Millie was the coach promoting the merits of oatmeal. The bushes—" He chuckled and held up a hand in apology. "Your translation missed a little. It is an adage—with bright eyes and a bushy tail. In college, when I went home with Paul Lulghum on a holiday weekend, his mother would tell us to come home early so we would have the bushy-tail thing going on the next morning. I do not know why women do this. If they want to call you a squirrel, they should simply do so. And the pigs, Zaki, are toes."

The older man immediately looked down at his feet.

Jeff laughed again. "I do not know the words to the pig story," he said, "but you should ask Millie to tell you. It has something to do with eating a roast and going to the supermarket."

"You have to go to the market *before* you can have a roast," Zaki corrected. When it came to food, you didn't argue with him.

Interesting, Jeff thought. Zaki and Millie had a great deal in common. Their uncanny ability to make him laugh. Their total disregard of his authority. Their love of cooking. Their adoration of children. Their ease in running a household and appearing absolutely unfazed in the midst of chaos. The list was much longer. Normally he might have thought of these commonalities in terms of relationship compatibility. Not in this case—or rather, not between these two.

What dominated his mind was that he'd *chosen* Zaki all those years ago. In an interview. The same type of interview in which he'd chosen Millie.

Zaki had lost his wife at a young age. He'd been farming his father-in-law's land and selling produce at the street market in town, but his heart was no longer in it. Jeff had visited the market as often as he could slip away from the palace, and Zaki had always saved him the sweetest tangerine or plumpest dates, the best of whatever was in season. While Jeff ate his treat, they would talk. And they had formed a bond—much like Millie had with Sam.

"Of course you are right," Jeff said. "Shop at the market before eating the roast. Now, we were discussing tin boats and fishing, which then hooked into oatmeal. Is there a more direct route I could follow?" He didn't recall Sam having a toy boat, and Mike wouldn't take them on the yacht without notifying him, so Jeff still had no idea where they were.

"That would be best," Zaki agreed. "It would spare me from relating the worm-gathering ceremony and the singing of a truly awful song to chase away early birds." He closed his eyes and gave a small shudder. "Any earth worm stupid enough to expose himself to *that* racket deserves to be fish bait. The last I saw them, Millie had taken the boat and oars out of the shed—"

"We have a boat? A real one?"

"Did you think I was making this up?" Zaki's incredulous tone rang with injured dignity. "I did not *ever* insult your toes when I served you oats. How could I think up this story?"

Jeff quickly raised a hand to his face, covering his mouth. He tried to look thoughtful while he fought to hold back his laughter. Evidently, it must have sneaked out through his eyes, because Zaki snatched a dish towel off the counter and flapped it at him.

"Get out of my kitchen." He turned his back and began polishing the countertop with the towel. But he wasn't quick enough, because Jeff saw the twitch of his lips.

"Which way shall I go out of your kitchen? Toward the beach?"

"I have been told to prepare tonight's menu around snapper." Zaki faced Jeff, the towel slung over his shoulder. "And they snap best around rocks—we received an education on the subject this morning, as Miss Millie's Pop was a fisherman. There are rocks close to the bay on the north bend. If you follow the bluff behind the house, you will come to a pathway that slopes to the bay."

"I know the bay, I will take the Jeep."

Zaki shrugged. "Suit yourself. Miss Millie claims it is only a short distance, easy enough to walk even with the added weight of the boat. I watched her myself. She tied a rope to that aluminum row boat and dragged it behind like a wagon. She is so small, but off she went, squabbling with Sadiq, who appeared to be insisting she hand over the vessel. She is quite independent and straightforward, and I do not think she wanted his help."

"Typical," Jeff muttered.

"She lost the tug-of-war," Zaki continued, "which is not surprising. Sadiq simply sliced the rope, plucked the boat from the ground and kept walking. It was very entertaining. If Sadiq had turned around, he would have seen an angel and two cherubs staging a pretend fencing duel with oars and fishing poles aimed at his backside.''

It was difficult for Jeff to imagine his son behaving that way. He wished he'd been there to see it. Armed with directions, he headed out through the back of the house. Since Zaki had made such a big deal over Millie's vigor and enthusiasm, there was no way in hell he was taking the Jeep.

Wet blades of grass clung to his shoes as he left a path of footprints across the manicured lawn. Beyond the grounds of the estate, he cut across a landscape that was a combination of evergreen forests and meadows.

From the pathway along the bluff, he could see for miles. The sea was calm, weak sunlight glancing off gentle swells too far away to build any momentum. The ground mist had lifted, but still toyed with the view of the mountains.

He hardly noticed the slope in the pathway that rounded the island's curve, spilling onto a finger of land where evergreens crowded the sandy banks of a serene bay.

The little row boat floated at the mouth of the bay, the oars secured in the oarlocks so that the shafts rested inside the boat and the blades angled upward like deformed grasshopper wings. By the time he reached the outer curve of the bay, where smooth rocks jutted from the water and lined the shore, he was close enough to hear the excited, happy chatter of the kids, and Millie's soft, encouraging praise.

Sam and Lindsey, wearing bright orange life vests, spoke in loud whispers that made him smile, since their normal tones would have been quieter. Two floats bobbed on the surface of the water, one red and one green, and despite the debate over snapping fish teeth verses lizards' teeth—he had no idea where they came up with these ideas—their eyes were glued to the floating balls as though they were luring the fish with mental telepathy.

Jeff shook his head. They were cute kids. He looked around, and although he didn't see Sadiq, he knew the man was close. Sadiq rarely hovered. He blended with the shadows, giving them as much privacy and sense of normality as possible.

The childish chatter stopped abruptly, replaced by a gasp, and adrenaline shot through Jeff. Sam shushed Lindsey, Lindsey shushed him back, then Sam, clearly vibrating with excitement, screamed, "I have a snap!"

For an excruciatingly long count of three, the little row boat seemed to turn into a tipsy bowl of chaos. Lindsey jerked her fishing line out of the water, shushing *everyone,* and in his excitement, Sam sent the boat rocking when he popped up from the plank seat as though he intended to dive overboard and seize the fish with his own hands.

Jeff was at the water's edge before he even realized he'd moved.

But Millie had everything under control. It was like watching a graceful ballet. Before Sam could fully stand, her hand was on the shoulder of his life vest, settling him back on the seat. Simultaneously, she snagged the pole from Lindsey's wild grip, laid it in the bottom of the boat, then with hardly a wiggle, switched seats so she was straddling the bench with Sam.

With his back against her chest, her hands over his, she steadied the rod and coached him as he reeled in the fish.

Jeff felt pride and sappy emotions lodge in his throat as he listened to his son laugh and shriek, watched him pull the flopping fish into the boat. Sam made several brave attempts to corral his catch, while Lindsey gave a superior how-to commentary from a safe distance.

Millie ducked down in the boat and Jeff had to stand on a rock so he could see better. When she sat up, she plopped the fish in Sam's lap and sent him into a gale of giggles.

Why hadn't he ever taken Sam fishing? Sure, his own father had never done so, but Jeff remembered the first time he'd caught a fish, and the joy he'd felt. It was Zaki who had taken him, and showed him the simple pleasure, which didn't require exorbitant sums of money to make a person glow with excitement.

Millie was giving his son so many new experiences that Jeff had convinced himself he didn't have time for. But the happiness on Sam's face was plenty of motivation, and he vowed he would make time.

Millie spotted him and waved. "Hey! Did you see your son catch that granddaddy snapper?"

He smiled and nodded, giving Sam a way-to-go gesture.

"I catched some, too!" Lindsey shouted.

"Caught," Millie corrected. "Hang on, we're coming in."

Acknowledging Lindsey's competitive spirit with an identical gesture of praise, Jeff watched as Millie secured whatever she had stored on the floor of the boat and settled both kids together in the center of the seat opposite her. He had to admit she handled the boat with confidence and skill, her hands steady on the oars as she maneuvered around rocks, paddled into a smooth turn, and glided safely back to shore.

Jeff kicked off his shoes and socks, rolled up his pant legs, and waded out to meet them. The shock of the cold water had him sucking in a breath. Needles of pain stabbed at his feet like hundreds of ice picks.

He grabbed the hull of the boat, dragging it all the way

onto shore, and tried not to embarrass himself by dancing from foot to foot or howling like a pitiful animal.

Millie grinned up at him. "Cold, isn't it? I had the same problem launching us. You can scream if you want to. It'll make you feel better."

"I think I can manage to control myself." He noticed she was wearing an old pair of canvas gloves to protect her hands from the icy water and the fish. She also wore a brown fishing vest, which she'd probably found in the shed, along with the boat. The front was covered with pouch pockets, and it looked as though it had been around for a good fifty years.

Her curly hair had turned to frizz, her nose was red and she didn't have on a drop of makeup. Yet as she sat in that poor excuse for a boat, looking up at him with a smile full of life, he thought she was the most beautiful woman he'd ever laid eyes on. The urge to cover those smiling lips with his, to drink in her joy, was nearly overpowering.

The kids brought him to his senses, clamoring to get out of the boat, both talking at once. He helped them out, trying to listen and appreciate, but he felt like a boxer dodging a series of confusing feints.

Worms were shoved under his nose and snatched away. The eyeball of a fish gaped at him from the palm of a hand, then disappeared behind small fingers squeezed into a fist. Nasty. A drop of dried blood on an elbow was pointed out but evidently didn't require any action from him, because both kids were off and running, squabbling over the worms left in the tin can.

"Who do those children belong to?"

Millie laughed. "See what you've been missing?" She thrust a cooler into his hands. "Dinner," she proclaimed.

"So I heard." He glanced at the kids, who were now

torturing Sadiq with their fish eyeballs and worms. "May I have a word with you?"

She opened her mouth, closed it, then astonished the hell out of him when she actually stood there and thought about it.

"You know, I really need to get the kids back to the house and get this fish cleaned," she said. "How would you feel about postponing until after dinner?"

"Nice to know you are seeking my opinion," he muttered. "Since we are all going the same way, I am sure the children and Sadiq will be happy to have a head start while the two of us secure the boat."

Millie sighed. He'd done so well yesterday, shedding some of his stiffness, but she had a suspicion he was about to backslide. Too bad she couldn't just tip him in the icy water to clear his head and help him stay focused.

"Not much to securing the boat, but I'll be happy to walk with you. Deke," she called. "Why don't you and the kids get started toward the house. Just don't get too far ahead of us in case Jeff needs some help."

Deke frowned, but rounded up the kids.

"What was that supposed to mean?"

"Just a nice gesture. When you get a certain look in your eyes and say you want to talk, it usually means we're going to disagree over something, which generally leads to a debate over our vastly different views on the issue." She shrugged. "You might need an extra man on your team, and I was merely being a good sport and making sure one was available."

The expressions crossing his face ran the entire gamut. Shock, insult, challenge, disbelief—they were going too fast for her to keep up. Then his lips twitched. He shook his head in good-natured defeat and chuckled.

"Millie Gallagher, I do not think there is another woman on the face of this earth who is quite like you."

"Well, I hope that's a good thing. I never did like the idea of them cloning poor Dolly. Even a sheep likes to know someone would recognize her in a crowd."

"It is a very good thing. And the Dolly sheep had my sympathy. Kasim was my carbon-copy twin. Or nearly so. Our personalities were opposite, but on the outside, we were true mirror images. Our mother was the only one who could tell us apart."

"What about your wife…before?" She gestured with her hand, not wanting to mention the affair.

He shook his head. "Not unless we spoke."

"Oh, that's ridiculous, Jeff. You can alter anybody's face, but you can't change what's in their eyes. I'll bet you cheated and made her stand across the room."

He lifted his hand to her face and slid his palm along her cheek, idly stroking his thumb along her brow and temple. His eyes softened with both resignation and tenderness.

"She was standing as close as we are," he said softly. "But thank you for giving me an easy out if I chose not to admit it."

She wasn't going to tell him his wife was a fool, because if she allowed herself to get started on that woman, she might never stop. And she wasn't going to let herself respond to his heart-stirring tone or read more into his captivating eyes than either one of them needed right now. One word of encouragement could easily have them rolling in the sand for all the wrong reasons.

Instead, she reached up and gave his wrist a squeeze. Easing his hand from her face, she held it between her own.

"If you ever run into a problem like that again, give

me a call. I promise I won't let anyone make you feel like the Dolly sheep.''

A slow smile grew into laughter. ''I spent half the morning looking for you, feeling justified and perfectly content with my less than charming mood, and now I do not think I could work up enough annoyance to step on a spider. I could well be losing my mind.''

She grinned. ''A little insanity is good for you. And you ought to know I wouldn't take Sam out unless Deke was with us and approved.''

''I know.'' He hooked an arm around her neck and urged her toward the path. ''We will leave the boat and I will send someone back to take care of it. And despite Sadiq's unquestionable abilities, now that you have perfected the alarm code, I would not age quite so quickly if you would make it a point to let me know when you are leaving the house and returning.''

''Sure, I can do that.'' She ducked from beneath his arm. She knew her limits when he turned on his charm. ''See how easy and nonconfrontational that was? Have you been watching the afternoon talk shows and boning up on relationship skills.''

''I do not need to watch afternoon television, Millie. I pay attention and I am a quick study.''

''Well, I'm impressed. From now on, you'll either know where we are at all times, or you'll be with us.''

He glanced sideways at her. ''That felt a little *too* easy.''

''Oh, stop looking for the ghost to jump out of the shadow. Why don't you come supervise Sam while he cleans his fish. You can even help him cook it tonight... Don't lower your brows at me like that. Some of the most renowned chefs in the world are men. There's nothing wrong with a guy working in the kitchen.''

"In Balriyad, it is most definitely wrong. You are teaching my son skills that are not befitting an heir to a kingdom."

Millie rolled her eyes and sighed. It was going to be a long day.

CHAPTER TWELVE

JEFF TOSSED his gold pen onto the desk, then watched it roll across the mahogany surface and drop to the floor. The sound of laughter and happy voices filtered from the courtyard through his open window, distracting him. This was exactly what he'd wanted for his son, for his household, but oddly enough, Jeff felt left out.

If he had any sense, he'd say to hell with work and let someone else take over. He wasn't accomplishing anything productive. He pretty much had the branch office in Seattle up and running, with good people in management. At this point, he could easily delegate his duties and spend the rest of the week with Sam. It's what he'd intended.

Funny, when Amala had been taking care of Sam, she'd been content to let him watch television and movies all day while she sat in a chair and stitched orange blossoms on fabric squares. And Jeff had kept his head buried in work. *That* was when he should have been distracted, and paid more attention to what was going on with his son.

Now that Millie was here, the TV was rarely turned on—mostly because she'd confiscated the remote and kept the children too busy to search out the manual power switch. They were constantly on the move, laughing, playing, going from morning until night.

Jeff wanted to be a part of that, too. He had the time to spend with Sam, but he didn't have the imagination that Millie did. He feared that if he took his son on a sightseeing trip, just the two of them, he couldn't compete. Not that entertaining Sam was a competition. But Millie had a gift. She brought out the joy in Sam, the joy that had been missing for so long. In fact, Jeff wasn't sure he'd ever truly seen the full depth of his son's spirit.

That was inexcusable. Why hadn't he known about Sam's teasing sense of humor? His streak of mischievous charm? His love of a good debate—even rhetoric? His irresistible silliness? He'd seen glimpses of that happy child when Rana was alive, but now he knew he'd only been looking at the first layer.

Millie had peeled back the tender blossoms and coaxed them to bloom.

She'd managed to strip away some of his own layers, too. That part gave him a twinge of unease. But the need to be with her, spend time with her, the crazy desire to do things as a family foursome was driving him nuts.

He drummed his fingers on the desk, glanced down at the yellow note pad, and found the perfect excuse to join the party in the courtyard—not that he needed an excuse to go relax on his own patio. He keyed in an electronic message to his secretary, forwarded all his calls to the office, left his cell phone on the desk and headed outside.

They sat at the round, glass-top table, surrounded by lush greenery and trickling water fountains. The low marble balustrade that separated the courtyard from the mosaic-tiled swimming pool was littered with dandelion flowers plucked from their stems, a book and a pyramid of orange peels.

Jeff pulled out a chair at the patio table. "Is this a private party or can anyone join?"

Millie beamed a smile. "Sit. It's too gorgeous out to be cooped up inside anyway."

"Yeah, Dad. Watch us play poker."

He wasn't sure which to react to first. Hearing his son use the more casual address of "Dad" or realizing they were playing poker. Dad felt okay—pretty good, actually. Gambling was another matter. What was Millie thinking? He opened his mouth to voice that very question—tactfully, of course, since he didn't want to start an uprising.

"Go fish!" Lindsey sang, practically crawling on top of the table as she wagged her head at Sam.

Jeff shut his mouth at the same moment that Millie gave him a wink as though to say, "Aren't they the cutest things, calling their card game poker?"

Bless Lindsey's timing.

"Any news yet on your broken drill bits?" Millie asked.

"The manufacturer is still testing. I have been told— very politely—that an entire team is assigned to the project, and harassing them with telephone inquiries will not produce a findings report any faster."

"Sounds to me like they're stalling so they don't have to admit fault." She caught the three of spades that flipped out of Lindsey's hand and passed it back without missing a beat. "I hope you bought your replacement part from a different company."

He shook his head and felt an inner smile warm him when she gaped at him as though he'd lost his mind. Her immediate leap to his defense and her genuine interest continually caught him by surprise.

"I have known the owner for many years, Millie. Chuck is a good man. If his factory is at fault, he will make it right. Meanwhile, he personally inspected and delivered new drill bits—and threw in drill collars for the rig, as well." He figured that information would appeal to her thrifty nature, and it did.

Her eyes softened. "Chuck is lucky you're such a sweet

guy. It's nice that you're not penalizing him for a possible mistake one of his employees might have made."

Sweet? He'd been called a lot of names in his life, but sweet wasn't one of them. Before he could set her straight, something else snagged her attention.

"Oh, look at the butterfly, guys. Isn't she pretty?" She pointed to the colorful insect that landed on the glass table, and the kids abandoned their cards, carefully leaning on their elbows and scooting as close as they dared to get a good look.

If Jeff didn't know better, he would suspect both kids were farsighted. They couldn't seem to watch television unless they were hugging the screen, and conversing—especially if they wanted to make a point—was an in-your-face contact sport.

"Why is her wings flapping?" Lindsey whispered.

"She's just resting for a minute, so she's keeping her motor running," Millie said.

"Pretty smart," Sam whispered.

Technically an insect didn't have a motor, Jeff thought, but that was a hell of a witty answer. He'd have said something generic like, "That's just what they do."

"There she goes," Millie said when the butterfly flitted off the table, heading toward the open sea. "All dressed in her pretty clothes. Where do you think she's going?"

"Shopping." Lindsey didn't even hesitate.

Millie smiled. "Off to Macy's sale? What fun."

"She wants a purse to hang on her wing." Lindsey's hands pantomimed her words. Jeff didn't need three guesses to figure out where she'd gotten that trait. "And shoes," she continued. "Boots with high heels so when the gardener waters the flowers, she won't get her feet all wet."

"Butterflies do not have feet," Sam said.

"Uh-huh!"

"Maybe she is going to meet the husband butterfly to buy a car." Sam poked his chin out, giving Lindsey a you're-not-always-right look. Obviously, Jeff thought, his son had inherited a few of Millie's traits, as well.

He found himself leaning back in the chair, folding his arms across his chest and nodding in agreement with Sam. *Good for you, Son. If a man's got to shop, by damn, make it for something practical and interesting.*

Drumming his fingers against the sides of his rib cage, he waited for Millie's response, primed to even up the sides if the mall shoppers dismissed the car buyer without fair deliberation.

"Oh," Millie said, beaming at Sam, "she very well could be. And she surely wouldn't want to keep Mr. Butterfly waiting for something as important as the family car."

Jeff's fingers stilled against his ribs. He'd girded himself for battle, gotten all worked up in the defense of men…on behalf of a butterfly.

"I bet they buy a truck," Sam said. "With off-road tires, and a lift kit and a cool stereo."

"No, a Volkswagen," Lindsey insisted. "A yellow one. With a flower on the steering thing so she can sit on top of it and see real good."

Sam's face scrunched up in disgust. "The husband is not going to drive a yellow Volkswagen."

"So." Lindsey shrugged. "He doesn't have to drive it. The wife butterfly is buying it with her check, and she only needs the husband butterfly to come because sometimes the men take advantage of the girls."

Sam frowned. "Why?"

"I don't know. That's what Mimi said. Sometimes she takes Dr. Jessup places to be her eye-candy on her arm.

He's big and he's a doctor, and people won't try to charge her too much money." Lindsey rolled her eyes. "All he does is just stand there. Mimi talks and buys the stuff. You better not do that when you grow up."

"Do what?"

"Act like girls are stupid!"

Jeff didn't know whether to laugh or hide under the table. He definitely wanted to know who this Dr. Jessup was and how important he was in Millie's life. But fascination with the two kids held his attention.

They agreed one minute and disagreed the next, segued from make-believe to reality without so much as a signal. Apparently, he was the only one who required notification. The rest of them had no trouble keeping up.

He leaned closer to Millie. "Where do they come up with these imaginations? A flower perched on a steering wheel?"

She chuckled. "That *was* a pretty good one."

She'd mistaken his question for a comment. But he really wanted to know. Not knowing the rules of the game left him sitting on the sidelines as a mere spectator.

He didn't want to be a spectator in his son's life anymore.

The kids had settled the price-gouging issue and were back to upgrades on their vehicles—except now Sam was buying his own truck, too.

He touched Millie's cheek to draw her attention to him. Her eyes widened, their color reflecting the ocean beyond. "I meant that literally, Millie. You have it, too. The ability to create a whimsical story out of nothing. My mind doesn't work that way."

"Of course it does." She shifted toward him and tucked one of her legs in the chair, pulling her bare foot flush against her denim-clad thigh.

The length of her shin crowded his knee as she leaned close, her expression earnest. Her scoop-neck peasant top caught the draft of an ocean breeze and bloused open just enough to tease. The cut was so modest that it didn't afford him even a glimpse of cleavage or hint at the type of bra she preferred—delicate lace or ordinary cotton.

The mystery was even more provocative. Smooth, unblemished skin, collarbone forming an elegant vee. It shot his concentration all to hell.

"For a man who claims he's lacking in the imagination department, you seem to be displaying all the typical behavior." She slapped a hand to her top and straightened.

His gaze rose to hers. "I was not speaking about sexual imagination," he said softly, conscious of the kids conversing on the other side of the table. "I assure you, in that arena, I am quite inventive."

She surprised him when she laughed.

"You can save the bragging for someone who's actually impressed, Sheikh."

His lips curved with a will of their own. About the time he thought he had this woman figured out, she threw him for another loop. Generally, blatant references to sexuality sent her into a tizzy she did her damnedest to disguise.

"You're hell on a man's ego."

"I think we've already established that yours is big enough to survive me. Now—"

"Mimi? Can me and Sam go water the flowers by the frog and see if the troll comes out of the bridge?"

"Yes, but stay where I can see you."

The kids scrambled down and took off like bullets. "What troll?" Jeff asked.

"The one who lives under the bridge," she said, her expression perfectly serious.

He had an overwhelming urge to haul her into his lap

and kiss her until neither one of them remembered their names or what the hell a troll was in the first place. Giving himself extra points for restraint, he raised his brow questioningly instead.

She grinned. "The first day Lindsey and I came, we were enchanted with the bridge over there." She pointed to the grassy area beyond the courtyard where a wooden pathway arched over the Koi pond. "When Lindsey saw Deke, she decided he might be a troll who lived under the bridge. Now, because he seems to blend in and out of the woodwork, I'm afraid she's halfway convinced he *is* a troll."

The image of Sadiq's face if he knew someone called him a troll had Jeff laughing out loud. "Please, do not tell him of this sleuth mission."

"Are you kidding? I wouldn't dare. He could probably squish the kids *and* me with one hand."

"I am sure it would take his entire arm for all three of you," Jeff countered. "But he would not harm you. Sadiq has skills that might require him to register his body as a lethal weapon in some situations, but you will not find a gentler, more caring man."

She leaned forward again, her leg bumping his, her hand resting on his arm for a fleeting moment. "I know, Jeff. He stole my heart the first day."

Jealousy winged out of nowhere. "You have feelings for Sadiq?"

"Not like *that,* silly." She whacked him on the leg and shook her head. "Sometimes you're so literal. I'm crazy about him. I'd trust him with my life and with the kids', and I had his number right away."

"Why did you need his telephone number?"

"Not his phone number. I figured *him* out—saw the snuggly bear masquerading as the grizzly."

He nodded, fascinated by her remarkable eyes, which reflected each shift of her emotions, tantalized by the way her generous lips drenched every word in sensuality. A possessiveness he didn't understand swept through his blood.

"Snuggly bear might not offend him as badly as troll, but I'd keep that one quiet, as well. What about the candy man? Jessup," he elaborated when she stared at him blankly.

Eyebrows several shades darker than her wheat-blond hair drew together. "Ben? What about him?"

"Is he merely decoration, or are you involved?"

She stared at him for a full thirty seconds before her enticing lips curved into a sexy grin. "Well, he's definitely gorgeous, single and a doctor—a decorative package. And I suppose you could say we're involved…" She raked her teeth over her bottom lip, then let out a delighted laugh. "He's also Lindsey's paediatrician, and his son used to attend Forrester Square Day Care. I told you, relationships take time and energy, and with my hectic schedule, I don't have either of those to spare. I appreciate the jealousy, though. It's a nice compliment."

"I merely asked a question. Jealousy had nothing to do with it." He half expected a bolt of lightning to strike him. Damn it, he didn't need this kind of complication in his life.

"Be a sport, Jeff. My life is devoted to children most of the time. Let me at least bask in the illusion of the compliment."

He felt a smile tug at his lips. He was going to miss her spunk. "You have an amazing gift when it comes to children, Millie. My son is proof. He is a different boy, happy and full of spirit. I do not know how I can ever repay you or find the right words to thank you."

Her smile was soft and genuine. "You just did. And you're very welcome."

He looked over at the kids frolicking on the grass. They tumbled, giggled, then scrambled up and tiptoed to the mouth of the arched wooden bridge, obviously scaring each other with whatever game they were playing. Lindsey clutched Sam's shirtsleeve and stealthily dogged his steps. They exchanged whispered words, had a couple of false starts, then ran like mad across the bridge, screaming the whole way. Next, they raced around the pond and lined up to do it again. He didn't understand how repetition could keep them entertained.

"I have no idea how to compete." He hadn't intended to voice the thought, but since it was out, he looked back at Millie. "When you are no longer here, how do I keep the spark alive in him? I don't have your gift of imagination."

"Oh, Jeff." She leaned in and squeezed his knee. "This isn't a competition. Sam idolizes you, and you adore him. You don't have to plan your relationship, just let it happen—let him bring out the child in you. Like when you pretended to be a scary alligator and chased him and Lindsey."

Now she was cupping his knee in both of her hands. His body and his brain battled over translations. The first chose sex, and the second recognized compassion. Millie never hesitated to open her heart and offer it to anyone in need.

Jeff was desperately in need. But he wasn't ready to give a name to that need. Putting a label on emotions could be powerfully destructive. He knew that firsthand.

"Didn't you pretend when you were a child?" she asked. "Imagine you were a famous race car driver sliding into a curve as you pushed your metal cars around a track, then maneuvered them into a hairy crash? Or played with plastic dinosaurs that were eating the earth? Battle aliens with your toy laser rifle?''

Absently, he dodged—again—as she flung her hands out a final time. When she stilled, all he could do was stare. His heart was beating faster. Under the pressure of adulthood, he'd forgotten. Her examples were so close to the target, she could have been a childhood playmate of his.

They were good memories. It felt as though another piece of his battered soul clicked back in place. Reaching out, he plucked her out of the chair, hauled her to him, kissed her and returned her to her seat.

She stared at him with the stunned look of a maiden who'd had her sensibilities compromised and couldn't decide if she should run or beg for more.

He wasn't in much better shape. The impetuous two-second kiss made him hard. But by damn, he liked being the victor for a change. Grinning, he leaned back in his chair and watched her try to gather her composure.

''Well.'' She took a deep breath and flicked her hair behind her ear. ''You're welcome...I think.''

He chuckled and pulled the yellow notepaper from his back pocket. ''Before we become sidetracked again, I have a mission to complete. Katherine called when you were out with the kids this morning. She said you did not need to call back, she just wanted to give you a weekly update. I was under strict orders to take meticulous notes, but they do not make a lot of sense to me.'' He glanced down at the message.

''I am supposed to tell you that everyone misses you, and that Hy is great, but he does not make double-chocolate, skinny lattes like you do.''

"It's all in the foam," Millie said. "I've showed him a hundred times."

Jeff wondered if she wore a sexy uniform when she served up designer coffees and advice. He looked back at his notes. "Russ Tidwell apologized to Carmen and actually thanked her. Evidently Carmen is quite suspicious of this apology and gratitude, because she is convinced that either the man has suffered brain damage or there has been divine intervention—"

Millie laughed, and Jeff looked up from his notes again. "If you'd met him, you'd understand," she said. "He's Amy Tidwell's father—Amy's a young girl who works as a teacher's aide at Forrester Square. She's eighteen and just had a baby. Her father, Russ, owns a business in Seattle—rich, very rigid and he expects everyone to live up to his standards. Amy's unplanned pregnancy didn't meet those standards, and he's been quite vocal about it. Carmen—she's the head teacher at the day care—has gone head-to-head with him several times on Amy's behalf."

"Mmm." He glanced back at the paper, searching for his place. He'd thought this would be a quick matter of reading down the list.

"Russ had a stroke right in the day care," Millie added before he could begin again, "and if he *does* have brain damage, it's the best kind. You know, I've heard that people's personalities often change after a life-altering illness."

"Yes, that would probably be a very good thing," Jeff said. "Because I have it written down here that Amy and Will are going to get married—and they are thrilled to have her father's blessing. He is going to help them financially, as well."

She whooped and leaped out of the chair before he'd

even finished his sentence, startling a sparrow into flight. "Oh, my gosh. That's so exciting. Those kids have been through so much. And they have the baby." She threw her arms around him, hugged him, then danced back to the chair.

"I'm beginning to wonder if someone's tampering with the water at Forrester Square," she said with a wink. "You wouldn't believe how many engagements and weddings there have been lately. And right before I came here, we hosted a wedding shower for Hannah Richards—she's the third partner of the day care, along with Katherine and Alexandra."

She leaned forward like a long-lost family member who'd just received word from home. "What else?" she asked, folding her hands beneath her chin. "I talked to Alexandra three days ago, and I can't believe how much has happened since then!"

Jeff found it difficult to concentrate. Her parents were gone, and the only other family she had that he knew of besides Lindsey was her aunt Flo, who gave her more trouble than help. Yet clearly, Seattle was her home, and these friends had become her family.

He scanned his notes. "Ah, this one is about your pal. The good Dr. Jessup has brought Doug back to the day care." He paused and looked up. "Evidently there has been quite a bit of groveling taking place at this day-care center." He realized that *he* was doing the commentary thing now and quickly got back to his notes. "Jessup admitted to Alexandra that the...something pricey did not work out. I cannot read my own writing."

"Well, if Doug's back at the day care, that means the au pair didn't cut it," she said. "There was a messy thing a couple of months ago with some jewel thefts in a store across from the day care, and the police set up surveillance at Forrester Square. Ben thought it endangered the kids and pulled out his son, Doug. It all got settled just fine—in fact, the detective on the case, Luke Sloan, ended up marrying Abby Douglas, who was working at the jewelry store. I'm telling you, Jeff. There's something about that day care. *Everyone* is falling in love and—um, well, there are a bunch of weddings going on, that's all.''

Jeff wondered why she'd stopped abruptly and stammered over that falling in love business. Since it worried him a bit, he decided to skip it, and focused on the paper in front of him.

''Katherine said I *must* tell you that Alexandra did not gloat when Ben came with his hat in his hand… I am assuming that is the groveling part,'' he said, and glanced at Millie for her opinion. She sat silently, carefully listening to each word he read, and Jeff realized he was actually disappointed.

Being a private man, he generally made it a point to stay out of other people's personal business, but Millie had dragged him in, telling him things he hadn't asked to hear. And now, damn it, he felt like he knew these people and had a stake in what was going on.

''Do *you* think Alexandra acts odd around Jessup?'' he asked.

She grinned. ''You're really getting into this. You'll fit right in the next time you come to Seattle. And yes, as a matter of fact, there is quite a bit of friction between those two. Katherine and Hannah will want me to see what I can find out the next time I'm plying Alexandra with a double-chocolate skinny latte.''

''I do not know why anyone would want to ruin a perfectly good latte with watered-down milk, but that is just my opinion.''

He folded the paper, concerned by the faraway look in her eyes. "Is something wrong?"

"I'm just worried about Alexandra. She's not sleeping, and I doubt she's eating properly, either. And now if there's something going on with Ben..."

He reached out and covered her hand with his. "Do not get me in trouble with Katherine. I was told this was a happy update, and if she learns it has made you sad, she will think I did not copy down her words correctly. She was very specific about this."

She smiled. "I'm not sad, and I won't tell on you."

"Good girl. I got the impression that a great many people depend on you for advice. You have a gift for that, as well, you know. You always seem to know the right thing to say."

"Not really. I just try to look with my heart and not with my eyes."

"That can be a dangerous way to live. Who do *you* depend on?" When she merely looked at him, two creases forming between her brows, he said, "Who eases your load?"

"That's not an easy answer, Jeff. I would have to say no one—and everyone. I have wonderful friends who would drop everything and come running if I called. Lindsey stays at the day-care center free of charge in exchange for my help in the kitchen, but I'm getting the better end of that deal. I *am* raising Lindsey on my own, so it's my load. But it's not a heavy one. It never is when it's about love. You should know that from your own feelings about Sam."

Yes, he did. But he had advantages Millie didn't. He had the money to make his life easier, and a staff to cook, clean and take care of everyday details. Millie didn't have that luxury. She was raising Lindsey without any help, and stayed busy from sunup until late at night. Hell, it exhausted him just to watch her.

She'd given so much to him, and to Sam. She gave so much of herself to everyone else around her.

He looked over at the kids, who were still on a troll hunt by the bridge. An idea took shape in his mind. It might be tough to pull off, but he did have some leverage.

By tomorrow morning, *he* was going to be the head coach in this house.

CHAPTER THIRTEEN

WHEN MILLIE woke the next morning, the first thing she noticed was that her bedroom was brighter than usual. Mmm, nice. No clouds today. Rolling over, she checked the time.

"Oh, my God!" She ripped the blankets back and jumped up so fast her head spun. Snatching up the clock, she held it to her ear. There wasn't a thing wrong with it, and she knew she'd set it last night.

Damn it! It was nearly eight-thirty. The kids would be up. She grabbed her robe and raced for the door. No. Jeff would be up, too. She changed directions, snatched jeans and a sweatshirt out of the closet, and charged into the bathroom. She managed to brush her teeth and pull on her clothes in about two minutes. Dragging a brush through her hair made matters worse, so she wet her fingers and ran them through the scary frizz. Not bothering with shoes, she sprinted down the hallway.

The kids weren't in Sam's room. Jeff's door was completely shut, which meant he wasn't in there. She ran down the stairs, through the dining room, and burst into the kitchen, her chest heaving. She felt totally disoriented. Her hands were shaking, and she was sweating at eight-thirty-eight in the morning.

Jeff sat at the breakfast table reading the newspaper. Lindsey and Sam were eating cereal. Zac barely paused, then resumed kneading his bread dough.

Relief nearly buckled her knees. Somewhere between the mad search of the bedrooms and her arrival in the kitchen, the embarrassment of having overslept had been subconsciously edged aside by an eerie, overwrought panic as though she'd been sucked into a virtual reality game of her worst nightmare. Losing her family.

After Mom and Pop died, she'd been ripped from sleep many nights by a horrific recurring dream. She would find Lindsey's bed empty, and a teasing hide-and-seek game turned into a hideously distorted race through a maze of endless hallways as she screamed Lindsey's name, but heard only the sound of her own voice echoing back.

She didn't need an analyst to tell her that these dreams were tied into her subconscious fear of dropping the ball on her responsibilities.

Jeff lowered a corner of the paper and spoke over the top of it. "Good morning, Millie. Did you sleep well?"

Was that sarcasm she heard in his voice? The back of her throat and her nose burned. A trembling, small voice inside her wanted to say, *I couldn't find you guys. It scared me.* If she uttered those words, she'd lose it for sure.

She didn't like feeling out of control like this. And she damned well was *not* going to cry.

"Evidently, I slept a little *too* well. Who's the wise guy who shut off my alarm?"

He lowered the paper, swiveled in his chair and frowned. "What kind of tone is that?"

Millie gaped at him, seriously afraid her eyeballs were going to pop out of her head. Talk about tone—if his got any more pompous, they'd have to strap an anchor to him so he wouldn't puff up like a hot air balloon and bounce around on the ceiling. Never in her life had she known anyone who could push her buttons as quickly as Jeffri al-Kareem could.

She clamped her hand over the knotted muscle in her shoulder and massaged as she counted to ten. She didn't know what was the matter with her. She was edgy, frustrated, annoyed.

And she'd like to know what the heck happened to Jeff every night between bedtime and breakfast. He'd retire as a nice, sleek, manageable tiger, and by morning be back to the grumpy lion with his tail on fire.

She lowered her hand, irritated that she felt so emotional.

"I am *not* taking a tone with you, Jeffri." Yikes. Maybe she was. "I'm just disorganized and embarrassed because someone turned off my alarm and I overslept. Is that okay with you?"

He studied her as though he could see every secret in her soul, every scar on her heart. Then he shook his head.

"Actually, no. I do not believe it is okay. And I am thinking that perhaps a time-out will improve your attitude some." He glanced at his watch. "Six hours ought to be a good start."

Her jaw dropped.

"That's a long time," Lindsey commented, a spoonful of milk halfway to her mouth.

"Do not interfere, little one," he said gently.

Lindsey shrugged and went back to eating her cereal.

Millie had her mouth open, primed to fire back at him, but he cut her off.

"While you are in your room, I will take the kids on a dolphin-seeking expedition."

Lindsey and Sam cheered and bounced in their chairs, sloshing milk and cereal.

Millie didn't even react to the mess. She looked at

Jeff—really looked at him. He was serious. They would be gone for hours.

I wish somebody would send me to my *room.* She'd said those words to him the first day she'd been here. He'd remembered.

He was doing this for *her*. She could take a bath in blessed peace without Lindsey knocking on the door. She could read a book, sleep some more, bake, do nothing, do anything. The time-out was her precious time.

Tears filled her eyes. She turned quickly so the kids wouldn't think Jeff was truly being mean. She figured he'd probably explain it to them anyway. Lindsey, at least, would hound him to death until he did.

Wiggling her fingers over her shoulder, she said, "Have fun dolphin seeking." Then she walked out of the room.

Jeff caught up with her at the base of the stairs. He stopped her with a hand on her shoulder, stepped in front of her…and saw her tears.

"Oh, no. No, Millie. I did not mean—"

She put her fingers over his mouth and smiled in the stupid, lopsided, lip-trembling way women do when they're crying, but aren't sad. "I know…" Oh, boy. She wasn't sure she was going to get through this without her vocal cords seizing completely.

Totally embarrassed to react this way—especially in front of Jeff, she looked away. It took a couple more false starts and deep breaths before she was able to push past the lump in her throat and get a grip.

"Thank you. This is the most treasured gift I've ever received—aside from Lindsey."

"Going to your room alone is a gift?" He thumbed away the moisture on her cheeks.

"I haven't had a solid six hours just for me, with no responsibilities, since the day Mom and Pop died."

He folded her in his arms and wrapped her close. Tunneling his fingers through her hair, he held her as though she were fragile, her cheek against his heart. "You should have days, not hours."

She felt the rumble of his words deep in his chest and wondered how many people took the time to look past the No Trespassing walls he'd erected to see the remarkable man inside. "I'd get bored with days."

His palm shifted to her back, stroking all the way down and back up. Her pulse skittered. His hold was meant to soothe—and it did. But with the muscles of his chest cradling her breasts and the fly of his jeans grazing the zipper placket of hers with every inhale or exhale, it also made her want. The tingling desire had very poor timing.

As though he could feel the shift in tension, he buried his lips in her hair and held on for a long moment. Just that. He didn't move a muscle, and neither did she. It was a poignantly tender kiss that lingered, soul stirring in its utter simplicity.

That was the exact moment she fell helplessly, totally in love with Sheikh Jeffri al-Kareem.

He stepped back and steadied her. "Go have your slice of heaven or paradise. No need to confine yourself to your room or the house. Sadiq is going with us and Zaki is flying to Seattle for supplies."

She swallowed, needing a moment, a distraction. Leaking tears down the front of his sweater over a really sweet, thoughtful gesture was drama enough for one day. To even their heights a bit, she climbed the first step and leaned against the wood railing.

"So, I could swim naked if I want?"

He winked. "The pool is heated, and your time is yours. Do me a favor, though. If you *do* swim naked,

please do not tell me. The images in my mind are already
so vivid I cannot sleep.''

With that, he left her standing at the bottom of the
stairs, her heart pumping, every sensitive nerve ending
throbbing.

His sexuality still overwhelmed her at times, and it took
every ounce of strength she possessed to keep that information to herself. He was a powerful presence, and she'd
like to think she was doing a good job of holding her own
with him.

But this incredible sexual tension was definitely an
elective course she hadn't yet attended. She'd only heard
others *talking* about it. And that was about as useful as
talking about baking a fussy, temperamental cake without
actually being present in the class.

Oh, good grief. She was being ridiculous. If they ended
up in bed together, they wouldn't be baking a cake. And
to begin her time-out on the right foot, she was going to
take a cold shower. Icy cold.

JEFF SIGNED the purchase agreement and sent it off by
special courier. He'd hated having to leave Sam before
their dolphin trip was over, but a sticky land deal he'd
been trying to finesse for almost a year had come within
hours of totally unraveling. All because of one document
that had slipped through unsigned.

Two other companies had bid on the drilling rights and
were still in the running if Jeff's deal went sour. He'd had
until the close of business today or the deal was up for
grabs. Luckily, Zaki had recognized the importance of the
fax and flown it out to him.

Sam and Lindsey had hardly batted an eyelash over his
departure. Probably because they knew they could sweet-
talk Sadiq and Zaki into doing what they wanted much

easier than they could him. The kids were cute, though, hanging on the railing of the yacht like little birds, watching him take off in the plane, waving and blowing kisses.

He looked at his watch again and felt at loose ends. Technically Millie had another forty-five minutes of her alone time. He went to the kitchen and opened the refrigerator. Man, it was quiet around here without the kids— or Zaki and Sadiq. He closed the refrigerator and drummed his fingers on the stainless steel door.

He and Millie were alone in the house. The torturing chant had taken possession of his mind and wouldn't let go.

He should at least let her know he was home. Maybe she was hungry. It wouldn't be polite to feed his face and not offer her something to eat, as well.

The contents of a refrigerator—and what to do with them—weren't exactly his area of expertise, so he'd stick to the basics. He snagged a bottle of sparkling wine, spotted the strawberries and grabbed them, too. It took him fifteen minutes to find a plate, stemware, cheese and crackers. There was no systematized organization to this kitchen. A person could walk five miles in here trying to put together a bowl of cereal.

It wasn't his concern, though. He hadn't been allowed to step foot in a kitchen as a boy, and he didn't plan to involve himself at this stage of his life. He dumped the little green plastic basket of strawberries onto the plate and ended up chasing most of them across the counter and onto the floor.

The berries took up all the room on the dish, so he loaded half of them back in the basket, starting with the ones that had rolled on the floor. Seemed he'd heard somewhere about a five-second rule. If you snagged it within five seconds, it was still good to eat.

He stuffed the container of extras back in the fridge, fanned some crackers onto the plate, tossed some cheese on top, and patted himself on the back when the cork came out of the bottle and he didn't spew the walls with foam.

On the way up the east stairs and down the hallway, he only lost one strawberry. Evidently, he had a knack for waiter-type duties. If his oil wells dried up, he'd have to keep that in mind.

Once outside Millie's bedroom door, he hesitated. He couldn't believe he was actually nervous. This was probably a bad idea. He stared at the ceiling. What the hell was wrong with him?

Juggling the plate, glasses and wine bottle in one hand, he reached out and knocked on her door. Just in case she was sick of her time-out, he told himself, he would offer her some company, see if she wanted to catch a movie down the hall or something.

"Come on in," she called, "I'm decent."

He stared at the door panel for a full two seconds, wondering why he felt like the wolf in the Red Riding Hood story. Probably because he hadn't expected to hear the word *decent*. Too late to back out. He'd already knocked.

He opened the door. The smell of fresh apples filled the room as though she'd just taken a bath in them. She was standing on tiptoe, her back to him, hooking a padded clothes hanger over the lip of the bathroom door.

He knew one thing for damn sure. Her definition of decent and his were *not* in the same dictionary.

She wore a simple T-shirt that hit at midthigh. To a woman, that might spell decent. To a man, it was a wide-open invitation with no speed bumps to slow him down. Nice and loose, two seconds and it's gone, or less than a second and your hand's underneath, touching skin.

Damn it! He was ruining himself here. He shifted the wine bottle, dangling the heavy glass front and center. It didn't seem like a good idea to have his body jutting out like a steel crane on an outrigger when he'd barely entered the door of a lady's bedroom.

Millie let go of the hanger, wishing she could grow a few more inches. Lack of height was such a pain sometimes. If she'd known Zac was back home, she'd have asked him to find her a stool.

She turned around. "I was just—*yaiiike*." The sound came out part senseless word, part yelp. She pressed both hands to her chest in case her ribs needed extra support against her wildly slamming heartbeat.

"Jeff!" Her voice sounded breathy, as though her lungs didn't have enough air to get the job done. "I—I thought you were Zac—I mean, I didn't know you were back. The, um…kids? Where are the kids?" Good grief, she could hardly put a coherent sentence together. A person would think she was standing here stark naked when she was modestly covered in her old water polo sleep shirt. No Tweety Birds this time….

Oh, Lord. She glanced down at her chest, and decided right then and there she was tossing every set of pajamas she owned and buying new ones.

The red silk-screening, which had held up nicely through hundreds of wash cycles, stretched across the upper swell of her breasts. *Goalie girls are hot… We get wet.*

Definitely not innocent or virginal.

"You were expecting Zaki to visit you in your bedroom?" Jeff asked. "I had it on good authority that the rules of a time-out did not include visitors."

She rolled her eyes. "I wasn't expecting him. I heard the plane come back and knew he'd left in it earlier. As for rules and visitors, it appears *you're* breaking that one."

"I am allowed since I am the head coach of this strategic play."

"So you are. And why do I get the feeling you're stalling about telling me where the kids are?"

"They are with Sadiq and Zaki. A fax came through that I needed to deal with personally, and the paperwork was here. The children wanted to visit the kids' museum and the zoo, and Zaki was moaning about a mushroom I dare not try to pronounce or none of us will want to eat the dish he prepares with it. Seattle did not have any of these vulgar-sounding fungi, but he has been promised they will be at the international market first thing in the morning." He set the plate of strawberries on the dresser.

"And?" she prompted.

"Would you like a glass of—" he lifted the bottle, glanced at the label "—sparkling wine?"

"I'll tell you in a minute. After you tell me about the kids."

He sighed and dropped his arm to his side, holding the bottle by the neck. "I flew the plane back to the island and Sam and Lindsey are enjoying the sights of Seattle with two highly trained bodyguards who are crazy about children *and* the zoo, and were likely more excited with the outing than the kids. Then the four of them are spending the night at my condominium in Seattle. Zaki will have them up with the sun, and there is no telling how long they will spend squeezing produce. After that, they will return in the yacht. Tomorrow morning," he added.

"I thought you had concerns about staying at the condo because of security issues."

"Sadiq has seen to that. And I trust him completely, otherwise I would not have let the kids go—nor, for that matter, would Sadiq have agreed if he thought it was not safe. I know I should have asked your permission for Lindsey, but there were *four* sets of pleading eyes, Millie. *Four*,'' he repeated.

At that moment, no one could have convinced her he had a propensity toward stuffy sheikh quirks. Scoundrel, she would have believed. A flat out charmer, absolutely. *She* was definitely charmed.

''Yes, thank you, I'd love a glass of wine.'' *Oh, Millie what are you doing?* They were alone in the house, alone in her bedroom. And despite his lighthearted banter, the sexy man walking toward her carrying two stemmed glasses of pale bubbly had a powerful hunger in his eyes. She might be inexperienced, but she knew strawberries, crackers and cheese weren't going to satisfy his craving.

Their fingers touched when she accepted the glass. It was deliberate. She saw it in the eyes that held hers, eyes that gauged her mood, her willingness, her emotions, eyes that asked a question.

''You smell incredible,'' he said. ''I've never thought of apples as a sexy scent, but I think you have ruined any possibility of me shopping for produce or enjoying a snack in public without embarrassing myself.''

She sipped the sparkling wine, felt the tangy fizz on her tongue, the gentle bite of the tart ice-cold liquid on the first swallow. ''Do you really expect me to believe you have ever, or *would* ever, shop for your own produce?'' She glanced down at his flat stomach, covered by another of his trademark cashmere sweaters, black this time, and paired with jeans today.

''I've never seen you snack between meals, or seen evidence of junk food. That's probably one of the ways you keep your body in such good shape.'' She forced her gaze back up to his. "But crunching an apple in public?" She shook her head. "Too undignified."

"You like my body?" A barely there, pleased smile twitched his lips.

She glanced at his stomach again, but this time her brain missed the signal to put on the brakes and her gaze admired a bit lower, as well. Her eyes snapped back to his. Too late to play coy. Although she felt her cheeks heat, she answered honestly. "Yes. I do."

His dark eyes flared. He set his glass on the round table by the reading chair, then took hers out of her hand, his gaze never wavering.

When his hands cupped her face, she knew where they were headed. Knew what she'd invited.

"I have an urgent need…to taste." His breath whispered against her face an instant before his lips descended.

For several long moments, Millie stood exactly as she was, too awed by the evocative sensations drawn from only a kiss.

As though truly satisfying a craving, he nipped and toyed and tasted, drawing her in by slow degrees. She focused all of her concentration on his mouth, not wanting to miss a single trick. In this, she was more than happy to let him lead. Fitting his lips to hers, he molded them like two halves of a perfect whole. His movements were gentle, but so sure. That self-assurance was an aphrodisiac in itself.

With the barest pressure of his thumb at the corner of her mouth, he asked for more, urging her to open wider. She gave without question, and he took. His tongue stroked the sensitive inner skin of her lips, traced the front edges of her teeth, giving her time to adjust.

Millie appreciated his restraint, his skill, but when his tongue met hers, the flash of heat that seared her body demanded more. She wrapped her arms around his neck, knocking aside his hands, which had been tenderly cupping her face. She stood on tiptoe and indulged in her own sensual feast. If she could have climbed inside his body, she would have.

Time lost all meaning. There was only this, bodies pressing, mouths dueling, hearts pounding, hands seeking. His arms were like bands around her, holding her close, lifting her. Her T-shirt rode up. She felt his fingertips on her bare skin, just below the elastic of her panties, where they'd ridden up on her behind.

As though he'd touched a live electrical wire, he tore his mouth from hers, his chest heaving, his brown eyes blazing, slightly stunned.

Millie stared up at him, trying to clear the haze of desire from her mind, wondering if she'd gotten so caught up she'd done something wrong.

"I didn't come here for this." His voice rasped, as if he'd just run a race with the devil. "I didn't expect—"

"I know."

He leaned his forehead against hers. "I want you so badly I ache with it. That is not a line, Millie. I do not understand it. You make me feel alive in a way I have not felt... Oh, hell. I should not be here. You have given me so much, yet all I have done is take from you."

"You're not taking anything I haven't been willing to give, Jeff." She'd always known that when the right man came along she'd give him her body and soul without hesitation.

In her heart, Jeff was the right man. It was just unlucky that he happened to be a man who could never be hers.

But he could be hers tonight. For one night only.

She buried her fingers beneath the silky hair at his nape, holding him, firmly rubbing her hips against his, making it clear she wasn't letting him go. He fisted his hand on the back of her T-shirt and pressed her even harder against his erection.

"I am attempting to dredge a shred of honor, sweetheart, but if you do that again, I will lose it. I have not been with a woman in over a year, and everything about you, from the top of those blond curls to the blue paint on your toes, drives me wild. I have seen and had all of you in my imagination in every way possible, and having you this close for real has put me right on the edge." He traced his fingertip over her cheek.

"I want to savor, enjoy, show you pleasure the way you deserve," he told her, "the way it is meant to be. I could easily seduce you. We both know that. But you are…you are special. So tell me to leave, and I will go. Tell me to take a cold shower and meet you for a movie, and I will be there. Or tell me to stay. I do not want to take from you, Millie. I want to give back. And I want to know that you are very sure. Tell me what you want."

You. "This isn't one-sided, Jeff. I don't want to keep score here, but you've given me so much more than I could ever reciprocate. You've given me my dream for Lindsey's and my future."

And she would seize this dream, too. A memory to take out and cherish, of a gentle sheikh who'd entered her life for a brief time and changed her world. A man who'd held her heart in his hands, but would never know how deeply he'd touched her, because their worlds and responsibilities were poles apart.

Expressing one's heart to a child was different from burdening a lover with the words. It only created guilt when both parties weren't in a position to make or accept promises.

She knew Jeff cared for her. It was there in his eyes,

his tender touch, the way he beat on his chest like king of the castle, yet still listened to her opinion. She knew he cared by the special gift of solitary time he'd given her today.

But he had a country to return to, to rule someday, in a world she knew nothing about. She had a job to do, too, a little girl to raise, and a promise to keep to herself. A vow to provide Lindsey with all of the Gallagher traditions and memories, to give her the same type of childhood that Millie herself had—in the Gallagher family home.

For a little while longer, though, she wanted to hold a piece of her own dreams in her hands. Some might say she was foolish, but Millie didn't feel that way. She knew herself, knew her limits. She was making a conscious decision, going in with her eyes wide open, without unrealistic expectations. That's what made the difference.

It was only foolish if she made the choice without considering the consequences, and she knew those all too well.

Still, she wanted to live *now*. To love now. And when the time came, she would pick up the pieces of her shattered heart and go on.

"Give me this, too, Jeff. Make love with me."

With a groan, he swept her in his arms, and was kissing her as he strode toward the bed. Millie clung to his shoulders, a little stunned, her heart racing. She'd experienced his gentleness and built her fantasies around what she knew. Now she was getting a taste of the sexual power she'd known he'd leashed, but hadn't fully understood.

Without breaking the kiss, he held her with one arm and supported her with his knee as he yanked back the quilt and blankets. He handled her as though she weighed little more than the pillows he scattered off the bed. The mattress gave beneath her weight. Cool sheets caressed bare skin not covered by her T-shirt, and the clean scent of lemon worked its way into her subconscious, a scent she would now recognize as sensuous rather than soothing.

Denim rubbed against the inside of her thighs as he knelt on the bed between her legs, tossed his wallet on the nightstand, and jerked the black sweater over his head.

Millie's insides trembled like mad, from both arousal and apprehension. She wanted to see, feel, taste and touch every inch of him. Her body throbbed with desire and anticipation. She'd figured this would be a snap—just follow his lead and go where he took her.

Now she was seriously afraid she might not be able to keep up.

He paused above her, closed his eyes, and swore. When he looked at her, she saw apology and self-recrimination.

"The stunned look in your eyes tells me this is not the first time you have been rushed and disappointed by a lover."

Here was her opening to tell him that *he* was her first. But something held her back. The fear that he would leave through some misguided sense of honor. So she kept it to herself, glad that she could answer his question truthfully.

She smiled slowly. "You're lousy at reading eyes, sheikh. If it won't swell your ego too much, try substituting awed for stunned and see what you come up with."

His lips canted in a slow and sexy smile. "Sweetheart, if anything swells any bigger, we'll *both* be in trouble."

"See?" she teased softly. "Bragging already."

"Mmm. So I don't make a liar of myself, I think I will keep my pants on for a while." His hands slid beneath her T-shirt, smoothing the material up over her panties to her waist. "You, however, need fewer clothes on."

CHAPTER FOURTEEN

JEFF LIFTED the nightshirt over her head and sucked in a breath. His limbs seized for several beats as wonder and raw desire collided. Spellbound, he stared at her small, curvy body. This was what perfection looked like, he thought. He'd never before been rendered motionless by the sight of a nearly naked woman.

Mesmerized, he lifted his gaze to her eyes. Did she know what she did to him? The T-shirt slipped from his fingers and fell to the floor. He sat back on his heels, absorbing the artistry of her delicate form inch by fascinating inch. She had the skin of an angel, he thought, unblemished, peach-kissed ivory. Faint lines from last summer's tan rode the graceful swell of her breasts and the taut plane of her abdomen. His hands shook with the need to touch.

"My imagination was not even close." He lifted her hand and drew it to his mouth. "You take my breath away, Millie." He closed his lips over her knuckles, watching her eyes flare as momentary shyness melted into desire. The scent of sweet apples perfumed her skin, tempting him to rush, to slake the ravenous hunger raging inside him.

But he held back. From the moment he'd laid eyes on her, she'd kept him off balance, tipped his world and sent it spinning. Time to turn the table, he thought. Here, they were in his realm, and he intended to make up the rules.

Pleasuring a woman was one area where he had plenty of imagination. Although he didn't mind a little input.

He released her hand and skimmed his palms over her belly, toyed with the edge of her panties, running his finger along the faded silhouette of her bikini. She was so tiny he could almost wrap his hands around her waist.

"Tell me what you like." He swept his hands over the backs of her thighs, the curve of her behind, his fingers gliding over her back as his palms molded her waist, her rib cage, the unbelievably soft swell of her breasts.

"Um...you're doing f-fine."

"Fine right now?" Using the flat of his palms, he grazed the tips of her nipples in slow, sensuous circles, gently increasing the pressure with each seductive pass. With his whole hand now, he massaged her, driving himself recklessly close to the edge. A flush of arousal shimmered over her chest and throat. "Or fine right..." He dragged his thumbs down the center line of her stomach, over the top edge of her blue satin panties, then pressed them against her pubic bone. "...now?"

Her gasp ended on an ardent whimper, her hips arching against the steady pressure of his thumbs. Still kneeling between her legs, he felt her thighs squeeze against him, saw her stomach dip, noted the slight quiver in the muscles of her abdomen. Fire erupted in his belly, scorching a path to his groin.

"Let's do this my way." Wrapping his hands around her hips, he hauled her to his lap and wedged her pelvis flush against his groin. Without breaking the erotic contact, he shifted forward, followed her down and closed his lips over hers. He swallowed her cry of surprise, tasting her need and her surrender, then tortured himself as he rocked against her, his erection straining behind the fly of his jeans.

Her hips bucked, rivaling his aggression with unrestrained verve. Her hands raced over his back and his hair as she kissed him back, taking him higher and faster than he'd intended. Her avid response blanked his mind and sent him reeling.

Supporting her neck with his hand, he wrestled for control of the kiss. With her legs straddling his hips, he lifted her right off the bed as he thrust against her, faster and faster, desperate to assuage the feverish need, yet not trusting himself to go skin to skin.

He tore his mouth from hers as her fingers dug into his shoulders. Tension shimmered in her straining muscles, and her heaving pants turned to short, breathless screams as she rode the ridge of his jeans. His heart thundered in his chest, but he held on tight, and when she climaxed in his arms, it was the most irresistible, arousing thing he'd ever seen.

Millie clawed her way out of the haze of euphoria, stunned by the riotous sensations pulsing through her. But as sanity returned, a wave of embarrassment flooded her. How could that have happened? She'd already finished and he hadn't even taken off his pants. "Jeff? I didn't mean to—"

He kissed her with a soulful, earth-stopping tenderness that created a yearning so deep she felt faint. He made her feel beautiful, cherished, desirable. And a little bit afraid.

"Do you have any idea what your responsiveness does to a man—to me?" he murmured. "You are incredible. I intend to redeem myself and prove to you that I have an excellent imagination."

Millie shivered. "I didn't doubt it," she whispered.

"Just in case." Molding her breast in his palm, he trailed a line of kisses down her throat to her collarbone.

"Consider yourself warned. I do not plan to give you respite for a good long while yet."

She wasn't sure what he meant by that, but she was more than willing to let him show her. She skimmed her hands over his chest, brushing the pads of her fingers over his nipples. He caught her wrists, kissed the center of each palm, then stood and stepped out of his jeans.

Midafternoon sun bathed the room with a honey glow, but she only had a brief moment to appreciate the masculine symmetry of his body as he retrieved his wallet from the nightstand and removed several condoms. Then he was beside her once more, fulfilling his promise.

Within seconds he took her right back to that exhilarating storm of frenzied passion she couldn't seem to harness. She was hardly aware that he'd removed her panties until she felt his hand slide between her legs, his fingers massaging, rubbing, inflaming.

Sensation after vibrant sensation ripped through her, and when he suckled her breasts, the sheer rush of need made her dizzy. She didn't know where to focus. Pleasure swept her from every angle. The scream was building inside her again, filling her chest, crowding her throat.

She held back, determined to go the distance. Needing to touch, she reached for him, her hands feverish as she mapped his chest, his flat stomach, then wrapped her hand around the hard, hot length of his arousal. Velvet layered over pulsating steel. With untutored technique, her curiosity fueled by mind-numbing desire, she stroked and squeezed and reveled in the leashed power she held in her hand.

"Millie, wait."

The groan that escaped his lips was the only thing she registered. The feel of him was incredible and intensified her own pleasure. She slid both hands around him, relishing the electrifying hum of energy that surged through her fingers as she stroked him.

He swore. It could have been a curse or a prayer. In a move that left her dizzy, he had her swept beneath him, her hips tilted, a now empty condom package flung across the room.

"I've got to have you." His voice was hoarse with need. "Now." In one powerful thrust, he drove inside of her.

Millie gasped. Her body went rigid and she clenched her muscles in an effort to temper the sudden invasion, to adjust.

Jeff froze and stared down at her, stunned, disbelieving. "Millie? You're not…?"

"It's okay." The euphoria of desire ebbed, but she didn't feel pain.

His eyes steady on hers, he slowly pulled back. She realized at the last second that he intended to withdraw completely, and she hooked her legs behind his thighs and snaked her arms around him. "Don't you dare stop."

She wasn't a match for his strength. He eased out of her, but he didn't move away. With his steel hard erection lying against her stomach, he pressed his groin hard against hers for several torturous seconds, his eyes closed as though he was in agony.

At last, he looked down at her. "What in the hell were you thinking? You gave me no indication that this was your first time. In fact, you led me to believe just the opposite. Damn it, Millie. I would not have made love to you this way had I known."

"Exactly." She could feel her body stirring anew, a sweet, steady ache that pulsed with the rhythm of her heartbeat. "And if I'd wanted generic sex, I'd have told you."

"Generic?"

"What else do you want to call it? If you'd known, you would have either put a mile's distance between us or treated me like fragile china. I've waited twenty-three years for this, Jeffri al-Kareem, and I want it done right."

Jeff stared down at Millie. He'd taken a precious gift from her and felt like a heel for his inadvertent clumsiness. Yet here she lay, his aroused body stiff against her belly, telling him she wanted it done right. He had the urge to laugh, and to cry. That surprised him, because he didn't think he was capable of tears.

"Why me?"

She gave him the dim camel look and he was helpless to stop a smile of masculine pride. She'd damn near insulted his manhood by suggesting he might not get things right, but she wouldn't say the actual words to answer his question.

The message in her stormy-blue eyes stroked his ego, and her silent challenge was too tempting to resist. Despite her small size, she was no shrinking violet. She met life with curiosity and enthusiasm—plenty of enthusiasm, he thought, which was what had misled him in the first place.

"Need some help with that answer, spitfire?" She remained mute, and his smile climbed higher.

"Is it because I turn you on?" He shifted so he could skim his fingers over her breasts. "Because you like the way my hands feel on your body?" He shaped the silky flesh in his hand and rubbed his thumb around her nipple. Her eyes glazed and she arched into his palm like a contented kitten. He'd never known a woman who responded so quickly and with such abandon.

Even if he *had* known this was her first time, he didn't think he could have resisted her. Her unrestrained passion made him feel invincible. It was his technique he regretted. He'd been careless with her when he should have been gentle, impatient when he should have lingered. He intended to make it up to her.

And not with generic sex.

"Yes or no, Millie?" He slid his hand between her legs. "Is it my hands?" Before she finished her whispered yes, he eased his finger inside. She sucked in a breath and arched her back. His mouth went dry and his hands actually shook. She had the body of a goddess, and a sensuality he'd thought only existed in his fantasies.

With no inhibitions, no hang-ups over showing her pleasure, she eagerly strained toward his touch—naked, open and vulnerable, letting him know he could do anything he wanted with her. She was giving him her trust, utterly and totally. The knowledge humbled him.

And it made him burn, so that he almost forgot her lack of sexual experience. The only thing that gave her away was the wonder and hint of fear in her eyes when pleasure engulfed her, sweeping her along with a will of its own. He had an urgent need to take her there again. And again.

He flexed his finger inside her, pushing deeper, faster, then watched as unrestrained rapture consumed her. Denying his own release was agony, but his need to appease her was greater. With both tenderness and fury, he explored her body with his hands, his fingers and his mouth, learning each of her curves, seeking out her most sensitive points of pleasure, determined to drench her in sensation.

The sweet fragrance of her skin was intoxicating. Her body was slick with sweat, her whimpers segueing into the breathless little screams that drove him mad. He would die if he couldn't bury himself inside her. Soon. But he wanted her good and ready to take him; he wanted her mindless.

He sat up, pulled her sideways across his lap and pressed his palm low on her abdomen, holding her still. Her eyes were filled with confusion, but the trust was there, as well. He didn't understand why that was so important to him, why he felt a compelling need to test it.

With the sweet curve of her behind in his lap, her shoulders and legs lying flat against the mattress on either side of him, her hips bowed upward, just the way he wanted her. Holding her gaze, he inserted one finger, then two, in and out, slowly, letting her adjust.

Her pupils dominated her eyes, and her nipples stood tight and erect. He pressed the heel of his hand more firmly against her abdomen, just above her pubic bone, and angled his fingers toward the front of her womb. Her impatient hands grew frenzied, touching him wherever she could reach, pushing him to within a razor's edge of sanity. His single-minded goal was to insure her pleasure, and now his own need was reaching a crisis point.

"Millie?" She looked up at him, her breath coming in ragged sobs as he increased the tempo. "I am going to make you scream. And then I have to be inside you. But I need you to hold on to the sheets, and do not let go. If you keep touching me with those sweet, clever hands, I will come apart. And I do not intend to disappoint you twice in the same day."

With her hands no longer touching him, he tilted her hips and took her fast and deep, his fingertips unerringly finding the exact pleasure point to drive her wild.

She screamed, and her body arched taut as the orgasm ripped through her. Only fierce concentration kept him from following. He didn't wait for her spasms to subside. In seconds he had her flat on the mattress. He kissed her, traced her lips with his tongue and carefully pushed just the tip of his condom-sheathed erection inside her.

"Shh," he said when her hips rose up, straining against him, urgency and impatience vibrating beneath her skin. "Do not move just now. Let me do the work."

He held her steady as he slowly, gently thrust in and out, a mere inch at a time, pressing a little deeper with each advance and retreat. Slick and fiery hot, her inner muscles clutched him, squeezed and released. Her utter responsiveness continued to amaze him. This woman was a man's perfect fantasy. Each time she peaked, it stroked his masculine ego a little higher, made him feel as though he could conquer the entire world.

Something shifted inside him, luminous and soft. He brought his hands to her face and kissed her with a tenderness he hadn't known he possessed. If he believed in love, this was what it would feel like. Deep and all consuming, emotions more powerful than anything he'd felt in his life. For *anyone*.

"Hold on to me, sweetheart."

Millie could hardly form a coherent thought. Her body was so sensitized, her heart so full, she didn't think she'd ever be the same again. She wrapped her arms around his back and tugged. "Lay against me," she whispered. "I want to feel all of you. On me. Against me..." Her breath hitched. "Inside me."

He groaned and lowered his chest to hers, using the momentum to carry him forward, slowly, carefully, so gently she could have wept. She was on fire, wanted to urge him to get on with it, but she also wanted to memorize every nuance of sensation—and oh, there were so many. This was a day she would remember for the rest of her life.

She held his gaze as he finally buried himself deep inside her. The realization that his body was now a part of hers, that they were no longer separate, was incredibly moving. He was touching her soul. Emotions welled inside her, so powerful they were frightening. She didn't know where to put them, how to hide them.

I love you. The words crowded in her throat, screaming for release. She focused on the miracle of their bodies, the awe-inspiring, exquisite fulfillment of being a physical part of another person. The man she loved...and couldn't keep. Tears leaked past the corners of her closed eyes.

"Millie...? Sweetheart, did I hurt you?"

She dug her fingers into his behind, holding him in place. "No. It's just so beautiful." She felt the now familiar ripple of passion, the sweet steady ache that throbbed in every pulse point. She undulated beneath him. "Stay with me this time. Can we do that...together?"

"I am afraid I might beat you to the finish line," he murmured, teeth clenched tight. He pulled back and eased forward, watching her.

"Not a chance." Her eyes were already rolling back in her head. She had a fleeting thought. Was it normal for a body that had been asleep for twenty-three years to burst out of its cocoon a full-blown addict?

He repeated the movement, except this time his thrust slapped against her, pushing her closer to the headboard. She gasped and clutched his behind. "Yes! Just like that. Do it again!"

Her urgent demand seared the air, igniting a storm of blind frenzy as he gave her exactly what she wanted, pumping his body against hers, hard and deep. She couldn't draw a breath. She could only feel.

As wave after wave of glorious pleasure flooded her, Millie lost all concept of time and place. And just when she thought she couldn't possibly survive another second of bliss, he reached between their bodies and did something incredibly erotic with his fingers...and he showed her ecstasy. She cried out as a kaleidoscope of brilliant, vibrant colors exploded behind her closed eyelids.

She was hoarse by the time he arched his back and shouted her name, shudders racking his body. Awed, she watched him embrace the pleasure and was astonished when he began to move within her again. Her concentration vanished in a haze of delirious desire as he slammed into her, again and again, pumping until the last tremor had subsided.

"THAT WAS INCREDIBLE," Millie said when she could find the energy to move her mouth. Jeff had propped his back against the pillows and pulled her up against his side. With her head resting on his shoulder, her leg sprawled across his thighs, she shifted to look up at him. "I've heard of multiple orgasms, but I had multiples *multiplied.* It's hardly fair that you only got to have one."

"Believe me, it was definitely multiplied. For a minute, I thought I had died in paradise."

She ran her hand over his chest, loving the solid feel of his muscles. "Mmm. I think we shared that experience. Except the white light everyone talks about was in color. Major fireworks."

He smiled and kissed her forehead. His hand was cupping her behind, holding her against his side as though she might disappear. The possessiveness excited her. She definitely needed a distraction, because her greedy body was good to go—again! She imagined Jeff would appreciate a rest period. "We never did get to those strawberries and wine," she commented.

"Sweetheart, after what you just put me through, that's not going to do the job. Which might be a problem, since Zaki is not home."

She gaped at him, her fingertips absently circling his

nipple. "Give me a break. Are you so helpless you can't fix yourself a meal?"

He flipped her on to her back and loomed over her. "I do not think I would starve. But I do not *cook*."

"Lucky for you, *I* am an expert." It was a wonder she could even speak past the thud of her heart. The way he so easily tossed her around, as though she was no more challenge than a paperweight, was disconcerting.

He looked at her. Just looked. "I *do* feel very lucky, Millie. I want you to remember that."

Her rapid heartbeat skipped into a bittersweet ache. There were deeper words he'd left unsaid, a deeper meaning. But this time, she couldn't read his expression. When it came to emotions of the heart, she wouldn't settle for anything less than clear-cut words. Because it would be so easy to assume what *she* wanted to see in his eyes.

She knew he cared. A lot. And he would miss her when they parted, maybe even call for a while. But busy lifestyles and other distractions—even a woman coming into his life—would merely turn her into a fond memory. The thought of him with another woman cut her to the quick, but she had no right to lay a guilt trip on him. This was what she'd chosen for herself. This day was for her.

And this beautiful man had made it all possible. He'd given her the opportunity to experience romance. Despite Jeff's sometimes-dark exterior, he was a romantic man, a man who made her feel like a woman, powerful, invincible, cherished, celebrated.

Reaching up, she hooked a hand around his nape. "Not that I'm trying to get out of K.P. duty, but how hungry are you?"

His smile was slow and seductive as his hand skimmed the curve of her waist, the outer swell of her breast. He scattered kisses on her breast, her nipple, her collarbone, sketched the contour of her throat with his tongue, nipped lightly at her chin.

She moaned, not sure which way to focus her energies. On food, or the incredible thing his clever tongue was doing to her ear. "Um…does this mean you're *not* hungry and I can give my insatiable hormones the green light?"

He didn't answer. With his lips and tongue, he trailed an erotic path back down her body—neck, breasts, navel. His hands followed, stoking the fire hotter, his silky hair feathering over her skin.

"I hope you're not teasing me because…oh!" His hands clamped around her hips and tugged her down the bed.

"Millie?"

She could only stare at him, eyes wide, heart pounding, just the tiniest bit afraid. Not of him. She trusted him completely. It was a…thrilling kind of fear. Because the hot intensity in his eyes was a threat. A very sensual threat.

"I—am—starving." Three words, resolutely spaced for emphasis, and then he feasted. Raising her hips to his mouth, he kissed her in a way that was far from anything she could have imagined.

An orgasm ripped through her. Three seconds was all it took. Three seconds to bliss.

THE SOUND of the yacht's horn pulled Jeff out of an exhausted sleep. He opened his eyes and found himself curled around Millie. Glancing at the clock on the nightstand, then at the window, he realized it was close to sunset.

Millie's warm breath feathered his chest as she slept in his arms. He hated to wake her, since they'd only been asleep for half an hour. The other five had been spent making love.

The feel of her naked body against him caused his groin to stir. He couldn't believe it. He should be satisfied for life. Hell, it would be a feat if either one of them could walk. Instead of quenching his thirst, making love with Millie made him want her even more, and he wasn't sure what to do about that.

He trailed soft kisses over her cheek, her temple, her delicate eyelid. She uttered a sensual moan and snuggled into him. Amazed, he watched her nipples pucker. It was as though she knew him even in her sleep. She trusted so easily. Why couldn't he do the same?

The yacht's horn sounded again. "Wake up, Millie. We're about to have company."

Her eyes fluttered open and she smiled. "Who?"

He sat up, grabbed for his jeans and pulled them on. "I suspect Sadiq and Zaki are bringing the kids back."

She shot up out of the bed, yanking the sheet with her as she searched for her clothes, and then remembered she'd been wearing a nightshirt. She raced for the closet, the bed linens trailing her like the train on a wedding gown. Stepping into jeans, she jerked a sweatshirt over her head without bothering with a bra.

"I thought they were spending the night in Seattle." When she came out of the closet zipping up her jeans, Jeff was already dressed and standing at the door.

"That was the plan. I'd better go down and see what's going on."

"I'm coming, too." She finger-combed her hair, glanced in the mirror and nearly faltered. Her reflection looked different. Not the wild hair and lack of lipstick—it was the blush in her cheeks, the glow in her eyes. Thank goodness the children were too young to know about these things, because it was pretty darn obvious she'd just had great sex. Five hours of great sex.

By the time they got downstairs and went through the alarm ritual, Deke and Zac were coming in with the kids. They were a solemn group, and Millie's heart started to pound. She quickly looked at Lindsey and Sam, but before she could determine why they were so glum, Sam broke loose and ran to Jeff, wrapping his arms around his dad's hips.

"Son?" Jeff gently cupped his hand over Sam's head, stroking the silky black hair, then looked at Sadiq for an explanation.

"You did not answer your phone," Sadiq said.

Jeff glanced toward his office door. He'd forwarded all the lines and turned off his cell phone. For the first time in his adult life, he hadn't even thought about checking his messages. He'd only thought about Millie.

A sense of foreboding tightened his gut. He had an idea what was coming, and his mind screamed, *No! Not now. It's too soon.* Looking back at Sadiq, he simply said, "No, I did not."

"I received a message from home." Sadiq glanced at Sam, then at Lindsey and Millie, his dark eyes apologetic. "The children overheard. It is your father, Jeffri. He suffered a massive heart attack this afternoon. I am sorry."

Jeff's fingers tightened on Sam's head, every muscle in his body taut. He didn't dare glance at Millie. *Not yet.*

"I have made arrangements for a morning departure. I did not think you would want to travel this evening." Sadiq's gaze dipped to Sam.

Jeff nodded. And then he *did* look at Millie. He saw sadness, understanding and acceptance in her eyes. They'd been making love less than an hour ago, yet she would not ask anything of him, would not beg him to stay. He almost wished she would. She'd told him she wasn't looking for promises. Subconsciously, he hadn't believed her, especially when he'd realized he was the first man to ever make love to her.

He watched as she walked to him and slid her arms around him, including Sam in her embrace. She was offering comfort and telling them goodbye.

"I'm so sorry about your father."

His hand trembled as he returned the embrace, and when Lindsey snuggled against his leg, completing their circle of four, he nearly came undone.

MILLIE STARED at the clock for hours, unable to fall asleep. She desperately wanted to spend this last night with Jeff, but they'd agreed it was out of the question now that the kids were home. It was probably just as well. Her heart ached enough. To sleep in his arms, knowing they were both leaving the island in the morning, separately, would be torture.

That wasn't the biggest problem, though. Now that he'd awakened her body, she didn't know how to shut it off.

She closed her eyes and must have dozed. A sound startled her awake. She nearly jumped out of her skin when she saw Jeff standing beside her bed, staring down at her. Dressed in a black shirt and pants, he blended in with the darkness of the room.

Without a word, he bent down and scooped her up in his arms. "Jeff?"

"Shh." He kissed her forehead and strode into the hall.

Millie came fully awake. She knew something was wrong even before he turned away from the main stairway. His touch didn't feel right. These weren't the same hands that had turned her body inside out for five hours straight. Her heart banged against her ribs, and since her eyes had already adjusted to the dark, she had no trouble seeing. Something was very wrong.

"Wait a minute!" She twisted against his hold. "You're not—"

The arms tightened around her like steel bands, the hands deliberately squeezing as they clamped onto her thigh and the side of her rib cage. Paralyzing pain shot through her, stealing her voice. Even when she stopped struggling, he didn't let up on the pressure and she wondered if her ribs were going to snap.

She couldn't even draw enough breath into her lungs to scream. He strode down a back hallway where the carpet had been ripped up and never replaced, then shouldered through a door that had been left ajar, and descended a stairwell she hadn't known existed.

Despite the horrendous pain of his fingers digging into her flesh, she renewed her struggle to throw him off balance. He flipped her around like a rag doll, clamping her under one arm as he shoved through the door at the bottom of the stairs. She was getting damned sick and tired of being manhandled.

She only had a moment to register the damp sea air hitting her face before she was set on her feet and shoved against the wall in a cavelike alcove at the side of the house. Moonlight spilled over them, then disappeared behind the clouds.

The eyes that bored into hers made her go absolutely still. And she knew. "Oh, my God, I thought you were dead!"

CHAPTER FIFTEEN

JEFF'S EYES snapped open. In seconds, he went from a sound sleep to a state of alert, his heart hammering in his chest. He wasn't sure what had awakened him, and he lay perfectly still, trying to hear past the drumming in his ears. Nothing stirred, but something didn't feel right.

The bedside clock read 3:00 a.m. He realized he'd fallen asleep with his clothes on. He sat up just as the connecting door to the sitting room opened. Another pure shot of adrenaline rushed straight to his head. He saw the outline of Sadiq's massive shoulders a second before the bodyguard stepped into the room.

Jeff recognized the tension immediately. "The kids?" he asked, pulling on his socks and stuffing his feet into the boots he kept beside the bed.

"They are safe. I put them in the hidden room behind Sam's closet," Sadiq said. "Zaki is with them."

Jeff noticed the blood trickling down the back of Sadiq's bald head. Every muscle in his body knotted. "What happened to you?" His voice was so low it was barely audible.

"There is no time to talk. I want you in the safe room with Zaki and the kids. *Now,* Jeffri. I have reinforcements on the way."

"I asked a question, Sadiq." He grabbed his keys, yanked open a dresser drawer, and unlocked the safety box that held a forty-five caliber, semiautomatic pistol.

"I got sloppy. I thought he was you."

I will be you. The words of the note flashed in his mind. "Who?" He shoved a loaded clip into the gun.

"Kasim," Sadiq said shortly. "He is alive. He disconnected the alarm on the tunnel that leads into the library. I walked in on him. I thought I was talking to you, and the next thing I knew, I woke up and found myself on the floor. Now, do as I say, Jeffri, and get in the room with Zaki and the children."

Disbelief crippled him for several seconds. Kasim was alive? With sudden clarity, his mind flashed on an image of the bookcase sliding away, and his hand grasping the doorknob that led to the passageway. He'd been so intent on finding Millie that morning, it hadn't even registered that the alarm hadn't sounded.

Millie. Dread scorched a terrifying path up his spine—she was alone in the other wing with a madman. "I have to get Millie." He was almost at the door when Sadiq spun him around.

"Damn it, Jeffri. You are as hardheaded as ever. At least let me go first. And try not to shoot me."

"Likewise," Jeff said through clenched teeth, "since you obviously cannot even recognize me." His gut twisted. He'd known Sadiq since they were boys; the man was trained to notice details.

It seemed to take forever to make it from the west hallway to the east. Jeff pushed past Sadiq. The bed he and Millie had made love in all afternoon was empty. They were too late.

"I DID NOT SPEAK, yet you knew I was not my brother." Kasim al-Kareem spoke in a suave, accented voice, a blend of slick charm and arrogance that made Millie's skin crawl. The minute he'd backed her against the wall, he'd pulled out a gun. It was in his hand now, against the wall behind her, where his arms bracketed her head, trapping her, deliberately intimidating.

"I am impressed," he said.

"Don't be. Only an idiot couldn't tell the difference between the two of you. You're nothing at all like Jeffri." She was shaking so bad her voice was breathy. She was also spitting mad and scared out of her mind. And she desperately needed to get a grip.

A man like Kasim would feed on fear. And Millie hadn't clawed for survival these past four years just to end up as the main course on a deranged man's dinner plate.

She'd bluffed her way through the first week with Jeff, she could damned well do the same with his brother. She lifted her chin. "If I were blindfolded, I would know him anywhere, in any crowd."

"How touching." His tone was a sneer. "I gave myself away. Had you not been in…shall we say a *fearful* situation, then I would not have been forced to hurt you."

"Get real, Kasim. That's the reason you tried to break my ribs—because I knew right away you weren't Jeff. You smell different—"

His brows snapped together. "I do not wear cologne."

"Neither does Jeff. Your skin still smells different. Besides that, your hands are rougher than Jeff's, your shoulder muscles are softer, and the curve of your chin is wrong—it's weaker."

"You are a plucky one." He glanced at her mouth, bent his arms and slowly leaned toward her. Inches away from her face, he used the momentum to push away from the wall. He stepped back, leaving her nauseous and trembling.

"Maybe I will decide to keep you. Most women prefer

a taste of sin. Brother dear's wife certainly did. I could take you back to Balriyad…how would you feel about living in a palace in another country? With a man,'' he added.

She straightened her shoulders and spine, needing every bit of her height. Inches were important for a fool who was taunting a madman. If Kasim was anything at all like his brother, there was a chance her boldness would distract him, giving her an opening to run like crazy.

"I would go anywhere for the man I love,'' she said. "All he would have to do is ask. But that man does *not* happen to be you.''

Unconcerned by the verbal slap, he shrugged. "Don't count on brother Jeff asking. He'll be dead.''

She tried to ignore the terrifying word and the way Kasim had uttered it with an eerily pleasant relish. "If that's your plan, why did you bother with me?''

"I watched you sleep. I was looking for the boy. I thought he would be in the opposite wing of the house— that is where children and their nannies are *supposed* to be. Since that is not the case in this house, it makes things more difficult. But I decided you would be my prize. That is why I came for you first. I have already taken care of the bodyguard—the kid will be next, and then brother dear.''

Deke. Every atom in her body trembled and cried out. Deke was supposed to be watching over the kids. Lindsey was in the room with Sam. Oh, God, did Kasim know that? Would he hurt Lindsey, too? "Why are you doing this?''

"There can only be one replacement for my father. I will not be cheated out of what is rightfully mine. It is well known that Kasim is already dead, so I will simply return home as Jeffri. No one will question me.''

"But everyone will expect Sam to be with Jeff when he goes home! If Sam's not with you, someone will get suspicious and you'll be found out. Jeff said no one could tell the difference between the two of you, including Sam. You can raise him as Jeff would." She couldn't believe she was talking as if Jeff's death was a given. But right now, she was a mother desperately trying to keep a predator away from her children. "And people love single fathers. You'll get more cooperation and adoration."

He seemed to consider for a moment, then shook his head. "It will not work. I know nothing about their lives this past year. The boy will become suspicious if I do not remember what he did yesterday."

"Tell him you hit your head and can't remember. He'll believe you. And then you can ask him to help you remember, and that way you'll find out about Jeff's life, as well."

"You are making quite a case," he said. "But you are a cute thing, which might be swaying me. I will make my decision on the way upstairs when my head is clear. And do not worry that you will not have an opportunity to say goodbye to Jeffri. That is why you are my prize. I have had every one of his women. I would not want to spoil my record. But when I take you, Jeffri will be there to watch."

Terror roared in her head. She was trying so hard to bluff, to hide her fear, but she was seriously afraid she was losing the battle. She could barely catch her breath. "Why do you hate him so much?"

"Because there has never been room for both of us in Balriyad. I was the firstborn, yet Jeffri was the chosen one. I should be him. And I *will* be him."

Even in the shadowy darkness, she could see the hatred glittering in his eyes, hear the malevolence in his voice.

I will be you. Oh, God, Kasim had written that note Jeff had found in Seattle. She couldn't let this madman walk up those stairs and hurt Lindsey and Sam. She had to think, to fight back.

The scent of peppermint wafted in the alcove. Millie's adrenaline surged so hard, white specks danced in her periphery.

Kasim grabbed her around the waist, holding her like a shield, the gun aimed toward the opening. "What is that smell?"

"Good grief, would you calm down. I'm the only one in this house who wears perfume." Her bruised ribs were on fire. "That's a candy cane flower. It grows on the island in the spring." She pushed at Kasim's arm, trying to get free. If Deke was dead, that meant Jeff was out there, and she couldn't help him or the kids if she was being used as a bulletproof vest. "We don't smell it every night—only when the wind blows a certain way."

He finally turned her loose, pushed her back against the wall and picked up a roll of duct tape. "I have dallied long enough. Forgive me if I do not trust you to remain here on your own." He ripped off a strip of tape, the sound echoing against the walls like a rapid machine gun blast. "However, before I tape your beautiful mouth, I will take a kiss for luck…and to whet your appetite for later."

Millie shrank back against the wall, wishing she could disappear inside it. Kasim laughed softly. "That is good, baby. I like it when you are afraid."

He leaned in and put his mouth over hers. Millie nearly gagged. Without thought, acting only on reflex, she opened her mouth and bit down hard on his lip. That's as far as her plan went. She just knew she wanted his mouth and hands off her. He jerked back and slapped her so hard she saw stars.

From the corner of her eye she saw Jeff coming toward them. She didn't know if she gave him away by her body language or if she'd actually glanced in his direction.

Kasim raised his gun and fired. Millie screamed as a bullet slammed into Jeff and knocked him backward—somewhere out in the dark where she could no longer see him.

OhGodOhGodOhGod. Her limbs were paralyzed in shock and agony. The world spun around her like the walls of a grotesque carnival house, black as doom and splashed with deadly crimson, trapping her in the deafening echo of gunfire. If she ran, Kasim would kill her, too. She had to stay alive, find a way to save the kids.

Deke walked in, pointing his gun. She tried to shout at him to stay back, but the words wouldn't come. Streaks of blood were dried on his bald head. His face wore a lethal expression, but his eyes were kind, urging her to step off the mind-numbing merry-go-round.

Thank God, Deke was alive. She glanced down at her side. Until this moment, she hadn't realized Kasim had fallen beside her.

There was blood on her Tweety Bird pajamas. This was twice now that she'd been caught in mixed company wearing these pajamas—and both times there had been a gun pointed at her.

Her gaze moved to Kasim and she let out a sob. He looked so much like Jeff...

"I am here, Millie."

Her head whipped up. "Jeff?" He stood at the opening of the alcove, watching her. Heart pounding, she ran to him. "Oh, God, I thought you were dead. You're hurt. Let me see. Sit down before you faint." His shoulder was bleeding. "What the hell were you thinking, walking in here like…like… Oh, damn it." A sob broke free. Tears flooded her cheeks as she wrapped her arms around him and held on tight, her body shaking.

"Shh. I've got you." Jeff's uninjured arm snaked around her. "You're okay now."

Her ribs were on fire, but she didn't say a word. She didn't want him to ever let go. He tipped her chin up and laid his hand gently over her injured cheek. His eyes were so savage it was almost inconceivable that his touch could be this tender.

"I am so sorry, Millie." His voice was raw with pain.

"I'm all right." She placed her hand over his, brought it to her mouth and kissed the center of his palm. "He hits like a sissy. I got beamed harder than that in water polo." Her attempt to erase the haunted look from his face didn't work.

"Let's move away from here," Jeff said. "I want you to go in the house. You don't need to see any more of this."

"Don't tell me what I need." Even as she snapped at him, she was contradicting herself, automatically following his lead. But she kept her arm around his waist in case his blood loss made him weak. "You're the one who needs to go in the house so I can get a look at your shoulder."

She reached for the stairwell door at the same time that Sam barreled out. Millie and Jeff froze.

"I heard the gun!" Sam was as pale as the moon, and tears flooded his eyes and face. When he saw the blood staining Jeff's arm, he went wild. His instant, piercing wail sounded like a siren. Wringing his hands, he shrieked, "No! No, Dad. Don't die. You can't die, too!"

"Oh, Sam, sweetie." Millie quickly swiped away her

own tears and reached for him, but he darted away, inconsolable. She glanced up through the open door of the stairwell, saw Zac standing at the top and Lindsey sitting on one of the steps, her hands over her ears, rocking.

"Kiss it, Millie," Sam screamed, slamming his little body into Jeff's legs. "You can make it better. Your kisses are magic! Please! Help him!"

She didn't know her heart could ache. He was remembering the fall on the kitchen floor. There hadn't been any injuries, but he'd believed she had the power to heal with her kisses alone. Oh, how she wished she did. To see Jeff's blood flow was like feeling her own life spill out of her.

"Sam," Jeff said softly. When he finally coaxed Sam to let go of his legs, he bent down and lifted the little boy. "I am fine." He kissed his son and murmured to him in soothing tones. "Shh. Do not worry, son."

Jeff finally managed to get Sam's attention and break through the hysteria. Tears rolled down his son's pale little cheeks.

Millie put her hand on Sam's back. "Remember when you and Lindsey fell, and I asked if you needed doctoring or kisses?"

Sam nodded, snuffling.

"Well, your dad needs both. Doctoring first. I promise I'll kiss it after. It's not all that bad, just messy. See?" She lightly patted Jeff's arm—well away from the injury site—to show Sam it would be okay. "If I put my mouth on *that* mess, I'd look like a vampire who forgot to wipe his face after dinner."

Sam hiccuped on a giggle. "Are you sure?"

"Yes, sweetie. I'm sure if I put the kisses before the doctoring, I'd be mistaken for a vampire with sloppy table manners. And I'm *very* sure your dad will be just fine.

He's tough. He's standing on his own two feet and he's holding you, isn't he?''

The little boy nodded again. Jeff buried his face against Sam's cheek and kissed him for a long, emotion-filled moment. ''I love you,'' he whispered. ''Go inside with Zaki now.''

''I love you too, Dad,'' Sam whispered back.

Millie blinked back her tears as she watched Jeff set Sam on the ground. Zac, holding Lindsey's hand, had moved down the stairs and was standing by the door, waiting. Sam appeared torn, as though he couldn't decide if he should go or stay—regardless of what his dad said.

Millie knelt beside him. ''Will you do me a big favor, Sam?'' she asked softly. ''Will you watch out for Lindsey for a while? She's not as strong as you are and she's pretty scared right now. Can you stick real close to her for me? But don't let her know what you're doing,'' she cautioned. ''You know how she gets when she thinks a boy's trying to be tougher than her.''

Sam nodded solemnly, as if he had ten years on Lindsey rather than just one. ''Don't worry, Millie.''

She kissed his cheek. ''You either, pal.''

MILLIE STOOD on the dock the next morning, looking up at Jeff. She wished he'd take off those damned sunglasses so she could see his eyes. And she wished she had a pair of her own to cover her swollen cheek—and any tears that might betray her. She knew the handprint on her face was part of the reason for his stoic behavior. He felt guilty and responsible.

Their bags were aboard the yacht. Lindsey had already kissed Jeff goodbye, clinging to him, and was now on the yacht whispering with Sam, who'd hopped on to keep her company for ''two minutes,'' he'd said. Millie figured they were plotting a way to accidentally take him for a ride to Seattle.

"I will have my bank send over your check," Jeff said. "It will be waiting on your doorstep by the time you get home."

"That'll be fine." She shaded her eyes with her hand and watched the seaplane taxi out a ways, engines revving as it skimmed the water's surface and lifted in the air. It circled the island, wiggled its wings. Millie forced a smile and waved to Zac, then looked back at Jeff.

"Are you sure your arm's okay? You have everything you need…medicine?"

He nodded. Zac had flown him to Seattle before dawn. The bullet had passed through his shoulder and thankfully hadn't hit any vital bones or arteries. He should be wearing a sling, but they'd already had that argument this morning, and she felt too fragile right now to go through it again.

"Well," she said, feeling awkward. She wanted to prolong the parting, but at the same time was afraid to stay much longer. Her throat ached, and no matter how many times she swallowed, it didn't ease. "I guess I should go."

"Would you ever consider making this a permanent position?"

Her heart lurched. Was he saying…? "What position?"

"Staying on as Sam's nanny. You could travel with us. Live in the best homes. Have anything you wanted."

Except you. She shook her head. How could she have thought, even for a second, that he'd been talking about marriage? She'd known from the beginning that a lasting relationship between them wasn't a possibility because of their different backgrounds and lifestyles, so she hadn't let herself get caught up in fantasies.

But the thrill and instant acceptance that had trembled on her lips in those brief seconds surprised her. It made her realize she *had* harbored that impossible fantasy. And he'd just confirmed its impossibility.

I don't want material things. I want the fairy tale.

She swallowed the words and placed her hand on his chest. Very softly she said, "Sam doesn't need a nanny, Jeff. He's got his dad back." Her eyes clung to him, her own image bouncing back in the reflection of his sunglasses. "Thank you for the job offer—both of them. Take care of yourself." Then she turned and joined Lindsey on the yacht, fishing Sam from beneath some stored cushions.

"Come on, pal. No stowaways on this trip."

He peeked out, his eyes welling with tears. "I don't want you to go."

"I know, sweetie, but remember we talked about this? You have my phone number, and friends are allowed to call each other any time."

"Why can't I come and live with you?"

"Because your dad would be lonely. He needs you, Sam." She lifted him and buried her lips in his soft cheek. "You take care of him, okay? And don't you stop laughing or I'll have to send the grinch after you." He giggled through his tears, and when she set him down, he bravely climbed up on the dock and ran to Jeff.

Millie looked up at Mike and put all of her mental energy into making him sail this damned floating hotel out of here. Her desperation must have shown. Diesel engines fired to life and men untied thick cables. She forced herself to turn and smile as they backed out of the slip.

Jeff stood with his hands in his pockets, the wind blowing his hair. The lump in her throat ached, and the sob was nearly impossible to swallow. She waved. He pulled one hand out of his pocket and returned the wave, but not the smile.

This was one time Millie couldn't stanch the tears of grief. If she didn't release at least some of the pressure from the emotional valve, she'd come completely apart. Sitting down on a padded seat, she let the salt air smear the tears across her temples into her hair.

She didn't look back.

Lindsey's fingers gripped the yacht's rail, her head resting on her hands. She looked at Millie. Tears streamed over her cheeks, and her nose was red.

Millie opened her arms and Lindsey raced into them. For the remainder of the trip they stayed just like that. Holding each other and letting the emotions and pain escape, precious teardrops added to the ocean's flow, perhaps one day finding their way to the small isolated island country of Balriyad, where a man and a boy would think of them and smile with gentle hearts.

As the yacht neared Elliott Bay, Millie saw Jeff's seaplane fly overhead, going back toward the island. Zac must have needed some kind of exotic fresh vegetable to take back to Balriyad with them, she thought with a smile The plane's wings dipped side to side, an aeronautic farewell. She put her hand to her lips, raised it and waved back as though sending a kiss, as well.

"Bye, Zac," she whispered. "I'll miss you."

It was still morning when they arrived home, but Millie was having trouble putting one foot in front of the other. This was what happened when you didn't shore up the cracks in the dam, she thought. Pain could suck you into its pit of despair and bleed you dry. She damn sure wasn't going to let that happen.

Squaring her shoulders, she put her hand on Lindsey's shoulder and squeezed. "We're home, pet. Tomorrow we'll wake up rested, and everything will be just like it's always been.''

"Okay." The sad acceptance in Lindsey's voice nearly shattered what was left of Millie's heart. "What's at our door, Mimi?"

"Looks like one of us got a delivery." She stepped onto the porch and examined the package. Wrapped in plain brown shipping paper, it looked like a huge painting. It had to have been hand delivered, because there were no postal markings or addresses. Just a white envelope attached with her name on it.

She lifted the flap on the envelope, unfolded the paper, and nearly fainted. A check for one hundred thousand dollars stared up at her, signed by Jeffri al-Kareem. Hands shaking, she read the handwritten note.

Millie, I know you, and I know you will be wanting to return this check requesting a replacement in the amount of our originally agreed upon fee. Please do not, as I will merely have to annoy you with my nasty habit of tossing my checkbook around, and will simply have the money deposited into your account. Millie pulled her lips between her teeth, a smile hovering despite her tears.

The tapestry is my sincere thank-you. You will never know how much you did for me in helping me see through the eyes of imagination again, showing me the way to repair my relationship with my son. You inspired me. J.

She peeled off a corner of the brown shipping paper. The framed tapestry of Apollo and the nine muses. The lump in her throat swelled even larger.

"What is it, Mimi?" Lindsey helpfully ripped away a chunk of paper. That's when Millie saw the inscription on the back.

For Millie. You are my goddess of inspiration.

The sentiment touched her heart. But why couldn't she be his goddess of love?

The ache in her throat was nearly unbearable, but Lindsey was suffering, too. Millie had to be the strong one. That was one area where she was a pro.

CHAPTER SIXTEEN

JEFF HAD HARDLY had a minute to himself in the two weeks since he'd left the island. His days had been a nonstop marathon of meetings, and public assurances that Balriyad's affairs were in order.

He'd gotten through two funerals, his father's and his brother's, and he had mixed feelings about both. An evil madness had consumed the man Jeff had known as his brother. Or had he ever really known Kasim? They were identical, yet they'd never shared the bond typical of most twins.

And their father…Faruq had eventually ended up pushing away both of his sons. Kasim wasn't good enough to rule Balriyad, Father had said. *He has a sickness in his brain, and a thirst for blood and power.*

And where Jeff was concerned, Faruq had never praised any of his accomplishments without tacking on extra words. "It is good," he would say. "But not quite excellent, you understand, my son. I need excellence to follow in my shoes, and my father's before me."

But in the end, Faruq's callousness had all but extinguished the brilliant glow of excellence. And the devastating consequences had spilled over into Jeff's world, leaving him emotionally numb.

Until Millie had breezed into his life.

But how the hell did he trust his emotions? He'd misjudged his wife—a woman he'd known since he was a boy—his own father, and his twin brother. Lousy track record.

He could not allow himself to be weak and vulnerable again. He could feel intimacy and affection once more, enjoy a woman—Millie had shown him that. But love, in Jeff's mind, no longer existed. It was a poet's word, four letters that could be used against you at a time when you least expected it, a time when your guard was down and you were weak and vulnerable.

Deep in his soul, though, a small icy block remained that Millie's warmth had not melted away. Inside were the buried remains of what he'd once believed was love. Frozen solid, never to be opened, it was his reminder.

The problem was, the reminder had never hurt like this before. And every time he pictured Millie's face, he felt the wound more deeply. He'd seen Millie looking at Kasim's body—the horror on her face. She'd thought it was him.

Did he *really* need her to recognize something special about him? He wanted to let go of the past. He wanted Millie.

He leaned his head back against the sofa. It didn't matter what he wanted. Millie had her home and she'd made it clear that she intended to raise Lindsey the same way she'd been raised. Balriyad had everything to offer that Seattle did, he thought—except for the Space Needle and the like—but the main thing it did not have was her family's home or her friends. There was no way she would come halfway around the world to live in a country she'd never even seen.

He realized that he desperately wanted her to see his home—or perhaps he wanted to see it through her eyes. He wanted that sense of belonging she had for her town and her friends. Balriyad was his now, and he intended to make changes. Accountability would be one of them. He would not allow a repeat of his father's actions. No one had the right to take a life arbitrarily—not even the highest ruler of the land.

Sadiq strode into the room, and he looked up.

"This is a surveillance disk from the island." Sadiq lifted his hand. "I think you should take a look at it."

"That is your area, Sadiq. I will likely sell the island. Kasim is dead, so there is no need…" He tossed up his hands and let them drop onto his thighs as Sadiq simply continued toward the wide screen television set, ignoring him, and proceeded to load the disk into the player.

What good did it do to be the ruler of a country, a sultan sheikh, if he could not even command his security man? Although in fairness, Sadiq could not shoulder the entire blame. The minister of security had been influenced by Millie.

The moment Jeff thought her name, her face appeared on the fifty-two inch screen. He shot to the edge of the sofa cushions, grabbed for the remote, and held his thumb on the volume control. He could hear her shallow breathing, crickets singing, the ocean's surf. She was wearing the pajamas with the birds on them. He wanted to smile, but his heart was racing.

Like a ghost from the grave, he saw Kasim on the screen, crowding Millie, taunting her. Jeff clenched his fists.

"Kasim dismantled the main security cameras," Sadiq said. "He missed this one."

Jeff didn't respond. He was frozen in place, forced to relive that night and witness Millie's terror. But it wasn't only terror he was seeing. She was spitting mad. My God, the woman would take on an army and threaten them with a squirt gun.

Kasim's voice blared from the speakers. "I did not speak, yet you knew immediately that I was not my brother."

Jeff's heart nearly stopped beating. He listened to Millie list all the ways he and Kasim were different, and without thought he raised his hand to his chin.

But it wasn't her ability to tell them apart that had his heart pumping and his gut clutching in hope. His hands shook and his thumb still squeezed the volume control button even though it was already full-blast.

I would go anywhere for the man I love. All he'd have to do is ask.

"But I *did* ask you," Jeff said to the screen. Sadiq snatched the remote out of his hand, and the sound of Millie's voice abruptly stopped. Less than a second later, Sam came into the room.

"Dad, what's going on? Was that Millie? Did she call on your speaker phone?"

Jeff automatically made room for Sam to climb into his lap. He wrapped his arms around his son and closed his eyes. Before they'd gone to Seattle, Sam would not have crawled into his lap unless Jeff had extended an invitation first. He had Millie to thank for the sweet, uninhibited boy he'd brought home.

"It was a security tape from the island, son. We don't want to go through that again."

Sam shook his head and his eyes dimmed. "I miss her a lot, Dad. And Lindsey, too."

Sadiq was still standing in front of them, the remote sticking out of his hand as he perched the back of his wrists on his hips. Jeff frowned. What was the deal with the sissy pose?

"What did you ask her?" Sadiq demanded. "You were talking to the television screen."

Jeff gave him a pointed look, nodding his head at Sam. Sadiq didn't budge an inch. The guy looked like a pissed-off sumo wrestler wearing an apron. Except Sadiq wasn't wearing the apron—although he damned well looked like he should be.

"I asked her to come home with me," Jeff said in exasperation. "She said no."

"What exactly did you ask her to come for?" Sadiq glared at him, and Sam looked up, both waiting for an answer. He'd asked her to be Sam's nanny. He didn't want to say that in front of Sam. It might hurt him.

Sadiq obviously didn't have sense enough to realize that. "I bet you asked her to be the baby-sitter."

Jeff scowled. Friend or not, this time Sadiq was going too far. But before he could open his mouth, Sam shook his head and said, "Oh, man, Dad. I hope you didn't do *that*. Even I know better, and I'm only six! Well," he amended, "me and Deke talked about it some, so that's really why I am smarter about the marriage thing. You have to ask her to be the wife. Then she can be the mom, and Lindsey can be the sister." He waved his hands in a gesture much like Millie would have done. "It is easy."

The rush of emotions went right down to Jeff's soul— a soul that was almost whole again. Almost. He wrapped his arms around Sam and laughed for the pure joy of it.

It really *was* that simple, he thought. His only excuse for idiocy was that his goddess of inspiration wasn't here to shake him up and clarify his thinking—which she dearly delighted in doing. He needed to get her back.

"We might need a little help on this, champ," he said to Sam. He reached for his cell phone and searched through the stored numbers. "Let's assemble the troops."

WHEN MILLIE stepped off the elevator on the Space Needle's observation deck, she was in a snit and trying like the devil to keep that information to herself. Holding the electronic doors open, she waited for Carmen Perez's day-care group of five- and six-year-olds to spill out of the elevator and go on ahead of her.

This was the last place she wanted to be. It had been two weeks since she'd left the island, and the pain of missing Jeff and Sam hadn't lessened at all. Sadly, even though they'd said goodbye, she really *had* expected Jeff to call her. She was such a fool. And this sky-high monument only made the longing worse.

But Katherine had insisted she needed one more chaperone for this field trip. She'd been in a huge tizzy because Rona Optiz had turned in her resignation notice and Katherine now had to find a new teacher for the two- to three-year-olds!

Good grief. It wasn't as though the toddlers were going to be left to their own devices to dismantle the cribs and paint the walls or anything. Besides, Meg Bassett-Taylor worked at the day-care center as a part-time music teacher and would be totally willing to fill in on a short-term basis, so Millie truly didn't see what all the fuss was about.

She glanced over at the kids, who were crowded in a messy line and taking up the entire walkway of the deck. Oh, for heaven's sake.

Pushing away from the wall, she started toward the children, intending to line them up in partners, then frowned because they were all snickering. And Lindsey was pointing her finger. Millie glanced down to make sure the zipper on her jeans was closed.

When she lifted her head, hands covered her eyes from behind. Lindsey's voice sang out across the observation deck. ''Guess who!''

Millie's heart gave one deep thud, then skipped into

triple time. She drew in a swift breath and went utterly still.

"Jeff," she whispered. The single word was hardly more than a puff of air. With her hand trembling like mad, she reached up and covered her mouth as though she could hold her emotions inside. She felt like an overinflated balloon about to pop. It didn't even occur to her to twist away or reach for the hands over her eyes.

"If you were blindfolded in a crowd, and I could not speak, how would you know me?"

She couldn't utter a single word. The balloon had just burst. Tears stung like acid behind her eyelids, burning her nose and her throat. The hand she held over her mouth couldn't hold back the sob.

"Millie?" Suddenly his hands were gone. When she opened her eyes, he was standing in front of her, blocking her from prying eyes—a human privacy screen.

He looked wonderful, aside from the terrified "guy" thing going on. And he was petting her—*petting,* for heaven's sake. What was it about a woman's tears that made a man panic? Didn't he know how sweet, how *touching* that was? That it just made a woman cry even more? She might have told him that, but she couldn't speak past the emotion in her throat. All she could do was stare at him, her heart full, her tears streaming, her mind scared to death to believe. She felt like an idiot. She sniffed and wiped her eyes.

"That was not a good opening line," Jeff said, his voice husky with emotion. "Let me try a different one. I love you, Millie Gallagher—oh, hell! You are not supposed to cry over that, too!" He hauled her into his arms, his masculine discomposure almost comical. She could hear his heart thundering in his chest where her cheek rested.

When she was relatively sure her vocal cords would

work, she lifted her head, held his gaze and spoke softly, slowly.

"If I were blindfolded in a crowd, my heart would know you, my soul would feel you, my senses would taste you…and my fist might slug you for giving me heart failure."

He laughed, a joyful sound that echoed off the windows of the observation deck. Then he lifted her right off the floor and soul-kissed her until she thought her heart *would* give out.

She reached up, twining her arms around his neck, and decided she didn't need the heart after all, because she had his.

When he lifted his head, his eyes were nearly black. She could read them so well, the love, the desire, and…

"Oh, my gosh, Jeff. Your arm. What are you doing picking me up? You should know better—" His lips stopped her words in midsentence. It truly was the most wonderful means of interruption, Millie thought.

This time when he broke the kiss, his eyes were dancing with love and amusement. "I love you, Millie. You cannot imagine how much. I think I stopped believing in love because I had never felt the real thing. I love the way you make me feel, and I love the way you scream when I make love to —"

"Jeff!" she whispered fiercely. Since he was still holding her off the ground, she peeked over his shoulder.

She saw Katherine, Hannah, Alexandra and Carmen all smiling and teary-eyed, as though they were watching Julia Roberts meet Richard Gere on the fire escape in *Pretty Woman*. Katherine—the faker—was as calm as could be. The day-care kids were lined up beside them, clearly anxious to continue their field trip. Millie's heart sang when she saw Lindsey and Sam holding hands, their faces wreathed in happy smiles.

Oh, yes, she thought. This was exactly right—for her and for Lindsey.

"May I continue my declaration?" Jeff's insulted tone made her laugh. "See?" he said. "The woman laughs at me when I am trying to be romantic. A man should have some respect."

With her arms still around his neck, she kissed him, then smiled with her lips against his. "I feel the same way. A man *should* have respect, and I'll expect you to show it on a daily basis."

He laughed. "Oh, we will argue, won't we?"

"Contradict," she countered. She leaned back slightly. "I'd rather you save the rest of your declaration for someplace private," she whispered. "Like maybe the bedroom in that penthouse I've heard so much about."

"Shame on you. I cannot take you home with me in broad daylight when I have not received a commitment of marriage from you. I am a sultan now. I have a reputation to uphold."

She bit her bottom lip because she wasn't sure if what she was feeling was going to come out as laughter or tears. She only knew that she loved this man to distraction. "A person can't very well give a commitment without being asked for it first," she said.

His steady gaze held her like the softest caress. "How would you feel about living in a palace in another country with a man who loves you so deeply he aches with it, a man who loves your little sister and desperately wants to be her father? How would you feel about making a family with this man and his son who loves you to distraction, as well? How would you feel—"

She put her fingers over his lips and repeated words she suspected he'd somehow heard. But they were words from her heart, and she wanted him to truly know that.

"I would go anywhere for that man, live anywhere *with*

that man. And he wouldn't even have to ask. I love you, Sheikh Jeffri al-Kareem. And Lindsey loves you. She doesn't want to live without you and Sam, and I don't, either. So will you marry us?''

He swung her around in a circle, laughing, and while Millie's adult friends sighed, the children all clapped their hands.

''I thought you'd never ask. Yes. Sam and I will definitely marry you.'' He kissed her then, a romantic kiss so tender there could never be room for doubts.

And when she looked at him, Millie knew she was the luckiest woman on earth. Because this man adored her. ''How about that bed in your penthouse?'' she whispered. ''Now that your virtue is safe, I wouldn't mind hearing you finish that declaration you started.''

''As it happens,'' he said softly, his voice filled with raw emotion, ''a very good friend of ours has offered to take our children on a field trip to the Space Needle. And another very good friend has agreed to fly them home for a few days so Lindsey can brag that she was in Balriyad first. That will give us four days to practice for our honeymoon before they return for us.''

She smiled down at him. ''Well, aren't you the over-confident one. If I didn't like your plans so well, I'd have to take issue with your tactics. And to be fair, I should point out that you're an injured man. Do you think you can keep up with me for four days?''

''Sweetheart, you will learn it is not wise to challenge me. You will be begging for mercy by the second day.''

''I think I'll take that challenge. Take me home, Sheikh. I've got some experience under my belt now, and I'm dying to wreck your virtue.''

* * * * *

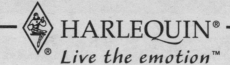

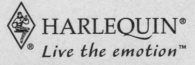

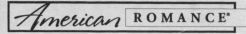
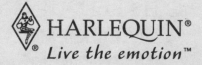

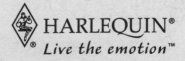

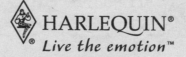

HH Harlequin® Historical
Historical Romantic Adventure!

Imagine a time of chivalrous knights and unconventional ladies, roguish rakes and impetuous heiresses, rugged cowboys and spirited frontierswomen— these rich and vivid tales will capture your imagination!

Harlequin Historical . . . they're too good to miss!

REQUEST YOUR FREE BOOKS!

2 FREE NOVELS PLUS 2 FREE GIFTS!

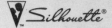

Silhouette® Desire®

Passionate, Powerful, Provocative!

SDES08R